THE WASTELAND

by Takako Takahashi

THE WASTELAND

by Takako Takahashi

TRANSLATED WITH AN INTRODUCTION BY

BRITTEN DEAN

East Asia Program
Cornell University
Ithaca, New York 14853

The Cornell East Asia Series is published by the Cornell University East Asia Program (distinct from Cornell University Press). We publish books on a variety of scholarly topics relating to East Asia as a service to the academic community and the general public. Standing Orders, which provide for automatic notification and invoicing of each title in the series upon publication, are accepted. Address submission inquiries to CEAS Editorial Board, East Asia Program, Cornell University, 140 Uris Hall, Ithaca New York 14853-7601.

Number 200 in the Cornell East Asia Series.
New Japanese Horizon Series Editors:
Michiko Wilson/Gustav Heldt/Doug Merwin

ISSN: 1050-2955
ISBN: 978-1-939161-10-9 hardcover
ISBN: 978-1-939161-00-0 paperback
ISBN: 978-1-942242-00-0 e-book
Library of Congress Control Number: 2018967224

Cover images: Jiris. Shutterstock 619465739; Anansing, Shutterstock 651863242
Cober design: Mai

I will lead her into the
wasteland
And speak to her heart

— *Hosea 2:14*

Contents

Introduction

This is a dark and troubling novel. It begins with a gritty Tokyo street scene where "the very ground itself seemed to be in agony" and concludes with a gruesome bathtub scene with "blood-splattered surfaces everywhere." In between we have infidelity, hatred, insanity, loneliness, lust, and cynicism. Withal, it is a Christian novel: its author was a devout Roman Catholic (indeed, a one-time nun), and the title page epigraph from the *Old Testament* book of "Hosea" unmistakably mantles the narrative in a religious message.

Dominating the story is Nobe Michiko. She leads an aimless existence in Tokyo where her husband, a successful corporate employee, has recently been transferred. Complicating her life is worry about her estranged and emotionally unstable sister, now a mental hospital inmate somewhere in the Tokyo area. Reluctantly, Michiko seeks to learn her whereabouts and resolve differences between them. Michiko also seeks to realize her oppressed inner self with extramarital affairs. A chance misdialed phone call introduces her to Sawamura Takuzō, a well-educated scion of an upper-class Tokyo family, who himself is drifting through life. His sincerity and apparent self-confidence attract Michiko. They become lovers.

Caught between Michiko and Takuzō is Muro Sawako, who enters the picture as Takuzō's casual girlfriend. A working-class girl, Sawako projects outward optimism and kindness as a "cheerful redcap," delivering goodness everywhere. Inwardly, however, she is tormented by unrequited love for Takuzō.

Woven into the narrative is Michiko's husband Nobe Keitarō. He is supportive of his wife's efforts at reconciliation with her mentally disturbed sister. He is obsessed with organization and control, yet too obtuse to realize his wife is having an affair. He represents the typical driven, single-minded salaryman and domineering husband of Japanese society in the 1970s.[1]

Finally there is Sachiko, troubled teenager who walks the streets seeking sexual company to compensate for her broken home. In a cruel irony, the name Sachiko literally means "happy child." We know her only through her telephone conversations with "LifeLine," an emergency psychological help telephone service. She is the product of a morally corrupt Tokyo, and her tragic life implies that Michiko's search for sexual fulfillment is likely also to end in disaster.

Takahashi Takako (1932–2013) would seem to be an unlikely author for such a novel as this. Born Okamoto Takako, the only child of a cultured and affluent Kyoto family, she graduated in 1954 from prestigious Kyoto University in French literature. Her senior thesis treated Charles Baudelaire (1821–1867), best known for his poetry collection *Les Fleurs du Mal* (The flowers of evil), often viewed as the product of a depraved and morbid mind. In 1958 she earned a master's degree, also from Kyoto University, with a thesis on François Mauriac (1885–1970), Catholic apologist and respected French novelist (Nobel laureate, 1952). This educational experience clearly presaged her future writing career.[2]

---

1. Keitarō neatly exemplifies the salaryman in the business world as described in Ezra F. Vogel, *Japan as Number One: Lessons for America* (Cambridge, MA: Harvard University Press, 1979), chapter 6, "The Large Company: Identification and Performance," pp. 131–157, written about the same time as *The Wasteland* (1980). What Vogel leaves almost unmentioned is that the drive for postwar economic reconstruction levied a heavy emotional toll on the family—long working hours, postings far from home, and often heavy drinking by the husband, and marginalization of the wife and her subordination in the male-dominated society. See Jon Woronoff, *Japan as—anything but—Number One* (Armonk, NY: M.E. Sharpe, 1991), pp. 179–186, 234–241.

2. Biographical detail is available in Takahashi's *Lonely Woman*, translated by Maryellen Toman Mori (New York: Columbia University Press, 2004), pp. ix–xv; and in Julia C. Bullock,

Shortly after graduation in 1954 Takako married Takahashi Kazumi, a fellow student, who himself was to become a prize-winning writer and university professor. Takako supported him for the first few years of their marriage while he was establishing himself in the literary world. In 1958 the couple moved to Osaka, where they lived until 1965. They then bought a small Japanese-style home in Kamakura, not far from Tokyo where her husband had obtained a teaching position at Meiji University. Takako was relieved to be able to leave what she considered the excessively patriarchal atmosphere of the Kyoto-Osaka area of Japan. Yet the restrictive social environment of her new home proved little better. A brilliant woman fully the intellectual equal of her husband, she was nonetheless excluded from his male study circles and reduced to playing the role of the silent and submissive housewife as her husband's career developed. One can imagine that for a sensitive young woman like Takako, the emotional pain thus caused may well have been excruciating. Indeed, she openly acknowledges experiencing serious emotional depression—neurosis (*noirōze*) as she calls it, which was to affect her intermittently for the next several years.[3] Just two years after moving to Kamakura her husband was offered a professorship at Kyoto University, which he accepted, not just because of the greater prestige of that university, but also to return to the city and surroundings to which he felt a strong attachment. Takako herself, however, remained in Kamakura, refusing to return to the repressive social and intellectual environment of Kyoto. Not long after taking up his position at Kyoto University, Kazumi contracted cancer, and in 1969 he rejoined his wife, who cared for him until his death in 1971 at age 39. She later published two memoirs about him.

During these years Takahashi Takako managed to begin her own literary career. She started a novel and published stories and essays. In 1963 the prestigious journal *Chūō Kōron* published her translation of Mauriac's novel

---

The Other Women's Lib: Gender and Body in Japanese Women's Fiction (Honolulu: University of Hawai'i Press, 2010), pp. 44–47. Takahashi's own "Jihitsu nenpu" (Chronological autobiography) offers yet more detail. See *Takahashi Takako jisen shōsetsushū* (Takahashi Takako's self-selected literary works; 4 vols., Tokyo: Kōdansha, 1994; hereafter cited as *Takahashi Works*), vol. 4, pp. 553–579.

3. Takahashi records her neurosis in "Chronological autobiography," pp. 557 and 559, and analyzes it in "Watakushi no noirōze no koto" (Concerning my neurosis) in *Takahashi Kazumi to iu hito, nijūgo-nen no ato ni* (Remembering Takahashi Kazumi: twenty-five years later; Tokyo: Kawade shobō shinsha, 1997), pp. 151–159.

Thérèse Desqueyroux. Its title protagonist closely resembles characters found in her own novels: women impelled to outrageous retaliation by what they view as suffocating social convention—in Thérèse's case, attempted murder of her husband.

Takahashi's first published novel, *Sora no Hate made* (To the end of the sky) appeared in 1973 and garnered a prize. Her literary star rose fast thereafter. She published prolifically, winning increased recognition and additional literary prizes. Her total output includes ten novels, numerous short stories, essays, criticism, memoirs, and spiritual writings. Most of her secular writings were produced throughout the 1970s and early1980s; her spiritual writings occupied her mostly during the late 80s and early 90s.[4]

Christianity made its impression on Takahashi as she studied the works of François Mauriac, and deepened during her first trip to France. That occurred in April through September of 1967, the result of a need to escape (to "race off"—*tobidasu*, as she puts it) from the anguish she felt over her willful decision to live apart from her husband. Thereafter she was a frequent visitor to France. Although, she later recalled, she thought it absurd that she might eventually take holy orders, she formally converted to Catholicism in 1975, moved to France in 1980, and indeed took holy orders to become a nun in 1985.[5]

Returning to Japan in 1989, she formally joined the Kyoto branch of the Carmelite Order as a postulant and, in conformity with the worldly isolation required by the Order, she requested her publishers to withdraw her works from publication. She thus set aside her very public writing career in favor of concentrating on the "charism" or spiritual focus of the Order. Thereafter she published no new fiction for several years, restricting her writing largely to

---

4. A bibliography of Takahashi's major publications is included in Mori, op. cit., pp. 149–152. Full bibliographical detail may be found in Takahashi's own "Chronological autobiography." For an exhaustive bibliography of works dealing with Takahashi and her writings, see Satō Kana, "Sankō bunken mokuroku" (An indexed bibliography) in Nakagawa Shigemi and Hasegawa Kei, eds., *Takahashi Takako no fūkei* (Takahashi Takako's literary landscape; Tokyo: Sairyūsha, 1999), pp. 225–236.

5. She humorously recollects the absurdity of suggestions she become a nun in her *Watakushi no tōtta michi* (The path I travelled; Tokyo: Kōdansha, 1999), pp. 290–291. The suggestions came from the well-known Christian writer, Endō Shūsaku.

spiritual subjects. But she left the Order after just a year; she found its spiritual life very appealing but she could not adjust to its "Japanese mentality" (*shinsei*), chafing, perhaps, under the Carmelite rule to lead a disciplined life of continual prayer. She may also have regretted allowing restrictions to be imposed on her writing career. In addition she seems to have felt a lack of stimulating, intellectually satisfying companionship at the convent. In any event, after leaving the Carmelites, she continued as a devout lay Catholic the rest of her life.[6]

She lived out her final decade in a private home for the elderly in Kamakura. Overly sensitive to noise, she had her bedroom soundproofed to assure an undisturbed night's sleep. Though quite the gourmet in her youth, convent life had accustomed her to simple fare, so her meals in the communal dining room were quite sufficient. Physically active and mentally alert to the very end, she died of sudden cardiac arrest at age eighty-one. She was interred alongside her husband.[7]

Takahashi Takako was one of only a handful of Catholic writers in Japan. Their influence, however, far exceeded their small numbers.

Arano, the Japanese title of the present work and translated here as "The Wasteland," clearly derives from the title page epigraph:

> I will lead her into the wasteland
> And speak to her heart.
> —Hosea 2:14[8]

---

6. Sources for this paragraph are Takahashi's "Chronological autobiography," p. 577; Suzuki Shō (Takahashi's longtime friend and amanuensis) in private correspondence with the translator; and Ogawa Yoshie (abbess of the Kyoto Carmelite convent) in private correspondence with the translator.

7. Suzuki Shō provides details of the final years in a postscript to Takahashi's *Owari no hibi* (My last days; Tokyo: Misuzu shobō, 2013), pp. 288–292.

8. This is a translation of the Japanese-language verse found in the original text of the novel. Takahashi based her Japanese version on a French translation of the Bible by Édouard Dhorme (1881–1966), *La Bible: l'Ancien Testament*; 2 vols., Paris: Gallimard, 1956–1959. More familiar to English-speaking readers would be the King James Version of the epigraph:

> Therefore, behold, I will allure her,
> And bring her into the wilderness,
> And speak comfortably unto her.

The "Book of Hosea" poses numerous problems of interpretation. Indeed, "Hosea" is considered one of the most troublesome books of the Old Testament, and has spawned a large literature far out of proportion to its own very modest length.

The book opens with God's commanding Hosea to marry a prostitute. This he does, marrying Gomer and caring for her children (scholars differ as to whether the children are the legitimate issue of Hosea and Gomer or the illegitimate issue of Gomer and her previous lovers). The marriage is traditionally taken as a metaphor of an apostate Israel, which has forsaken God in favor of the licentious Baal cult of neighboring Canaan, and which has made unholy alliances with foreign powers—Assyria and Egypt. God is punishing Hosea and Gomer and the children for their waywardness, representing the waywardness of Israel. The punishment is harsh: Hosea suffers the humiliation of marriage to a prostitute, and God threatens to deprive Gomer of grain, wine, wool, and flax—the necessities of life—and to strip her naked and expose her lewdness. Later God forgives her, leading Gomer (or, according to some translations, "alluring" her—an appeal to the licentious side of her character?) into a wasteland, a quiet environment free of distraction, and urging her (in Hosea's phrase, "speak to her heart") to return to the true God.[9]

This traditional interpretation of the text has come under attack by critical, especially feminist, scholarship during the past several decades. That God should command the prophet to marry a whore is found to be an outrageous notion, so outrageous, indeed, that some scholars question whether "Hosea" should any longer be regarded as sacred scripture at all.[10] The wasteland to which God will lead Gomer is an "arid land" (*arano* in the Japanese version of the Bible) where God will "slay her with thirst." At the other extreme, the wasteland may symbolize, one scholar has argued, the "pristine relation" between God and his people.[11] Be that as it may, the interpretation available to Takahashi in the 1970s would have been the traditional one.

---

9. This traditional interpretation is presented in, among others, *Life Application Study Bible* (New International Version), Grand Rapids, Michigan: Zonderman, 1991.

10. See Alice A. Keefe, *Woman's Body and the Social Body in Hosea* (London: Sheffield Academic Press, 2001), p. 151.

11. Yvonne Sherwood, *The Prostitute and the Prophet: Hosea's Marriage in Literary-Theoretical Perspective* (Sheffield, England: Sheffield Academic Press, 1996), p. 208.

Even so, Takahashi has her own particular take on "wasteland." For her it is represented by Tokyo: the impersonal metropolis, the city of sin, the source of psychological pain. The neurosis she complains of in her autobiographical writings results partly from her distaste of Tokyo, which in turn is one source for *The Wasteland*.[12] Tokyo is described throughout the novel in negative terms. Dust blowing everywhere, buildings gray and dismal, deafening traffic and stifling weather, filthy flop houses and nauseous greasy spoons, lurid neon signs advertising the seemingly ubiquitous love hotels. It is, she writes, "a huge metropolis where human beings don't relate to each other in a human way."[13]

Michiko's own apartment is an oasis in this hellhole: air conditioner humming efficiently, snug-fitting windows ensuring tranquility within, spacious layout and comfortable furniture. Michiko lives languorously, but she is skirting the edge of the wasteland. After all, the very name "Nobe Michiko," commonplace though it may be, literally means "she who walks the path along the edge of the wasteland." Will she stumble into it? The denouement suggests she will.

Michiko is not an appealing character. In physical appearance, Takahashi offers only a minimalist description of her. From scattered remarks here and there, we learn simply that she has double-fold eyelids, slender wrists, is beautiful, but little else. She is presumably well educated, and leads a life of leisure as the wife of an international trading company employee. She is self-centered, lacks any humanistic or religious ideals, and passes tedious hours lazing on the living room sofa leafing through women's magazines.

---

12. See, for example, her essay, "Kono yo no 'arano'" (This world as a "wasteland"), in *Takahashi Works*, vol. 2, p. 545. Tokyo as a source of neurosis is elaborated in Yamauchi Yukito: *Kami to deau: Takahashi Takako ron* (Encountering God: essays on Takahashi Takako; Tokyo: Shoshi Yamada, 2002), p. 92.

13. Quoted in "Female Sexuality and the Male Gaze: A Dialogue between Takahashi Takako and Tsushima Yūko" in Rebecca L. Copeland, ed., *Woman Critiqued: Translated Essays on Japanese Women's Writing* (Honolulu: University of Hawai'i Press, 2006), p. 129. Takahashi's unflattering descriptions of Tokyo are by no means pure fiction. In the name of economic reconstruction following World War II, Japan's industrial complex spawned severe air pollution and other forms of environmental degradation, several instances of which are scattered throughout the novel. See Woronoff, op. cit., pp. 165–166.

She has only two concerns. One is to locate her mentally ill sister and resolve differences between them, in pursuit of which she is reluctant and ineffective. The other is to open up her inner self through perfect sexual pleasure with the ideal man. About this she is positive and enthusiastic, and for a while her lover, the male protagonist Sawamura Takuzō, comes close to epitomizing the ideal. She has no children and desires none, for they would interfere with her sexual goals. Willingly, indeed happily, she rejects the ordinary standards of Japanese society. Her own standards, if generally accepted, would of course wreak havoc on the traditional Japanese family and transform Japanese society. She thus embodies a narcisism of monstrous proportions. More than that, being only slightly described, she lacks particularity, and lacking particularity she becomes Everywoman. Indeed, as Michiko proclaims, every woman possesses a hidden inner self which demands to break away from conventional constraints and burst forth into actualization. "That [inner] woman—naked, greedy, frenzied—would not hesitate to destroy everything for her own sake." Extreme though Michiko is, Takahashi nonetheless insists that she is not sick or perverse.[14] Takahashi's fiction often reveals a dichotomy between the "maternal woman" (*bosei*) and the "demonic woman" (*mashō*).[15] *The Wasteland* clearly offers examples of both: Michiko exemplifies the self-centered and destructive aspects of the demonic woman, while Muro Sawako, the self-described "cheerful redcap," exhibits aspects of the maternal woman. In *The Wasteland* neither experiences a happy ending.

With such wild ideas as these, is Takahashi simply immersed in some "psychological dreamworld"?[16] The events in *The Wasteland* are not the stuff of ordinary life and most of the characters lack verisimilitude. Is Takahashi working out some inner psychological conflicts? To some degree, probably so. Despite a privileged youth, lifelong conflicts arose due to her sensitive, independent spirit in contrast to the constrained and stifling social and intellectual environment in which she lived, as well as to the

14. "Kono yo no 'arano,'" p. 548.

15. For an elaboration of the maternal versus the demonic, see, for example, Mizuta Noriko, "Zettaiteki na tasha o motomeru fumō jiga no enkan—Takahashi Takako no tsumi to yume" (The cycle of the barren ego in search of the absolute other—sin and dream in Takahashi Takako), in Nakagawa, op.cit., pp. 13–23.

16. The phrase is Joan E. Ericson's; see Copeland, op. cit., p. 118, note 4.

general marginalization of female intellectuals, especially in the Japan of the 1960s and '70s. Her outrageous protagonists are usually her own alter ego, she says. She once identified herself with Madame Bovary, the tragic heroine of Gustave Flaubert's novel, who, suffering from social constraint, commits suicide in the end.[17]

To interpret the novel at a higher level of abstraction, is Takahashi taking the role of the "resisting woman,"[18] pushing back via a willful Michiko the boundaries imposed by the patriarchal society in which she lived? Is Takahashi openly challenging the traditional notion of a woman as good wife and wise mother? The "good wife, wise mother" concept (*ryōsai kenbo*),[19] deeply rooted in patriarchal practices, was given official encouragement in the 1890s by Japan's modernizing government as a way for women to contribute to nation building. The concept was given new emphasis in the 1930s as Japan mobilized for total war. In the postwar era, this "housewife feminism," as it was dubbed, became more assertive, arguing for (relatively superficial) social reforms such as consumer protection. It was challenged by a new "radical feminism" which promoted major redefinition of traditional gender roles, with the intent of altering core Japanese social values. Many of Takahashi's early works, like *The Wasteland*, reveal not just a dark inner self, but reflect similar virulent antisocial attitudes. Thus considered, Michiko is not a simple debauchee, but a heroine who shakes off the sacred mother myth by not having children and by using men for her own gratification. Takahashi would thus seem to fit in the radical feminism group.

On a yet higher level of abstraction, Takahashi may be telling us that without God, Everywoman will stumble into that wasteland and be destroyed by it. Do we not need God to speak to our hearts to prevent us from committing egregious errors, to keep us from walking dangerous paths? Michiko has

---

17. "'An-ya' o tōtte" (Passing through the "dark night") in *Takahashi Works*, vol 4, pp. 534–535.

18. For the "resisting woman," see Joan E. Ericson, "The Resisting Woman Writer," chap. 4 in Copeland, op. cit.

19. For the "good wife, wise mother," see Joan E. Ericson, "The Origins of the Concept of 'Women's Literature,'" in Paul Gordon Schalow and Janet A. Walker, eds., *The Woman's Hand: Gender and Theory in Japanese Women's Writing* (Stanford, CA: Stanford University Press, 1996), pp. 106–107, note 22; Julia C. Bullock, op. cit., pp. 2–3 and p.169, n.3; and Noriko J. Horiguchi, *Women Adrift: The Literature of Japan's Imperial Body* (Minneapolis: University of Minnesota Press, 2012), pp. 21–22 and passim.

occasional misgivings about the hurt she has inflicted on others and reservations about her lustful life, "gradually slipping morally downhill." When God, expressing himself through Hosea, says, "I will … speak to her heart," does Takahashi interpret this to mean that God will speak tenderly to Michiko, encouraging her, like Gomer, to abandon her life of sin? Probably not, for God, Takahashi asserts, does not speak to the self-satisfied living a life of plenty.[20] More likely, Hosea, as God's oracle, is actualized in the sympathetic voice of LifeLine, speaking tenderly to Sachiko. Michiko is apparently beyond salvation, but there still remains a chance for Sachiko.

It's a slim chance, though. The novel concludes with the heart-rending scene of Sachiko's dialing LifeLine, desperate to lay out her troubles. The stark hopelessness of these lines suggests that not merely Sachiko, but Michiko as Everywoman, will continue her moral descent to disaster. Sachiko cries,

"Hello? Will you please listen to me again today? Please listen. Oh, please listen …"

~

20. "Kono yo no 'arano,'" pp. 549–550.

Notes on the translation

In Japanese personal names, the surname is placed first and the given name second. That convention is followed here.

To protect the identity of people and places, the author often indicates place names by a single capital letter. I have discarded this usage as unnecessary and distracting, replacing the letter with the actual word or one that reads plausibly within the context. Thus, "S Station" becomes the actual Shinagawa Station (easily identified as such) and "R Hospital" becomes a hypothetical Riverview Hospital.

Arano (The Wasteland) was first published in 1980. The edition used for this translation was published by Kawade Shobō Shinsha, Tokyo, 1984.[1]

1. "Arano," by Takako Takahashi. © The Museum of Modern Japanese Literature. Kawade Shobō Shinsha, Tokyo, 1984.

Acknowledgment

The translator wishes to thank the California State University Emeritus and Retired Faculty and Staff Association for its generous financial support for this publication.

THE WASTELAND

One

NOBE MICHIKO HAD GONE OUT TO BUY A MAP OF TOKYO and was now back in her apartment. There was an address she had to locate.

It was the end of summer and, moreover, late in the afternoon, a time when she felt herself surrounded with things that were somehow particularly difficult to face. Such a feeling was not limited to the present. She had felt the same way since childhood. Wasn't that because, whenever a season or a day had come to its end, what had occurred up to then seemed to cling to her, to weigh upon her? She associated the feeling with having a burr in her throat, though a burr with neither color nor odor. All things must come to an end, and since nothing can be done about that, it gnaws away at one, she was thinking. As if intentionally to experience those sensations, then, she had gone out to a bookstore in the heat of the day to buy a map.

The streets were unfamiliar. It wasn't really necessary that she walk this route. There was a bookstore across from the train station nearby, but it was on a major east-west thoroughfare and large trucks continually rumbled by, so she decided to go to a bookstore located on a side street. On the way there, however, she actually did encounter a large truck. Only once previously had she come this way and there was nothing then, but now there was a large construction project going on. An old building was being torn down with something else apparently to be built in its place. A truck loaded with old plasterboard was attempting to leave the construction site. Trying to negotiate a tight turn into the narrow alley, the driver made repeated attempts, none successful. And so Michiko had no choice but to stop and wait. Yellow plaster dust was flying everywhere in the wind. The truck, the driver, the very ground itself all seemed to be in agony. Time and again Michiko had to wipe away her sweat. Then, for some reason or other, she felt a heavy anguish gradually overtaking her. What had been here before, Michiko did not know, for it was only the month before last, in July, that she had moved to Tokyo. This was the first time she had lived in Tokyo.

And yet, venturing out to buy a city map was not simply for the purpose of learning about streets now unknown to her.

When she returned to her comfortably air-conditioned apartment, her sweating began to ease. Recalling the yellow gusts at the construction site, she washed her hands and rinsed her mouth. Her hands and mouth were now clean, but she had the feeling those yellow gusts were still whipping about her, spreading out and covering all Tokyo with dust. The entire city was stained with the color of that dust.

Michiko took a jar from the refrigerator, poured out a cup of cold barley tea, and drank it down at a single stretch. She glanced at the wall clock—it was two minutes after four. The previous week her husband, Keitarō, had been sent abroad on business, so she had no worries about dinner preparation. For perhaps another week she could continue to live just as she pleased, eating what she liked when she liked. Yet during that week or so, before he returned from overseas, there was business that, one way or another, had to be attended to. It was business her mind dwelled on every single day. As if to get this preoccupation to recede into the distance, Michiko now left the map she had bought on the dining table and went into the bedroom and lay down on the bed face up.

She lay there vacantly. There wasn't anything in particular to do. Her husband was away, and in this great metropolis she had not a single friend.

When eventually she tired of lying down, Michiko got up and stood by the window, which looked out onto a large terrace. There was also a narrow balcony off the living room, but since the balcony closely fronted another apartment building, this was the only window where one could stand without being seen by others. The terrace, more than just large, was really too large—about the size of a twelve tatami-mat room. Such a terrace was attached to only this one apartment, which was at the far end of the building. Below it was the machinery room servicing the entire building, and its roof was put to use as this terrace.

The western sun was bursting in. The continued heat burned the concrete surface of the terrace like a frypan. Beyond there was nothing but building after building, the color of one differing from another, thus putting the entirety in discord. There was nothing resembling greenery, though one could see some garden plants in those private homes still remaining in the canyons between apartment buildings, but one could hardly call them green for they had been utterly wasted by heat and dust. Opening the window a crack, she felt the hot air instantly blow into her face, compelling her to close it immediately.

It was not a pleasant view, yet the bright reflection from the terrace nonetheless always hit her eyes. Scenes from the past floated up before her.

Wouldn't it be better not to have such an oversize terrace? I won't feel comfortable with it, Michiko had remarked the day they had moved in.

Really? I rather like it. Just because there is this terrace, I decided on this apartment, replied Keitarō. Apartment hunting had been entirely his affair.

It would be a perfect play area for children, though. But since we don't have children, then this ... And I really don't at all want children, continued Michiko with a pout.

Actually I have a splendid idea, said Keitarō, resuming a cheerful voice.

Michiko did not inquire.

Don't you think we could put a ping-pong table there?

Huh? And play ping-pong with whom?

Isn't it obvious? You and me, smiled Keitarō, patting Michiko on the shoulder.

Because Michiko did not actually say that it was a good idea or a bad idea, Keitarō before long sent for a ping-pong catalog. For several evenings after dinner he pored over details of color and style. He could have placed an order for it and made the purchase immediately, but since it was to be set up outside, a waterproof cover had to be specially made for it. That would take time. He concluded arrangements for having a cover made, and by the time he returned home from his two weeks abroad the ping-pong table and cover would probably have been delivered.

It was not that Michiko had any reason to dislike ping-pong itself.

Her eyes were fixed on the reflection of the western sun off the terrace as her thoughts wandered aimlessly. That's the way it was: the brightness gradually would die away and darkness would steal in, but until then the glare spread even more broadly across the sky, and this long day seemed to have no end.

Then there were dinner preparations she had to get through, even eating alone. The map of Tokyo was where she had left it, on a corner of the dining table. After dinner she again sat vacantly for a long time, elbows propped on the tabletop.

When night came, even with the aluminum-sash windows closed, the noise of the trains reached her ears. Their apartment was near Shinagawa station on the Tōkaidō line, a station where quite a number of routes converged. Both day and night the unending rumble of train traffic flooded in, but when night fell the sound became particularly grating. The trains passing through were coming from some distant place or going to some distant place, giving her the feeling that she was not here at all but somewhere else, and wherever that place might be, she had no special desire to visit it. The city of her birth, or the city where she grew up, or the city where she had lived for four years with Keitarō, or, thereafter, the city which she had occasionally visited when he was transferred and for two years living there alone—whatever the city, they were all places in the past, and, she thought, they were all borne on the noise of those gloomy heavy trains.

"Yes, yes, I've got to look at that map," said Michiko to herself.

She got up and went into the bedroom and took from a locked drawer a slip of paper on which an address was written, then went back to the dining table.

At last she took the map in hand.

It consisted of countless pages with a thick fold-up map of Metropolitan Tokyo at the front, which she was inspecting now for the first time. Opening it to the sound of crisp new paper, she was confronted with diversity and complexity, like a complicated schematic whose meaning she would somehow have to figure out. Innumerable tiny ant-like ideographs covered the map. Lines representing train routes, some straight others curved, ran out in all directions. There lurked on this dense fishnet-like surface a vertiginous exercise in futility for anyone trying to meet another, even if he did manage to slash through the netting.

She refolded the full-view map and then flipped through the panels ward by ward, opening it at Suginami Ward. That single ward was now spread out before her like a fishnet.

Finally the reason for her impression of a fishnet became apparent—the designations of the neighborhood precincts were marked everywhere. It seemed that the absence of any indication where one was to meet another amounted to an indication where one could not meet. In similar fashion the map booklet continued from one ward to another, each and every one having its own precincts, and each of those containing how many hundreds of residences, and in each of those residences there were how many people—a pattern which repeated itself endlessly over the map. It was not just that there was such a large number of marks, but that there was such a repetition of them. In Suginami Ward, there was Ogikubo district with its 1st precinct, 2nd precinct, 3rd precinct, 4th precinct, 5th precinct, and so on, and after that there was South Ogikubo district with its own 1st precinct, 2nd precinct, 3rd precinct, 4th precinct, and on and on.

Studying the slip of paper she had taken from the drawer, she figured out where the address was. Riverview Mental Hospital: such and such precinct, such and such district, Suginami Ward.

After that she began searching for the street block. Like a warplane circling overhead in search of its bomb target, she bent over the map, tracing across it with her right index finger. There was a special symbol to mark post offices. There was another symbol for high schools. She felt she was now becoming actively involved in that map, which up until just a while ago she had deliberately kept pushing to the back of her mind. Indeed, she thought, was she not in fact becoming rather obsessed about what she had all along been avoiding? There was a symbol for Shinto shrines. There was a symbol for tax offices. And then … yes, there it was, Riverview Hospital. There was no special indication that it was Riverview Mental Hospital.

As if she were actually walking there herself, her breath started coming in pants. She lifted her head from the map.

"Tomorrow, I'll go," she said aloud.

But what would be the best way to go? She had no idea. According to the map, by the looks of it the address of her destination was rather far from either the Ogikubo station or the West Ogikubo station or from the Asagaya station, all of them on the Central Line. Or, if she went either by subway or bus, what might be the best route to take? She had no friends whom she might ask.

So she spent yet another ten or twenty minutes studying the map. She sensed that the person whom she wanted to visit was getting buried in the mesh of the net. She ran her eyes over the map again, searching.

Finally it occurred to her to telephone the hospital and ask directions. She looked at her watch: it was already almost nine. A night watchman or somebody would probably be there to answer the phone. She looked up the number in the phone book, found it after a long while, and dialed.

"Hello?" A woman's voice answered.

"Hello … is this … Riverview Hospital?"

Michiko spoke very hesitantly. She had now suddenly become connected with that place, and, forced to confront her situation, she would do so. "I should like to come to the hospital tomorrow, so wouldn't you be kind enough to give me directions to it?" Conscious of her Kyoto accent, Michiko spoke in a very businesslike manner.

"You're an out-patient?" asked the attendant.

"An acquaintance of mine is staying there." The phrase "acquaintance of mine" pricked her like a thorn.

"Visiting, then."

"Yes."

"Visiting hours are afternoons from two until five, so if you come outside those hours, I'm afraid a visit would not be possible. Name, please?"

"Huh? You mean me?"

"The patient's name."

Michiko hesitated for a moment. Finally, "Murayama Kaori," she said.

It was acutely painful for her to utter the name. And yet, the reality behind the name was coming hazily into view. I don't want to remember, thought Michiko.

"That individual is no longer here," replied the attendant simply.

"What's that? She's recovered, then?" Having been discharged from the hospital, she might have gone anywhere at all.

"I have no information about that particular matter. In any event she's moved."

"Moved?"

"To another hospital."

Michiko asked the name of the new hospital, but the attendant didn't know. Inquiring further if there wasn't someone there who did know, the attendant replied that only she herself was there on night duty.

With a vague sense of having lost her bearings, Michiko hung up and just stood there. The object long weighing on her mind, which she had finally confronted, she felt now to be dissipating into a dense fog.

She stared at the map, still spread out on the table. She flipped through the panels—Suginami Ward, Shibuya Ward, Ōta Ward, Shinjuku Ward, Toshima Ward, Itabashi Ward … She looked, but without seeing. Every ward consisted of an enormous net, in appearance all alike, each proclaiming Tokyo to be a vast metropolitan expanse.

In any event, she was resolved to go to Riverview Hospital the next day to inquire about the situation. It then occurred to her, however, that she had forgotten to ask directions to the place.

She sat on the living room sofa and with nothing better to do she began thumbing through a women's magazine. Each and every page was covered with glorified objects appealing to self-indulgent women, giving her the feeling of something like a growling beast rising up from the pages. She soon put the magazine aside. She felt utterly exhausted.

After that, she simply sat there, sat there doing nothing.

The telephone rang, forcibly rousing her from where she had slumped down. Had she been just blankly sitting for two, even three hours? Without getting to her feet, she looked toward the telephone, just letting it ring and ring. She had not a single friend in Tokyo and it was unimaginable that anyone in Kyoto would be making an expensive long-distance call to her. Nor could she imagine that Keitarō had returned to Japan earlier than planned. Mechanically she counted the number of times the phone was ringing, and on the fifteenth she finally raised herself from the sofa. On the seventeenth ring she lifted the receiver. It flashed through her mind that perhaps Riverview Hospital was now calling to tell her the name of that other hospital, but since she had not given her name or telephone number, she realized it couldn't be that, and so without even saying a "Hello," she just kept the receiver pressed to her ear.

"Hello," came a man's voice, a voice, it seemed, straining to exude a bit of swagger.

There was a slight pause, and then the voice continued.

"This is LifeLine, isn't it?"

"What?" queried Michiko in return. This was altogether different from a caller who normally would say, Is this the Nobe residence, or, substituting some other name, Is this the So-and-so residence, and she realized that she had just heard a somehow very curious phrase.

"This is LifeLine, isn't it?" the man repeated.

"No," said Michiko. LifeLine—it was a phrase she had not heard before.

"This is 264-4343, isn't it?" the man continued.

"No; it's close though. This is ... 462-4343." Having only just moved to Tokyo she was still a little unsure of her own telephone number.

"Damn, I must have made a mistake," the man said, his strained voice instantly relaxing. "And I really did want to make this call. Well then, I guess I'll just have to hang up. I'm listening to someone with a different voice and so superfluous things are intruding between the LifeLine person and myself—that's what it's about."

"By 'different voice,' you mean my own?" For some reason or other Michiko felt inclined to respond to this caller.

"Yes," the man said somewhat sternly.

Though his tone possessed a certain youthful quality, to Michiko it seemed to fit more a person already in his thirties.

"What is this thing you call 'LifeLine'"? She really did want to know, and she was also interested in carrying on this phone call.

"What? What are you asking?" Caught off guard, the man seemed puzzled.

"What in heaven's name is this 'LifeLine' you're talking about?" Michiko was becoming obstinate.

"Why are you asking these kinds of questions?" The man was now on the offensive.

"I'd just like to know. It's an odd term."

"Hey look, I'm the one who mistakenly telephoned you. Ordinarily I'd just hang up. People are all busy because they're trying as hard as they can to manage their own affairs. It's that way just trying to put food on the table, and they're trying as hard as they can just getting along. That's the way it is. If you live in a place like Tokyo. But anyway, it was you who started this conversation. Here in the dead of night. What for?"

Two

"I'D REALLY LIKE TO KNOW."

"I don't know anything definite about LifeLine—its organization, its purpose. Really, I haven't the slightest idea about such things," said Sawamura Takuzō to the woman on the other end of the line.

"Isn't that what I've been saying?" he continued. "I'm trying as hard as I can just to get along. Everybody's that way. And you, when you walk the streets of Tokyo, don't you feel it? I go walking in places, whether it's Shinjuku or Shibuya or some other place where lots of people walk, and I often think that it does seem as if every one of them is carrying a piece of heavy luggage containing their inner being. In the case of women it's a handbag or a shopping bag, and in the case of men they're clutching an attaché case or file folder; and although it looks very appropriate, well, as I say, it's just camouflage. What they're really carrying is something quite different. And although it's heavy, they can't check it anywhere. And if they can't check it, I suppose it just gets heavier and heavier."

When Takuzō had spoken this much without pause, the woman on the other end uttered a vague "Ah." It was an utterance neither surprised nor restrained, but one which somehow commanded his attention. She was not a particularly young woman, thought Takuzō; he supposed her to be about his own age.

"As for me, for a long time now I've been following a regular discipline. Discipline of the mind, that is. By dint of that I ought to have reached certain objectives. And while there's no reason to say I've failed, it's gotten now to where the goals themselves have become vague."

With this, Takuzō realized that while he had intended to talk with LifeLine, he in fact was trying to strike up a conversation with this woman, whoever she might be. The woman said nothing, though she seemed to convey the impression she was listening. Her presence, he felt, was one not of vapid silence but rather of meaningful silence. Even such uncommunicative people as these would certainly respond to a LifeLine call if they received one, would they not?

"Actually, I've never spoken to anyone about these things before. A matter of discipline. Ever since I was in grade school, they've been going through my mind by fits and starts for about twenty years. And I've had plenty of social life. So there's no reason not to have had a friend I could talk to. And yet in talking with you like this for the first time, there's no doubt it's because I don't know you in the slightest. But more than just being somebody I don't know from somewhere I don't know, you don't even have face or form for me."

"But I do have a voice."

The woman finally said something.

"Yes, and that's a relief, all right. There must at least be a voice," said Takuzō.

"Yes, but a moment ago you said you had made a mistake and were listening to another voice. What you really seemed to be wishing for was someone with a pleasing voice. And mine just wouldn't do."

There was a bit of humor in the woman's voice.

"What do you mean, 'just wouldn't do?' I may have spoken a bit rudely earlier, but you have a very nice voice." Takuzō was aware that he seemed to be mouthing quite a line.

"Forgive me for not having the pleasing voice you wanted. It seems to me, though, that something must be seeping out through it."

"Huh? What a strange thing to say."

Takuzō felt like continuing the conversation with this unknown woman.

"Well then, so you think my voice is not pleasing?" said the woman, as if provoking him.

"It's not that at all. Didn't I say it was a nice voice?" Takuzō was at a loss how to respond.

"Because now I'm talking very politely. Because I'm being careful not to let something slip out."

"So what kind of voice is it, usually? Let me hear a bit of it, won't you?"

"Well! I certainly will not."

Whether that was to be taken as glum rejection or gay coquetry, the utterance was somewhat hoarse, and Takuzō was for a moment taken aback. And yet when her voice stopped short, he felt such feelings quite unwarranted, and that the woman was perhaps implying that she simply didn't like speaking too openly.

"Your voice now—that's the way it is," he ventured.

There was no reply.

Surrounded by the late night stillness, Takuzō suddenly felt oppressed.

The woman laughed. It was neither a laugh to lift his male spirits nor a laugh to make fun of him. It seemed to be a laugh turned around and directed at herself.

"Everyone is that way," she said, now resuming her argumentative tone of voice. "Whether one has a voice that projects or that is restrained, one speaks with a restrained voice quite without thinking about it."

"Yes, that's right."

It crossed Takuzō's mind that for this unique situation—this LifeLine—he felt fortunate that someone was listening to his restrained voice. He would try to convey that to the woman.

"Do you follow me?" she asked.

"What's called 'restrained,' that's probably just using reason. It might be called reasoning or social consciousness. How would it be if you just altogether set aside this restraint? Aren't there times when you're in such a mood?" said Takuzō, thinking that for himself recently things were extremely restrained.

"Well, that depends on the person," said the woman, assuming an unexpectedly decisive tone of voice.

"Why is that?" he asked, taking an increasing interest in the woman's reactions.

"Because when you let up on the brakes, something terrible can happen."

"What?" he queried, sensing he'd lost something of her train of thought.

"I know perfectly well."

"What is it you know?"

"Because I myself have sometimes let up on them."

"On the brakes?"

"But it's not that I'm speaking negatively."

"What is it? What are you referring to?"

Just as Takuzō was on the point of explaining LifeLine, he was bewildered by the unexpected flow of words coming forth from this woman. The woman apparently took "set aside this restraint" to have a different meaning.

"I'd really like to know more," he urged.

"Like desiring?" asked the woman simply.

"Who, you?"

"No; in general," said the woman, retreating.

"Well, haven't you somehow brought up these matters not just in general but about yourself?" Sawamura Takuzō was seized with an urge to know about the doings of this unknown woman.

"Well then, take for example an insane person—someone who has 'let up on the brakes.'" The woman was aware that she seemed to be exposing herself, and suddenly tried to avoid the subject.

"So you know someone who's insane," said Takuzō trying to pin her down.

"No, no … A hypothetical case." The woman's voice instantly stiffened.

"Oh," she said, changing the subject, "I just remembered. In Suginami Ward—what's the best way to get to … umm …"

"Where are you going?"

"I'm concerned because I don't know the route, and I have to go tomorrow."

"May I ask the name and address of the place you want to go to? It may be rather near where I live."

"Name? … Address?" she stammered. "Never mind," she went on. "I'll look them up myself and go there."

The woman suddenly turned cold. She said a good-bye and hung up.

Takuzō had the feeling that this changeable and utterly unknown woman kept lurking about his telephone and yet, he considered, she was after all a flesh-and-blood woman and was no substitute for some impersonal voice on LifeLine. As it turned out, he never did provide any explanation to the woman what this LifeLine was all about. When his eye fell to the memo pad next to the telephone, he saw 462-4343 written on it. The woman, correcting his mistake, mentioned her own telephone number, and he had absent-mindedly jotted it down.

He sat down on the sofa. The ashtray on the small table before him was heaped with cigarette butts from the previous day. He got up, grabbed another ashtray from atop the bookcase, and sat down again. In it too were five or six cigarette butts that had been lying there for more days than he could remember. That was not necessarily due to lazy housecleaning habits. It was in fact a reserve should he be seized with a craving in the middle of the night when he had run out of cigarettes, requiring a twelve- or thirteen-minute walk to the nearest vending machine. Not that twelve or thirteen minutes was so important but, remembering the days before the vending machine had been installed, that late-night craving would really get the better of him, so he had gotten into the habit of accumulating a few half-smoked remains. He poked his fingers into the ashtray, soiling them with ashes as he searched for a cigarette butt he could still smoke. He lit up a short one; the match flame leapt up, almost burning his lips. He smoked hurriedly, but as the smell of ashes and the odor of burning tobacco passed down his throat, that craving still kept its hold on him.

This evening there were fresh cigarettes. He lit one and inhaled the smoke. Stillness returned to this spacious and empty room—formerly a painting studio, it was said. Only the lamp on the writing table was lit, leaving the corners of the room cast in darkness, a darkness which continued into the gloom beyond the door. The ceiling light was not turned on, and with the table lamp providing the only illumination, the brightness of that one point of light seemed to diminish slowly into space—a sensation he rather liked. Contrariwise, the gloom beyond the door and the penumbra of the corners within the room collected toward the light of the lamp, and that one light source somehow seemed to become the central point of the universe. A hushed silence came over the entire universe, converging into that single point of light. And thus, his innermost self emerged. That self, he thought, would talk to LifeLine. He dials the number. Someone answers. Only voice can be heard. It is as if it were neither a man's nor a woman's voice, but a somewhat dehumanized voice and thus a voice which, as the woman had said, is "pleasing." Voice only; no face, no form. He knows utterly nothing of the person who produces the voice or what the room is like where the voice is produced. Indeed, there may not even be a room at all. Perhaps his call just goes to some vague open space.

He had learned of the existence of such a telephone service just a year or so ago at some snack bar, when he overheard a conversation of five or six boys and girls, high school students apparently, who were seated nearby. One of them happened to mention the telephone number, which had etched itself in his memory. Just to make sure, he looked it up in the telephone directory and it really was listed there. He thought that rather odd, because he was sure such a number would not be listed. Nonetheless, buried in the minutely detailed classified section of the Tokyo telephone directory, there was indeed an entry for this number. And although those high school kids were saying it was just personal advice by telephone, in Takuzō's imagination some other significance was attached to it.

Just now when quiet had returned to the night, with the sound of his breathing gradually becoming more and more the only impurity to be heard, he had the feeling he could endure it no longer, but when suddenly he tried dialing the number the feeling evaporated. It was probably on account of having just chatted with that woman.

Well then, he abruptly resolved, tomorrow he would try telephoning her again.

He had now finished his cigarette, which had taken a rather long time since he was not inhaling continuously. He went out into the hallway. Next to the toilet at the end, a small modular kitchen unit had been newly installed, where he now put on a kettle of water to boil. There was a toilet downstairs as well, which was available for the use of lodgers like him. The house entrance was shared by both lodgers and owner, but the toilet and kitchen upstairs were quite separate, so he rarely bumped into his landlord. For the two years he had been renting here, he'd been quite pleased with the arrangements. When the water came to a boil, he returned to his room, put in some tea leaves and added whisky.

Although he had said to the woman that he had meandered through twenty years of discipline, he realized on second thought that in fact it was not exactly twenty years.

To be precise, twenty-one years ago, that is to say, when he was eleven years old, he had an experience that affected him immensely. After the event had been entirely forgotten, it was unaccountably recalled to mind when he was a college sophomore. Indeed, that was the time when his discipline really began. And yet, doubtless even before then his discipline had been lying dormant. At eleven something like a seed seems to have been sowed within him.

On that day when he was eleven and a sixth grader, he was tracing his way back home after school. Walking for a while along a shop-lined street just beyond the school, he came to a section where nothing but poor homes were huddled together. His mother had warned him not to pass that way. There was another street which, though longer, was lined with large homes like his own, and his mother had told him she would "feel easier" if he would take that other route. Even among those large houses, his own home counted as one of the largest of them all. Why she had said "feel easier" he could not understand. In any event, he was disobeying his mother's instruction when he did sometimes walk through that poor section. He happened to be passing through there on that particular day. Walking just ahead of him was a boy two grades below him in school. The boy was from the poor section, though Takuzō did not know which house. Every so often they would come together as they walked along, but midway the boy left the narrow street of humble houses and veered into a side alley, barely wide enough for one person. Sewage oozing along the alley had the stench of rotten food. When Takuzō might brush by him, the boy had the same smell about him. The boy, walking a few steps ahead, stopped in front of a stationery shop. Previously there had not been a single store here but just recently someone from another area had come in and opened up this stationery shop. The boy was hunched over just in front of the show window peering in. Takuzō also walked up and stopped there and looked. Two different styles of toy autos were on display. Thinking back on it now, it was a period when Japan had just broken out of its postwar poverty, and in this neighborhood new shops of all kinds were appearing, apparently reflecting the trend of the times. Standing there side by side, the boy smiled sweetly at him. His face was full of joy. He then drew back from the window and casually stepped into the store, grabbed an eraser, slipped it into his pocket, and, not even rushing, continued walking at his previous pace. Astonished, Takuzō started out after the boy. How could the boy's guileless smile of a moment ago and his behavior just now be reconciled? Coming to the corner, the boy quickly turned into the street. A moment later when Takuzō turned into the street, the boy was crouched in front of one of the houses. He was scooping dirt out from an orange-crate placed next to the entrance in which morning glories were planted, making a spot to bury his eraser. Noticing his presence, the boy suddenly straightened up and ran off down the street. Startled by Takuzō's appearance, the boy hadn't done very well in hiding the eraser, which poked up out of the dirt. Takuzō stood there blankly, wondering why the boy didn't take the eraser home with him rather than hiding it in such a place as this. Only long after did he understand: at the boy's home quite a few family members would have been living in cramped quarters where there would not have been even a desk for the boy's own use and of course nowhere at all to hide things. But at the time, Takuzō just stood there next to the orange-crate of morning glories considering various explanations, when from behind him came a man's voice. The owner of the stationery store and a woman from the house opposite were standing there glaring at him. Their gaze alternated from his face to the eraser poking up from the dirt. Then they began yelling something at him. Due to the man's heavy regional accent and the shrillness of the woman's voice, he wasn't able to make out very well what they were saying, but that they were accusing him of stealing something was clear enough. The stationer dug out the eraser and thrust it before his eyes, and with fists clenched started hitting him hard on the head. For a moment Takuzō felt the entire world splitting asunder like a globe, with huge fragments flying everywhere. The pummeling came a second time and then a third. Why he suffered this beating in silence was something he thought about later. He resigned himself to the notion that it was a situation for which there simply was no explanation. It was certainly not as if he felt he'd martyred himself for the boy. What were his feelings at the time? He sensed he had become utterly naked, or rather, that he had been stripped naked by someone else. As the eldest son in a large family, a child in a household surrounded by caring parents and kind sisters, a good student with top grades, and a young man of clean-cut appearance, as a person, in short, blessed with every advantage, the attributes accorded to himself had been thoroughly stripped from him by this beating. It was as if his inner self were standing there alone, naked. It was not an agreeable feeling; it was cruel. It was a cruelty altogether different from other cruelties he had tasted in his life. Neither his explanations nor the resentment he felt toward the boy, the stationer, or the woman from across the street made sense any longer. The incident had not exceeded five or six minutes. Indeed, by small degrees his emotions cooled throughout the entire day, and by the following day he had almost completely forgotten about it. And so thereafter he slipped back into being a person blessed with every advantage and many attributes.

When he was a sophomore in college the incident was unexpectedly recalled to mind. He pondered it for some months. He could by that time understand a little better his mother's words about "feeling easier" if he walked only those streets lined with large homes. He understood that the meaning was different from what she had said. Thus, he chose to deny for himself the condition of "feeling easier." He resolved to strip himself of any extravagance that clung to him. This, then, was his self-proclaimed "discipline." It had continued from his sophomore year in college down to the present day. Now, approaching his apparent limits, he would come to a stop. And yet, why did there have to be limits at all? It was because of this that he had to carefully reconsider the point of departure and the course of a new life.

Three

EMERGING FROM RIVERVIEW HOSPITAL, NOBE MICHIKO walked toward the subway station. Following the directions she had been given, she turned left, then took the second right, and came out onto a main street.

Unexpectedly, as if she had walked into an extensive factory area, a cacophony of sound assaulted her from all sides, emphasizing the secluded residential location of the hospital. When she had come to the hospital, she had gotten off at Ashikaga station on the National Line and then had taken a bus, after which there was quite a long walk. For the return, however, she was told it was better to use the subway, so she was now following a different route on her way back. Yet this return route was so very similar that she almost wondered if she hadn't made a mistake. A certain sameness in the scene persisted throughout and it oppressed her, both going and on the return.

Everything erodes, she mused, each according to its nature. Even a city, where some single phenomenon dominates, will deteriorate. And because the city was deteriorating, she too, as she walked along, seemed to be deteriorating.

Tokyo was the only place that made her feel this way. She felt it continuously ever since moving here, and she felt it all the more as she made this trip to and from Riverview Hospital. The unceasing flow of traffic on the main streets, the frightening din pounding her ears, construction sites everywhere, the dust, the filth. In addition, there was the sameness of the office buildings, the sameness of the residential homes, the sameness of the streets. Even just walking along she had the feeling that she was not encountering humans at all. What she was really encountering were people being swallowed up by their environment.

Let me find my way quickly to the subway station, she thought, hastening her pace. Catching sight of the subway sign across the street, she started across on a pedestrian overpass.

A hot wind blew up from below and her skirt billowed out. She stopped in the center of the bridge and stood there absentmindedly. She was in mid-air while below her all that could be seen was a thundering river of flowing metal. Malodorous exhaust wafted upward in bilious impurity.

Finally she boarded a Shinjuku-bound subway. As the train pulled out from the station, she heaved a sigh of relief, and began recalling the interaction at Riverview Hospital.

I was told that the person whom I had thought to meet is no longer here, but I still should like to learn of her present whereabouts, which is why I have come here.

So she had inquired, speaking in a roundabout way without even mentioning her own name.

And what is the patient's name, please? asked the receptionist mechanically.

Murayama Kaori.

Forced to mention the name somehow irritated a festering sore, so she hardly wanted to utter it at all. Nonetheless, she simply had to do it. Yes, there are things in this world that simply cannot be ignored. That name was becoming like a knife sewn into her flesh.

Mura … yama … Kao … ri. Hmm. As the receptionist pronounced the name she bent over the register and leafed through it. Not finding the name she went out a door at the back of the office and returned with another register.

Michiko's gaze drifted to the waiting room. Seven or eight people were seated in chairs waiting their turn. If they were not visitors, they must be out-patients, she thought. They did not seem to be mentally ill, and to all appearances they were no different from people one sees on the street. As she looked at them, the very name Murayama Kaori kept her heart pounding. Having finally come this far there could be no turning back.

Here it is, said the receptionist. Edgewood Hospital in Yashio City. She moved this spring on April 22, according to the entry.

Why did she move? queried Michiko.

Doesn't say, replied the receptionist, her eyes still on the register.

It must have been very serious, then? said Michiko somewhat hesitantly.

And who are you, ma'am? The woman abruptly raised her eyes and looked straight at Michiko.

Michiko felt she was under something like an interrogation, so she let it all out in a rush.

The person in question, Murayama Kaori, is my elder sister. She'd been living in our hometown, but she ran off to Tokyo by herself and after that I heard she'd been admitted to this hospital. I've only recently moved to Tokyo, so this is the first time I've come to visit her.

You must be very troubled, the receptionist said, her gaze softening.

Troubled ...? Well, um, troubled ...? Michiko stammered, taken aback that the receptionist should have inflicted anything like "troubled" upon her. Such manner of talk was simply not done.

The receptionist suggested asking the physician in charge about the patient's condition, but, after getting directions to Edgewood Hospital in Yashio, Michiko immediately left.

Michiko had used the expression "the person in question," aware that she was trying to keep her emotional distance.

Shinjuku station was announced and Michiko stepped out onto the platform.

Although it wasn't rush hour, there was a wave of tightly packed people heading toward the stairway from the subway platform. At street level even more people were crowding around the wickets to the National Railway, while other crowds of people swept along the passageway beyond the wickets. What might those people be doing? All seemed as active, indeed as ferocious, as wild animals. Each person was advancing singlemindedly in his particular direction. Just a while ago on the way to and from Riverview Hospital she had the feeling that she hadn't encountered anyone, whereas here, to the contrary, there was nothing but people. Were they not like beasts of the forest, urged by hunger, swarming from their crowded lairs in search of food?

Michiko separated herself from the human wave and pushed through the wicket toward the private Odakyū Line and bought a ticket for Yashio City. She had been told that the special express did not stop there. Somewhat confused, she managed to find a local express; she boarded and the train soon pulled out.

Even so, had she not been compelled to pass tediously all over the landscape from her apartment to far-off Riverview Hospital, and now again tediously from there to Edgewood Hospital, located in some little town?

When she got off the train at the station she had been told, there was a relaxed suburban-like atmosphere, and she felt a refreshing breeze blowing in on her. Yet, when she emerged into the open and walked along the shadeless streets, the late summer sun baked her as if her face were bent over a pot of boiling-hot tempura oil. Because of this year's interminable heat a lassitude had accumulated in the very landscape.

A pine grove came into view ahead. She had been told to turn right just before it.

As she approached the hospital building, emotions welled up within her much as they had shortly before at Riverside Hospital. The people in there were humans, but humans who had lost their humanity because, she thought, they were imprisoned. It was all very well to say that having utterly lost their humanity they had become birds or lions or some such. Still, they were after all humans at bottom, and as humans there were a great many instances where one could communicate with them.

Edgewood Hospital differed from the concrete structures of Riverview Hospital. It was of wood construction, just as in the old days, with white-painted clapboard. From a pine woods in back came the leaden noise of locusts sounding en masse.

At the reception window she announced quite clearly this time that she had come to visit her sister, Murayama Kaori. But the receptionist replied that they had no patient by that name. She went in back to look it up, and soon returned with the information that no such person had ever been here.

Michiko was bewildered. She had spent half the day getting here, and now had the sensation of being suddenly swallowed up by that very expanse of land she had traversed. Standing there, Michiko felt she had lost her way.

The quiet sound of slippers drew near.

"Excuse me ..." came a drawling voice.

Michiko looked around. Standing there was a middle-aged woman, who just a moment ago was seated on a bench. With a pleasant, knowing expression, she caught Michiko's eye.

"I believe you're referring to Mrs. Yamakusaki Kaori," said the woman to Michiko.

"Really?" said the receptionist speaking from behind her window to the woman.

"You see, I was Mrs. Yamakusaki Kaori's roommate. After recovering I was discharged and now I come here as an out-patient." The woman, with that same expression in her eyes, was speaking not to the receptionist but to Michiko.

"Yamakusaki ...," mumbled Michiko. It was a name she hadn't heard before. She knew that during her sister's marriage she was Sanada Kaori, but apparently she was no longer using that name.

"There's no doubt about it. When she was admitted to this hospital she changed her name." The woman patient spoke with a confident voice.

"But I was told she had moved from Riverview Hospital," said Michiko.

"In the case of Mrs. Yamakusaki, yes, that's what she did," said the receptionist, checking the register.

"Yes, yes, that's exactly it," the woman burst in excitedly.

And with that outburst, Michiko wondered, wasn't that woman's former insanity erupting again? She fixed her eyes on her.

"I'm quite familiar with the situation." Having calmed herself, the woman began explaining. "This Mrs. Yamakusaki was constantly saying someone was pursuing her, so she left the previous hospital and came fleeing here. In order that the person who was after her wouldn't be able to find out about her, she went so far as to change her name. She appealed to the doctor, who let her make the change."

"So who was this person who was pursuing her?" queried Michiko, feeling very troubled.

"A woman, she said."

"What sort of woman?"

"She wasn't very clear about that. It was a woman, but apparently a person without eyes or nose or mouth, she said. An abstraction, she said. And yet, it really was pursuing her, she said." The woman paused a moment, then continued, "How odd. I mean us. I've already recovered, at least I think so. But she, she was positively tormented."

"Yes, I understand," said Michiko. "Anyway, I just wanted to know where she was living. Well, then," she said, addressing both the woman and the receptionist, "I'll be leaving now," and she left the hospital.

She walked blankly along the hot street heading back in the direction of the station, accompanied by the thought that this woman without eyes or nose or mouth was Michiko's own affair. The leaden sound of the locusts from the pines behind carried across to her. It was as if one could hear the moaning of the people confined in that sanatorium.

She again took the Odakyū Line and got off at Shinjuku. Thinking she'd eat out and then return home, she walked about in the neighborhood of the station, but there were so many restaurants and cafés packed together she simply couldn't make up her mind which one to enter. And so she walked around for nearly an hour, finally going into a cheap Italian eatery. Compared with the appetizing models in the display window, the real thing tasted awful. Insipid like her own insides, she reflected. Leaving the place and walking toward the station, it occurred to her to have some fruit to cleanse her mouth. But there was such a plethora of snack bars she couldn't make a choice. The one she finally ventured into was crowded with men and women whose expressions gave no hint as to what they were thinking. When she had finished a fruit salad with its syrupy red dressing, she once again had the feeling that the same red color was dying her very insides.

As soon as she emerged from the snack bar with its frigid air-conditioning, she had the feeling that the city was suffering from a virulent fever. Wiping away her sweat, she headed toward the station. Every year in September cool breezes begin to blow, but this year the midsummer heat persisted, and according to weather forecasts there was no end in sight.

And so she walked along, rather unsteadily, yet not a single man approached her. She was inwardly depressed, that was the reason. What was the point of a man's being sexually alert if at such a time as this he never approached her. But if she could project an aura of warmth, surely any number of men would hail her.

Yet, if even in so bustling a quarter as Shinjuku Michiko tried to attract men's attention, at nearby Edgewood Hospital, her sister, with quivering antennae extended, would instantly sense it and would almost certainly never forgive it.

"Oh these entanglements—how troublesome they are!" cried Michiko aloud, as she melted into the noisy crowd.

She took the National Line from Shinjuku, and twenty minutes later when she had arrived at her apartment the telephone was ringing. As she was about to pick it up, after ringing for how many times, it stopped.

She changed into a housedress, washed her hands with soap and water, and rinsed her mouth. The phone rang again. As she picked up the receiver the previous evening's caller suddenly came to mind. It couldn't possibly be, she thought, but it was indeed the same voice. Not that she didn't have a premonition since, after all, perfect strangers have struck up very personal conversations with each other.

"I'm the person who called you last night. Is it all right to phone again? If you object I'll end the call immediately. But I think you won't object," said the man rather brazenly. His manner may have been brazen but his voice had a certain decency to it.

"This isn't LifeLine," said Michiko laughing lightly.

"You're living alone, aren't you. You answered the phone yesterday, and today too. Just now I telephoned twice but no one answered," said the man with that same brassy tone.

Indeed, Michiko was not displeased. After all, she had just spent the entire day running back and forth and was now feeling quite at a loss.

"I do have a husband," she replied. Asserting she had a husband did in no wise extinguish her feeling of being quite at a loss.

"At any rate, he's not there now, is he." Being informed that there was a husband did not alter the man's style of speech.

"He works for a trading company and he's in the U.S. now on business. Nor are there children. I've just moved to Tokyo so I don't have any friends either. There's no one. I'm quite alone."

To this unknown man, whom it was inconceivable she would ever meet face to face, Michiko, who as a habit would never talk to strangers about her personal circumstances, was now actually saying such things as "I'm quite alone".

"Yes, I know," he said provocatively.

Was this man being reckless, or was he just self-confident about women? If the latter, then she would surely be self-confident about herself, she thought, so Michiko charged her own voice with the strength to push back.

"And what makes you think you know that?"

"It's perfectly clear, isn't it? Aren't you responding for as long as you like to this kind of phone call from a perfect stranger like me? You don't consider me impolite. It was this way yesterday, and it's this way today as well."

"So?"

"Actually, it's the same with me, too."

"Really?"

"Look. It's that tone of voice of yours. It seems you're very interested in me so you're asking all these questions."

"Yes, I do have some interest, in men."

"What a wonderful thing that is. When I said, 'it's the same with me,' I meant that I have no one to talk with either."

"Nonsense! I don't believe it."

"I've got a lot of friends. But even so, I'm the person who had to dial LifeLine yesterday. Unfortunately, or perhaps I should say fortunately, instead of getting LifeLine, you answered. This LifeLine or whatever—it's only people at the end of their rope who dial it. At the end of their rope … What this all means is, I look upon you as a very understanding person."

"What is this LifeLine?"

"Let's meet and I'll explain it to you."

"Meet?"

"Let's meet and talk. It certainly can't hurt you any." And, in his high-handed manner, he decided the time and place.

Four

MURAYAMA KAORI WAS LISTENING INDIFFERENTLY to the sound of the locusts coming from the pine grove. With her futon pushed up against the wall and her pillow rolled up into a bolster, she had sunk to the tatami and was now just sitting there. From time to time she would cast a glance at Takeda Miyo.

Sitting on her own futon with her back hunched forward, Takeda Miyo had been sobbing the entire afternoon. It was the fault of the locusts. The coming of summer brought the sound of locusts from the pines, day after day after day, and though it was now early autumn, summer seemed still at its height and the sound of the locusts had not abated.

Turn off that noise, Takeda Miyo would say to the nurse every day.

It's not noise, it's the sound of the locusts, the nurse would reply.

If you'd just turn off that noise for me, she would plead, I could live. Please, please.

How many times do I have to tell you. It can't be turned off—they're locusts. If summer ever ends, they'll stop of their own accord. The nurse answered patiently the same way every day.

Let me live!

That's exactly what you're doing.

No, there's a limit to what I can listen to, and I can't take it any more. I'll die!

Now, now, stop whimpering like that. Pull yourself together. Finally the nurse would scold her in a stern tone of voice.

Sometimes the nurse would appeal to Murayama Kaori, who was in possession of her faculties, to lend support.

Well, that's so, isn't it. There are some things in this world that simply can't be turned off—like the sound of locusts or the soughing of the wind. There's just nothing that can be done about it. Period.

And with that, Murayama Kaori put on a smile.

I guess so, Takeda Miyo would blubber; there's nothing to be done about it, and precisely because there's nothing to be done about it, it's cruel, and the fact, as she says, that no one, however kind a person, can turn off the sound of the locusts that's tormenting me so much is really quite dreadful, whereas, say, if you find the sound of a person's talking to be objectionable and you complain about it the person talking should be kind enough to stop talking, or, say, the music is playing too loud and you find it objectionable so you complain, someone should be kind enough to switch it off … but the sound of those locusts is a matter of a different sort, isn't it, and if even the kindest person would climb the tree and kill one locust, it wouldn't change the situation in the slightest, because there are dozens or even hundreds of them and they'd still go on buzzing, buzzing away every day as long as summer lasts, and there's nothing to be done about these summer days themselves, and because you can't cool off the weather by splashing water up into the sky, there's nothing to be done about having summers, and as long as there are summers there is nothing to be done about locusts … yes, that's right, even given the power of mankind there is nothing to be done. And with that, Takada Miyo pulled the covers over her head trying to fend off the noise.

Sometime during the course of this soliloquy the nurse had disappeared.

Murayama Kaori heard the sound of the locusts, though without really listening. Along with the buzzing sound that ascended to the heavens, she too had the feeling that she was somehow expanding upward into the heavens, and so she settled down.

Uji Kyōko, unmindful of the heat, was snuggled into her quilt asleep. Facing away and curled up with her small fanny just a lump of roundness, it hardly appeared, even though a wisp of her hair poked out the top, that anyone was actually sleeping there. After all, the futon, the quilt, and the pillow were all bundled up inside white covers with not a bit of color showing. The whiteness of everything had always bothered Murayama Kaori. The walls and the ceiling were white, too. There was a resemblance to the white attire of a corpse.

"You have a visitor, Mrs. Yamakusaki," the nurse announced. "It's Mrs. Yoshino."

"Really. How very unusual."

Murayama Kaori rose to her feet. Yoshino Masako had occupied this room prior to Takeda Miyo's admission at the beginning of summer. Masako, now an outpatient, apparently came by every week, though she rarely talked with Kaori.

When Kaori reached the reception room she found Yoshino Masako standing there, wearing a red skirt and white blouse. Such a garish red, as if fluorescent paint had been added to it, particularly displeased Kaori. In general, red and white simply formed too sharp a contrast.

"Although I'm in a rush, there is a small matter I'd like to inform you of," said Masako rapidly, without even taking a seat.

"You seem well. Isn't that a wonderful skirt!" Murayama Kaori mouthed the words with a smile.

"Just a moment ago somebody came to visit you," whispered Masako, drawing up close, "but she has already left."

"Who might that have been?" The image of a man flashed across Murayama Kaori's mind, yet who it might have been was hard to say, for the image was simply that of a male, nothing more.

"So you have a younger sister, do you. I hadn't known anything at all about that."

"Oh? Sister?" The world seemed to come crashing down upon her.

"Good heavens, what's come over you?"

"My sister? What did she say?"

"That your being here put her at ease. And that she would go back without seeing you."

"What was my sister wearing? What shade of lipstick was she using?"

"What's come over you, Mrs. Yamakusaki. You're behaving rather queer."

"Queer? They say we're all queer, and so we are. Is there anyone here who's not queer?" Murayama Kaori had the feeling she was becoming hysterical.

"You don't look like her very much. The eyes are different. You've got narrow single-fold eyelids, while your sister has large double-fold eyelids. And you're very light skinned, while your sister seems a bit pasty in complexion. So you're the prettier of the two. And yet your sister is … how shall I put it … is more attractive to men. She doesn't really stand out, but there is something about her that seems coquettish." All this Masako said in a rush as she was moving toward the doorway.

"Attractive to men?"

Murayama Kaori snatched at Yoshino Masako's handbag.

"Hey, what are you doing? Don't startle me like that. You're like a great big frog lunging at me. And right now your eyes look like a frog's."

Yoshino Masako hurriedly headed toward the door.

"That woman," said the receptionist, who had overheard Masako's remarks, "—something seems to be happening to her again. I saw it just now. She certainly had a strange look in her eye. I'll report it to the nurse."

Murayama Kaori suddenly felt herself getting depressed. In that state she walked along the corridor back to her room.

White futons in a white room: it looked inordinately abstract. Curled up on one of the futons, Uji Kyōko; seated weeping upon another, Takeda Miyo. It was the same scene as a moment ago, but now devoid of all human semblance. Murayama Kaori slowly settled herself down onto the tatami.

"It's starting up all over again," she said aloud.

She felt as if her head were drooping, drooping lower and lower. It seemed to droop right down inside her, where it opened out onto an unlimited space. A moment ago she had felt the world was crashing down upon her, but in fact that was just an event taking place inside herself. And then there opened up a bottomless pit. She entered it as if duty bound. It was frightful, perfectly frightful. Not that she felt any particular object to be frightening; the fright, rather, was that her own contours were dissolving and disappearing. And although her contours were disappearing, she herself still existed, indeed an ever more substantial self existed. From then on, that same scene appeared before her endlessly.

The scene was a theater and, though the seats were closely arranged to accommodate a large audience, no one was present. She was alone, seated stage center. She had no desire to be there; she had been coerced into being there. Her freedom had vanished; she was unable to stand up or to flee. The stage was bright to the point of over-illumination. There were three characters on stage—one actor and two actresses, and one of the actresses was herself. The man she sensed to be highly abstract, and the other woman even more so. She had no memory of either, but the two nonetheless seemed curiously familiar.

The play begins.

I'm tired of you, the man says to Kaori.

I don't know why, she replies. It's not even a year since we've been married. Finally we were able to start living together, weren't we?

Suddenly I've gotten tired of you. I'm sorry.

But I really would like to know the reason. As a wife I have the right to know.

Right? Right as a wife? No, not a single individual has the right to interfere—not parents, not wife.

I can't stand this. What on earth do you mean? Tell me! Talk, I'm listening!

I don't care to talk about it. Rather, I can't talk about it. I'm confused. If I talk about it, I'll get even more confused.

What in heaven's name is it?

A scalding whirlpool. I'm trapped in a scalding whirlpool.

What! Coming up with something so preposterous as that will drive me crazy. I hate nonsense explanations like that. If you won't talk reasonably, I can't stand it.

Do you want me to give you an explanation you can understand? Do you really want me to?

A strong spotlight comes on, and a solitary woman floats up on the stage.

I lost my heart to her, said the man, motioning toward the woman. I'm sorry. There is nothing to be done about it.

Who is she? asks Kaori.

Isn't she someone you know quite well?

No, I don't know her.

Really? If that's the case, it's just fine. Let me introduce you. I think you'll know her. Her name is ...

"Ow!" Murayama Kaori cries out, for just then an electrically charged terror settles over the entire theater, and the charge increases by the moment. Although both dialogue and action become totally abstract, there is a strong sensation of reality.

The play continues.

You love me, don't you, the man says to the woman.

The woman does not reply.

You do love me. Even though you don't say so right out.

The woman still does not reply, but glances skyward and smiles. That smile is like a momentary flash of light and spreads across the entire stage.

How dare you to have done such a thing as this! says Kaori to the woman.

What do you mean, "such a thing as this?" I do live here, you know, says the woman, finally addressing Kaori.

Kaori is dumbstruck.

If such a thing were not permitted, I'd have no other choice but to end my life.

Having said that, the woman walks off stage.

The man follows her.

Kaori is riveted in place.

The stage darkens. Soon a bell rings. Then the curtain rises. There are three characters on stage. The same play is performed in its entirety just as before.

The play ends, the bell rings again, and then the performance begins. The sequence repeats itself. Three times, four times, five times …

Without her being conscious of it, everything had become extremely blurry, and Murayama Kaori dropped off to sleep. She was only vaguely aware that the nurse jabbed a hypodermic needle into the fleshy part of her shoulder.

Well, then. There's nothing to be done about it, and yet, precisely because there's nothing to be done about it, it's so cruel, and being in agony over it, the fact that not even the kindest man can stop that play is positively frightening, and even supposing some kindly person just did lower the curtain so the play couldn't be seen, the situation wouldn't change in the slightest, because for me at least whether the curtain is down or not, the whole thing is very visible, and so long as I exist that play is inside of me, and actually for some things, there is nothing to be done about them. I have been seized by something which human power can do nothing about, and so there is hardly any point in clinging to some kindly person.

As Murayama Kaori was muttering her monologue, she began to emerge from her drowsiness. It was already evening by the time she was fully awake and refreshed. Both the white room and the white bedding had become the color of diluted ink. Kaori had been sleeping on her own futon, probably spread out for her by the nurse.

"Were you having a dream?" asked Takeda Miyo, who had stopped weeping.

"No, it wasn't a dream."

Kaori shook her head. Even though she said it was not a dream, it certainly did seem like a dream, and somewhere vaguely within her there was something ebbing away, like a receding tide. Although she could still scoop up the fragments, they had already lost their electric charge.

"You were talking a lot about something or other," continued Takeda Miyo, who was as yet unaccustomed to hospital life.

"It's nothing. Really, it's nothing," said Murayama Kaori with a smile.

"I suppose so. Are you sure you're okay?" With puffy eyes Takeda Miyo looked at her anxiously.

"Quite aside from that, it's you who ought to be feeling more comfortable because the sun's already gone down and the locusts have stopped."

Kaori felt herself to be very considerate toward others.

"Locusts?"

Takeda Miyo looked at her wide-eyed. With her change in facial expression, her youth became apparent. She was four or five years younger than Kaori.

"They've stopped making noise now. Do calm down."

And the play is not starting up again, so do calm down, she told herself at the same time.

"The locusts were making noise, you say?" asked Takeda Miyo.

"No, no. There aren't any locusts." Kaori restrained her with her hand.

"Would you care for some rice crackers?"

Takeda Miyo held out a large paper bag of rice crackers.

"But it's already dinner time," said Kaori, taking a few crackers that Miyo generously offered.

"Have some, Mrs. Uji," said Miyo to Uji Kyōko, who was curled up on her futon.

No answer.

"She's always sleeping," said Miyo glancing at her meaningfully.

Murayama Kaori was not very familiar with the circumstances of Uji Kyōko's having moved here from another room about two weeks ago. Previously the two saw each other from time to time in the dining room where all the patients took their meals together, and the color of Kyōko's pellucid eyes had left a particular impression on Kaori.

"I've just eaten a whole bagful. And yesterday I ate three bags," said Miyo, smiling listlessly.

"One bag alone would seem to be bigger than your stomach," returned Kaori with a smile, as she nibbled a cracker.

"There's nothing to do here except eat," said Miyo, as if talking to herself.

"That's right. There isn't anything to do here," chimed in Kaori agreeably. And, she thought, having nothing to do formed the content of her present existence. Indeed, it was no more true in the entire world than in this very place that there was nothing to do. If it were a physical ailment, then the patient would work together with the doctor to achieve recovery, and the results of their efforts would be observable to the eye. But a mental illness was different. Whether the patient improves or deteriorates depends solely on the illness.

"Yesterday my sister was kind enough to come for a visit and she gave me these." And Miyo held up a bag of crackers.

Kaori endured the use of the word "sister." That was as much an effort as she could make.

"My sister's name is Sachiko, and she's just fourteen," continued Miyo, quite without regard for Kaori's feelings, "but she has a part-time job, and so she's made some money and gives me as much as she can." Miyo's face seemed to reflect deep happiness, and she closed her eyes behind puffy eyelids.

"There's nothing to be done about it, you said?" repeated Kyōko, as she raised herself up.

Kaori and Miyo exchanged glances.

"I wasn't sleeping at all. I'm never sleeping or anything like that. I live in so spacious a place here that it's beyond all comparison. So sometimes I meet people," said Uji Kyōko. But whom she met she did not say.

Five

RETURNING HOME FROM HIS PART-TIME JOB at a department store, Sawamura Takuzō stopped on the way to have supper, after which he would spend the evening in his room. There was a period once when he did not read at all, but recently, because disorder had somehow intruded upon his life of discipline, he had taken to reading philosophy and religion. Could it be, perchance, that disorder existed from the beginning? He needed to recall the beginnings of his discipline, and he wanted someone to fill the role of listener. It was for this reason that he had suddenly got it into his head to dial LifeLine. He felt that for him, the real him, such matters as these were more embarrassing than nakedness. He could hardly speak to a perfectly visible person about them, he thought.

Passing along the narrow walk from the front gate to the entrance of his lodging house, he could see his own room and he had the feeling that someone was there, but in the entranceway there were the shoes and sandals only of the people who lived in the place. And yet when he went into his room it was clean and tidy, a sure indication that someone had just been there. Looking around, a plate of sushi rolls, homemade it would seem, had been left on the table. There was a hastily written note.

Gone out to get some things I forgot to buy. Be back shortly.

Muro Sawako

Its penmanship was careful and the wording conveyed sincerity. There certainly was no awkward formality here; rather, there was an appealing tenderness in the overall effect. And Muro Sawako herself was perfectly reflected in her writing. But then he'd never had much opportunity to see her writing. She always telephoned from her place or came over to visit. Even if he said please don't come, she would come. And even if he got angry on such occasions, she'd just dismiss it with a laugh.

Reflecting thus, Takuzō recalled to mind another woman.

Yesterday evening at eight he was waiting for that woman in a coffee shop. He did not even know her name, nor did he know the features of her face or figure. He had told her he would be sitting by the window on the first floor. He had also said he was a man in his thirties and would be wearing a dark-colored sport shirt. But the woman never showed up.

Now Takuzō suddenly got the idea to telephone the woman again before Sawako returned from her errand. He would invite her to meet at the same place tonight at nine o'clock. Accordingly, he dialed immediately, figuring if it was worth doing, it should be done without delay. He could sense that her mere existence was somehow a good thing for him. He felt that the woman seemed to be opening up something within himself.

"Hello?" said a familiar voice.

"Hello," said Takuzō, hoping she would recognize his voice.

There was a momentary silence.

"I'm sorry about last evening," she said.

Takuzō was amazed. Because there were few women who on the spot would accept an invitation by an unknown man to go out on a date, one might think it only to be expected that the woman break the engagement.

"Well, you intended to come, then?" he inquired, somewhat encouraged.

"No," she said flatly.

Takuzō, buoyed by the remark "I'm sorry about last evening", realized that she was going to be difficult to deal with after all.

"I'm not in very good spirits these days," she said in a way that seemed not to be mere excuse, "so it wouldn't have been very enjoyable even if we had met."

"Not in good spirits? What's the matter?" asked Takuzō, who felt from the very beginning warm feelings developing toward this woman. Perhaps it could be ascribed to the magical power, so to speak, possessed by the telephone, since it linked him directly to an unknown person. The fact that he knew nothing about this woman posed no obstacle; rather, not knowing anything about her was fortunate, for it enabled them both to express their unvarnished feelings.

Yes, that was it. He sensed strongly that he would like to meet this woman and let her hear him talk about discipline. Having to some degree already revealed his inner self to her, this would probably be possible.

"Yes, something is the matter," she said rather mysteriously.

"Would you like to tell me what it is?"

"It would take hours to talk about it. No, it would take days. If I were to write about it in a letter, it would be hundreds of pages long. How can I talk of such things in just a word?"

"Yes, of course," he interjected. He could probably say the same thing about his own discipline, too. Nonetheless there would be nothing irksome in talking about it even if it took days, since for that duration they would continue to meet.

A noise came from the entranceway; he looked around to see if Sawako had returned. No, apparently it was the landlord's wife going out, and indeed a moment later her yellow blouse, reflected in the afterglow of the evening sky, could be seen as she walked along the narrow path to the gate.

Takuzō regretted he had chosen this constricted time before Sawako's return for making such an important phone call as this.

"If you're not in very good spirits again today, we really wouldn't be able to manage to meet at nine this evening at Sakura Coffee Shop?" he said, inviting her.

No reply. Finally, after a long pause, "Well, then, shall we decide on that?" she said.

"Oh? Then you're coming?"

"Anything's acceptable to me, so I might just as well go," she said, and, assuring him she would be there, hung up.

Immediately thereafter the phone rang, and Takuzō picked up the receiver.

"I'm back now," came the voice of Okada Heisuke.

"Indeed you are!" replied Takuzō. At the same time he recollected Heisuke was a man who invariably telephoned whenever he returned, and yet granting he had indeed returned, there was absolutely no way of knowing from where he had returned and where he was now.

"While you were away," said Takuzō, "I had a dream about you. As I was walking along what seemed to be a subway platform, you came hurrying from the opposite direction. It was that usual broad and bouncy stride of yours. I had the definite feeling that it was a large Tokyo subway station, though not a soul was about. You were carrying a briefcase or something squeezed under your arm. It seemed to be square, thin, and light. 'Hey!' you called out with a wave, but you walked past without even pausing. I had the feeling you were just floating on by. Struck by some inexplicable emotion, I turned back to look. What seemed to be the subway platform disappeared into the distance, and I could see you walking off with those great bouncy strides. You were visible for the longest time."

"Really? Is that so," Heisuke exclaimed somewhat breathlessly.

"Because you are kind of always that way."

"You didn't dream that, aren't you just making it all up?" said Heisuke with a laugh.

"Really, I dreamt it."

Takuzō recalled the sharp contrast of that vast Tokyo subway station as it swallowed up Heisuke's small retreating figure.

"So what exactly do you think I was carrying in that briefcase?" asked Heisuke, catching him by surprise.

"Yes, I was thinking myself I really ought to try to figure that out."

Takuzō had been acquainted with Okada Heisuke for about a year now, but still knew nothing about what he did. In age they were about the same or perhaps Heisuke was a bit older, though he looked younger.

"I think you must know," said Heisuke with a laugh, "because otherwise I wouldn't go to the trouble of always telephoning you." It was his vague way of expressing himself.

"I'll regard it as homework," said Takuzō. "A hasty reply would not do you justice."

"You have an exceptionally keen eye. I have never once shown you such a shape as that, and yet you know that I always carry a square, thin, light briefcase. Furthermore, it was a Tokyo subway, you say? Well then, hmm … ."

"Hey, by the way, where can you be contacted?"

"Ask at my regular place," said Heisuke, and he ended the call.

That regular place was a bar in the suburbs.

"Who was that?" Muro Sawako was standing right in the middle of the room.

"Okada Heisuke. You may have met him once." Now what did that guy really have in mind when he telephoned here, Takuzō thought to himself. Of course, it was to let me know that he had returned.

"He's kind of a strange guy, really."

It happened every time: Heisuke would make a hurried phone call, as if to satisfy himself by making voice contact that Takuzō still existed, then suddenly disappear somewhere. Even when they met from time to time at his bar, after an hour or so he'd suddenly jump up and leave.

"It'd be nice if he could come here, though," said Sawako, smiling sweetly. "He must be hungry. Then he could have some of the sushi I made."

"How do you know that he must be hungry?" asked Takuzō, who sometimes felt slightly exasperated when talking with Sawako.

"Absolutely everybody is that way. I've got to stand up for him." Sawako went to the table and uncapped the beer she had apparently just brought back. Her plump fingers moved dexterously.

"Oh, beer; but no thanks. I've got to go out on an errand. And I've already had my dinner."

What did this woman really want coming here like this to visit, wondered Takuzō, realizing that a moment ago he'd asked himself pretty much the same question regarding Heisuke.

Any number of people had come to his place. Although he had never invited them to come, they came. Having no title, no status, and no money, he understood that they did not come seeking such things as those. Yet in the end there was not a single person who had ever entered Takuzō's innermost life.

"I'm going to eat. Why don't you have a little something, too?" And without regard for his constraint Sawako poured two glasses of beer.

"If I had already finished a meal at home and then went visiting and some appetizing food was put on the table, I'd force myself to eat it out of politeness—that sort of thing happened often when I was a kid. Times like that were torture. If I hadn't just eaten, of course, it would have been a great meal, but that's the way it was and it became unbearable. That's what I mean. Eating something special became a torture." Takuzō spoke almost uncontrollably.

"Well, then, please help yourself," said Sawako cheerfully as if she hadn't heard a word he'd been saying.

"I'll keep you company with just the beer." And he raised his glass and drained it all.

"Mm, this is good. Try it."

Squinting her eyes into a smile, Sawako pushed a plate of food toward him. Her cheeks were soft and plump. Her hairline was sharply defined, and her hair as always was done up to perfection.

Yes, that's what it was, reflected Takuzō: hers was a face without a trace of doubt. Although they had been acquainted for fully two years, it was only today that this thought particularly occurred to him, probably because the strangely stiff voice of that woman with whom he had talked on the phone was on his mind.

"What's the errand you mentioned?" asked Sawako through a mouthful of sushi. "Did you find a job?"

"Possibly," he said. He had a premonition, depending on that woman, that his own future might be opening up.

"Honestly, I don't understand you in the slightest."

"What don't you understand?"

"If you'd gotten a job as soon as you finished college, you'd have a fine life by now. You graduate from the best department in the best university, but it's your quirk to work at nothing but meaningless odd jobs. For heaven's sake, what are you planning on doing?"

"Planning on doing?"

"Really, what are you going to do? I guess there's nothing for it but to just take you under my wing."

"Hey, now, please don't confuse the issue."

"Okay, okay!" said Sawako getting excited. She had somehow gotten wind of his academic background. "You don't understand what it means to be fortunate."

"It's gotten to be extremely difficult."

"This sushi, for example. It's such a simple thing," she said, beaming.

"Well, I've got to go out now," said Takuzō, getting to his feet.

"Eating my home-made sushi together—now isn't that some kind of blessing? For sure one of these days you'll understand the significance."

"A blessing?"

"As for me, I'm a cheerful redcap."

"A what?"

"A porter who carries cheer around."

"Yes, of course," he laughed, thinking the phrase somehow suited her. "If you say so."

"Ah! So you do understand."

"Yes, as far as the words go."

"Have I ever once put on a disagreeable face? Have I ever once spoken a disagreeable word?" From her place at the table Sawako had twisted around toward Takuzō to talk with him.

"Well, I guess not," he replied, standing in front of the closet as he changed into a black sport shirt.

"And why do you suppose that is?" she asked.

In the mirror on the inside of the closet door, Takuzō detected perspiration breaking out on his face, the consequence of there being no air conditioning in the room plus the fact he had just drunk beer. Looking at his perspiring face, the mirror reflected his thick eyebrows knitted into a frown. It was a rather irritable expression, superimposed on which was the vagueness he had been feeling the past two or three months about the direction his life was taking.

"Yes, why do you suppose that is?" he asked after a long pause, turning the question around.

"Well," she giggled, "as for me, I believe in myself."

"What about yourself?"

Takuzō wiped the sweat from his face with a handkerchief, tossed it to the back of the closet, took out a fresh one from a small drawer, and put it in his pocket.

"And as for you, you're such a bother," said Sawako. I have to say everything exactly point by point. You know what kind of person I am, don't you?"

"Sure. You're a person who does nothing but good, who's kind, and always cheerful. Well, then, I've got to be going."

Takuzō, irritated by Sawako's prying remarks, slipped out of the room.

"I'll leave soon," Sawako called out after him. "I wouldn't stay in someone else's apartment forever."

If it had been the Sawamura Takuzō of former times, it would probably have been totally impermissible that someone else remain at his home when he himself was not there. That he was accustomed even to the likes of what had now just happened was the result of his new life of discipline. This was because he had become utterly naked, thanks to his exertions to strip away his extravagant attributes. In those former times, his room belonged to him alone. According to his aim in those days, a part of him he kept on his person, and after he went out, a different part of him remained behind. It would have been unthinkable that some other person enter, for that other person, who might touch his own desk or books or clothes, would be touching the self which had been left behind.

Sawako worked for a tax accountant running errands. Because it was Takuzō's choice to make, he had tried not to select an extravagant woman. The tax accountant's office was located two doors away from a cheap restaurant where, some three years ago, he lived while working as dishwasher. Every morning she would poke her head in at the rear door. The restaurant owner's child was attending kindergarten and she had taken it upon herself to escort him there.

It's so difficult because you've got your own job responsibilities too, but you really do love children. That's what Takuzō had remarked to Sawako back then. It seemed to him to be such a troublesome thing for her to do every day.

Children? Well, I suppose it's love of humanity. And because of love of humanity, I do it for the sake of that person. And because it's love of humanity, that surely is a good thing. Sawako's round face beamed.

Because of love of humanity, that surely is a good thing, Takuzō said to himself. Of course. I hadn't been aware of that kind of thinking. Yes, of course.

That Takuzō should recall this conversation of so long ago was perhaps because he would soon be meeting another woman, and was anticipating what kind of remarks he might exchange with her on this first occasion. When he got off the subway train and went up to street level, he had the feeling he'd emerged into a tropical night sky languidly alit with neon lights. Simultaneously those lights seemed to heighten his anticipation. Their glitter accompanied him as he walked along, for it seemed the woman who at last would be entering his life was waiting for him.

Pushing open the glass door of the coffee shop and standing in the doorway, he looked about. Since he had formed an impression of the woman only through their interactions over the phone, he had not particularly considered the woman's outward appearance. With this thought in mind, from a seat by the window a beautiful woman suddenly rose to her feet. Wearing a loose-fitting one-piece sleeveless dress, she cast a keen eye his way—a look far different from the languid telephone voice.

Six

NOBE MICHIKO HAD ALREADY BEEN WATCHING for a while through the coffee shop window and saw the man approaching. Although he had said on the phone only that he would be wearing a black sport shirt, she knew for certain that the man who was approaching, a tall man with agile step and lithe figure, a handsome man of favorable impression, could be none other than he. In his high-handed tone of voice over the phone she could feel the man's self-confidence, and yet Michiko knew that men who talked in a presumptuous manner could in fact be quite the opposite. She was relieved that such would not be the case here.

One can understand men by the way they handle their self-confidence. Michiko was acquainted with various men, one man's self-confidence differing subtly from another's in degree and in temper, and it was such diversity that created the differences between one man and another. Her husband Keitarō had what might be termed an animalistic self-confidence while her sister's husband, Sanada Misao, had what might be called an artificial self-confidence, and so on. As she was musing about such things, sure enough a man wearing a black sport shirt crossed the street, approached the coffee shop, pushed open the glass door, and entered.

"Ah!" she uttered, rising to her feet. She had been about to wave to him, but did not, for to have gone to the extent of casually waving her hand would have reflected the intimacy of their telephone conversations. Here was this stranger, a man with whom she certainly would never share her feelings face to face, but because she had unwittingly gotten to know him through their phone calls, they had developed a relation, she felt, that was in fact more than simply a relation between strangers.

"I recognized you immediately," said Michiko, greeting him face to face.

"I haven't worn black in years," said the man, casting a kindly gaze on her. "If it had been some nondescript color, you wouldn't have been able to single me out."

He's a very genuine person, decided Michiko. Of course that was not to say he was naive or that he was overly serious. Indeed, though she knew not why, he seemed unsullied by the outside world and, furthermore, was resolute in character.

"It's really very becoming. There are few people who wear black well." Michiko's comment was but the flattery she was accustomed to using with men, flattery which, she realized, she had no apparent need to use with this man.

"No—this is something I was wearing ages ago. Before I chose to erase my identity."

"Chose?"

"It's the discipline I was talking about. Cutting out extravagances."

A consequence, perhaps, of that resolute quality, Michiko thought to herself.

"But, do please sit down."

With the man's courteous urging, Michiko became aware that she herself was discourteously still on her feet. Always there were these lapses on her part. It was something she was ever being reminded of by her husband. When she was listening closely to someone, she would entirely forget her manners. It's not at all lady-like, Keitarō would say.

When the two had seated themselves, the man took a slip of paper from his shirt pocket and placed it on the table.

"Here it is," he said.

"What's that?"

Michiko noticed the man's long fingers as she reached for the paper.

Matching her silver-gray dress, the large black pearl ring she was wearing glimmered softly with the movement. That glimmer seemed to illuminate the woman herself, imparting to her a certain light-heartedness.

"It's the LifeLine telephone number. Oh, yes; and my name is Sawamura Takuzō."

"And I'm Nobe Michiko. This telephone number is…yes, it's very similar to my own."

Michiko read the numbers on the slip of paper: 264-4343. The term "LifeLine," just as she had heard it the first time, now again struck her as rather peculiar.

"But really, why does LifeLine hold such interest for you?" she asked.

Takuzō again cast a kindly look at her. He leaned slightly toward her over the table.

Directly in front of Michiko was the unexpectedly bright color of her companion's eyes. This was the man who had said he was at the end of his rope, but he did not give that impression now, she thought. Rather, it was she herself who was at the end of her tether. And yet, she could not say what or how she had come to be this way. Of course there was the situation regarding her sister, but it was not simply that. The totality, of which that was one part, weighed heavily upon her, and the cause behind that totality was, apparently, herself.

"As for me," she said, "I'm living such an unsettled life. It's meaningless. A person like me might sometimes happen to get a chain letter or something, or learn about things like LifeLine."

Takuzō laughed pleasantly. Michiko could see a mole on his right nostril. When speaking in such a manner, she reflected, there was a certain type of man who would certainly respond.

"Did I say something peculiar," she asked quite deliberately.

"Not at all," responded Takuzō agreeably, showing his interest.

"Such things never happen to someone who lives a well-ordered life," she said. "The other party—the letter writer or telephone caller—would surely have gotten wind of it."

That was phraseology to which a certain type of man would certainly respond, Michiko thought again.

"Has a chain letter ever arrived at your home?" asked Takuzō after ordering coffee for himself.

"A malicious crank letter, you might say, came once."

"Oh? Malicious? You're strangely evading the issue. It was like that on the phone, too."

"But it's true. Let me tell you about it."

One day, she began, she saw mixed in with the mail a postcard addressed to Keitarō bearing this strange message. "To you who have received this letter of ill tiding: Please immediately write a letter with the same contents addressed to someone else and mail it. If you disregard this or if you delay in mailing the letter, misfortune will assuredly befall you. One elderly woman who was neglectful of this obligation died as a result. Please fulfill your obligation without delay." The letter was unsigned. Michiko was petrified. At the time she suddenly sensed a vacuum stretching out everywhere around her, a vacuum in which she was standing quite alone under the watch of an evil spirit. Had the postcard come addressed to her, she shuddered at the thought of what she might do. More than just the unease caused by the postcard as such, there would be the unease of groping blindly in the dark, of not having the slightest idea what action to take. When Keitarō returned home that evening and saw the postcard, he just laughed it off. "It's the same as when a questionnaire comes," he said. "You fill in the blanks and just send it back. It's all the same." He picked out someone from his elementary school alumni list to be the next recipient. He wrote the same message, likewise omitting his own name as sender, and mailed it the next morning on his way to work.

"What do you make of it?" asked Michiko after finishing her account.

"Well, nobody knows where it came from or where it'll end up, but the reason why it exists may be to make sure everyone carries out his obligations. If the letter had come to me, I'd have thought it best just to forget about it." And as if conforming to that judgment, Takuzō raised his eyes in an expression conveying his good sense.

"Just forget about it?" she inquired in return, sensing this to be a matter of some critical importance.

"Because you think you're going to lose something, you're scared."

"No, I'm not at all like that."

"If there is nothing to lose, then there is nothing to be afraid of. If there are no things nor any person which one can say are one's own; if there is no job, no family, no money; if there is only the person's mere existence; if one can think that even that person's existence after all amounts to nothing. In short, that's the case with me."

His manner of speaking seemed to be in the nature of self-introduction. It was wreathed in nuances of arrogance.

"But do consider this, please. Although there are over one hundred million people living in this country, that letter was directed to just one person from among those one hundred million. Supposing it had been delivered to me, not to anyone else. Not to any of those people out there, for example," and Michiko motioned toward the scene beyond the window. Though late at night, throngs of people were nonetheless incessantly milling about in front of the subway station. Pedestrians and the countless lights seemed to interweave then unravel then interweave again.

"Though there's a crowd of nameless people out there, the fact that somehow that postcard knew my name and came to my house makes your flesh creep, doesn't it? And what's more, it was unsigned."

"But in fact it did not come addressed to you. What on earth are you afraid of?"

Takuzō smiled slightly. Smoke from the cigarette he was holding was wafting right into Michiko's face. Having recently quit smoking altogether, Michiko brushed the smoke away with her hand.

"I too have nothing. I think maybe you don't believe me that I have nothing."

"And since you have nothing, there is no reason to be afraid."

"No … it must be a bit different from that. Perhaps …" Michiko hesitated. Beyond the window, she watched the pedestrians jostling like breaking waves, then she continued. "You said nobody knows where it's coming from and where it's heading. It's not just that single letter. That kind of chain letter is like an evil visitation, traversing the world invisible to the eye. How I personally should act regarding that visitation is like groping in the dark, and I haven't any idea. That's it, in a word."

"You're reacting very emotionally."

Takuzō shifted his position slightly so that finally the cigarette smoke drifting toward her was diverted.

"If you encountered such a visitation, could you just say 'no'? I can't. It gets into my very flesh. Then, I don't know what I'm supposed to do," said Michiko.

"You're getting more and more emotional. I don't understand you, so it's very interesting for me."

Takuzō's face flushed slightly.

"Ah, now I understand. It's this phone call," she said, her eyes falling to the slip of paper she had been clutching all the while.

"What is it you understand?" asked Takuzō. Whether it was his interest in Michiko or his fondness for expressing himself with precision, he pursued the subject methodically.

"So at such times, I mean, when I don't know what I'm supposed to do, this is the number I should call then, isn't it," said Michiko.

"Exactly."

"Did you telephone after that?"

"No, just that once."

"But why? You said you were at the end of your rope."

"Yes, it certainly seems so. But that's just the way I am. Besides, doesn't everybody have this thing called life? Somehow I can get comfortable with everyday life."

"Yes. Yes, that's the way it is. Men are very good at adjusting to circumstances."

"Aren't you the same way yourself? For a person like yourself at wit's end, LifeLine and crank letters form the subjects of your conversation, whereas that attractive dress or that ring … well …"

Takuzō hesitated as he thought of what next to say.

"Good heavens!" exclaimed Michiko. Abruptly, from within her subconscious mind, a sensual voice rose up, rather like a woman waking from sleep. And when she was feeling depressed, she knew for a certainty that the woman was sleeping within her. Or rather, the woman was only wearing the outer garments of depression, and when the garments were undone, sometimes a sensual "Good heavens!" would issue forth from her.

"What is it? Your face seems to show you've discovered something just now. What is it then," he said, responding to Michiko's exclamation.

"Trying to get you to discuss things accurately and in detail."

"Really? Hmm, someone else told me the same thing, too. Quite recently."

"When?"

"Just today, actually."

"Hmm … You're a single man?"

"Yes, of course."

"Really? Well, then … that's a great relief."

Michiko was aware of the awkwardness of her comment. Actually it resulted from a trivial incident. Just a moment ago when gazing out the window, Michiko had noticed a woman standing nearby on the sidewalk looking intently at her. A number of people were waiting at the bus stop there. Wasn't that woman too just waiting for a bus, thought Michiko, though when the bus did come she did not board it. But since several different busses stopped there, she also considered that the woman was waiting for a bus bound for another destination. She appeared to be about the same thirty-some years of age as Michiko. Notwithstanding the woman's appealing plump round face, for some reason or other her expression seemed much like that of a spy staring this way and that. In Michiko's mind, that expression and the expression in her sister's eyes were superimposed on each other. The doings of her ever high-strung sister, who was trying not to lose her husband Sanada Misao, were vividly brought to mind by means of the look of this unknown woman. Michiko once more turned her eyes toward the bus stop, but the woman who so concerned her had disappeared. It seemed, after all, that she had boarded a bus headed in a different direction.

"Would you care for a drink?" asked Takuzō. "I came here today thinking you would listen to what I had to say. I have now definitely come to realize that you would be my best listener."

Takuzō had stood up, and so Michiko too rose to her feet, feeling somewhat lost. Thinking back on her sister intensified her own sense of being at the end of her tether, for her sister reminded her of who she herself really was.

"People know me here; let's leave. If we're overheard, it would be awkward. This is a rather special conversation, after all." And Takuzō started walking toward the door.

You would be my best listener. While he was paying the bill, Michiko mulled over his words. There was a certain type of man who would certainly see that quality in Michiko, indeed would see that there was no woman who understood a man's remarks better than she. Thus in the safety of a good listener, she might inadvertently be caught off guard.

"Or do you refrain from alcohol?" queried Takuzō as he opened the door, his earlier question having gone unanswered.

"Anything is fine with me, and since anything is fine with me, we might just as well go." Michiko went out the door, and thought she had said the same thing on the telephone.

Stagnant heat enveloped her the moment she stepped out of the pleasantly air-conditioned coffee shop. Accompanied by a man about whom she knew absolutely nothing save his name, Michiko walked out into the midst of the city's interminable feverish late summer. The bodies of the innumerable pedestrians had undergone a complete change from what she had been gazing at a moment ago from inside the cool coffee shop, each now panting as he walked along.

"Such a crowd of people—I wonder why they are all walking around," said Michiko. Since coming to Tokyo, that was for her one of the strangest things.

"Because everybody has to live," offered Takuzō, with a ring to his voice like a lover. He somehow flavored his speech with nuances of self-satisfaction like a lover.

"It's amazing. Everybody is so active, like energetic animals. And yet … I don't care, I don't care at all."

Saying that, she suddenly could hear the voice of her sister. Her infuriated sister had spoken such words any number of times. You're just that kind of woman, she would say, opening up a hole inside yourself. And for sure some artsy fellow will fall right into it. It's as if you were a trap for luring men, and it's as if you had a void opened up inside yourself to lure them in.

"Oh!" exclaimed Michiko, casting a hurried look to her left. She had the feeling she was being watched. But just then a group of young men came rushing forward, brushed by blocking her field of vision, and when they had passed on, the traffic light at the intersection changed and a great throng of people went crossing over to the other side and a great throng of people from the other side came crossing her way. Michiko completely lost sight of the person who seemed to have been looking at her. And yet among the milling crowd of people, that round-faced woman who was standing there just a moment ago apparently waiting for the bus seemed to linger before her eyes.

"Someone you know?" asked Takuzō, tracing Michiko's line of sight as she looked back over her shoulder.

"No; I was just reminded of somebody." Michiko was thinking not of that round-faced woman, but of her sister who seemed to be shadowing her.

So the conversation was dropped. We'll be there soon, Takuzō said several times.

They turned from the bustling thoroughfare into a side street and walked along. The red neon lights of cheap love hotels floated up into the night like blood oozing from a wound. As she looked at the signs, it seemed perfectly natural to be going there with this stranger. She actually felt accustomed to walking late at night with some man and recognizing these signs. However much she tried to deny the feeling of going to a love hotel, the feeling persisted. Just about anything was okay, and so for her own sake as well as for her companion's, she really would feel sorry not to go into one of them. Since she could not offer any hope of a future relationship with him, this was the only gift she could offer right now.

Having passed by the red neon signs without incident, Michiko heaved a sigh of relief.

Seven

TAKEDA SACHIKO DIALED 264-4343.

"Hello?" answered a voice.

On the previous occasion it had been a woman, but today it was a man's voice. Even so, the voice was somehow different from what one would ordinarily expect in the voice of either a man or woman.

"Hello? I … ," began Sachiko, but she was unable to continue.

"Just talk about anything," the voice said. "Please say whatever it is you really want to say. Then we'll be able to have a good talk together."

The previous woman's voice was much the same, though this man's enunciation was uniformly slow.

"Well, I telephoned about two months ago. I called because I wanted to die. Second-year junior high student. Fourteen years old."

Sachiko held the receiver in her left hand, cupping her right hand around the mouthpiece as she spoke. Although no one was at home, she felt it would be extremely awkward if she were overheard.

"Yes, you telephoned because you wanted to die, but you are indeed still alive. How good it is to be living." His voice seemed to be full of gratitude.

"Oh no, it's not as simple as all that. There's more, something …"

Sachiko's words were choked off; sobs were stopping up her throat. Why should she be sobbing? Although as a child she never cried even when being scolded, now when her deepest feelings were brought out this way in front of another person, she couldn't hold back the tears.

"I see," agreed the voice. "So there is much more."

Because Sachiko said nothing further, a strained silence came across from the other end. At the same time, in this neighborhood where homes and shops were built closely together, even though it was past midnight the signs of activity nearby suddenly pressed in on her. And yet the silence from the person at the other end seemed even more intense.

"Well, sometimes I feel I want to die. But when I called before, after she'd listened to my story, I ended up not dying. It's not that I'd gotten to where I didn't want to die; it's only that the feeling went away a little. But about two or three days ago again I began to want to die, and so I'm telephoning now. I'm wondering if the feeling will go away again."

Sachiko had already been thinking what she might say and how she might phrase it, so now she blurted it out in a single breath. And having done so, she now felt she could convey the things pent up inside her to the person on the other end of the line in a calmer manner. Even though she was in her own home, she nevertheless had the feeling she was standing somewhere else. Yet there were no obvious indications of that somewhere else, for invariably people's voices, traffic noise, and so on in the vicinity were mixed into the background noise.

"Why is it that you want to die? There must be some particular reason."

It was a kind voice. A very kind voice, a voice one would not think even human. Sachiko certainly had never encountered such a voice from either family or friends.

"Reason?" asked Sachiko, rather more to herself than to the voice. The previous time she had telephoned she hadn't talked about reasons, because that was the first time she had called and she was incoherent, complaining only of her wish to die.

"And the reason for wanting to die …" the voice repeated.

"It's a really crazy situation, but …"

"No. Whatever the situation may be, it's not crazy. Whatever it is, the things people feel are not crazy. Things that are called crazy simply don't exist. That's because they're things which people feel."

"But when I say how I feel, people just make fun of me."

"Who are they who make fun of you?"

"My friends, my mother, my sister, my brother."

"And your father?"

"I don't have one. He died a long time ago. But I do have a stepfather. My mother got married again. They say my father was very intelligent. My sister and I take after our father. But my sister's weak points are also like his. She's in a mental hospital now. My brother takes after Mother. Both my brother and my mother are not a bit like me." Sachiko again blurted it all out in a single breath.

"Hmm, is that so. Then you're quite lonely, aren't you." As usual the voice projected deep concern.

"Lonely?"

He probably has no idea at all how lonely I am, she was thinking, and she continued speaking in a somewhat defiant manner.

"It's not on that account I'm lonely."

"I see. Well then, please do tell me what it is. I'm listening to whatever you want to tell me." The voice was flexible in following Sachiko's changing mood.

An irresistible urge to sob moistened Sachiko's eyes, and that in itself prompted her to speak out.

"It's really crazy, but… Sometimes, y'know, I suddenly get the feeling the things that are covering me are peeling off one by one. It seems like the clothes I wear fall off one piece after another and then my flesh falls off, with just my bones still standing. And so I get freezing cold. Now, even though it's hot out, I can't help still feeing cold. When I want to die, it's always at times when I feel like this."

"So when you're lonely you get cold."

"That's the final stage of being lonely."

"But why do you suppose you're lonely? There must be a reason. There's always a reason why people feel as they do. There are different reasons for different people. Please talk to me about anything. Let's put our heads together and try to think about those things which you cannot think about alone."

"Reason?" echoed Sachiko. "Speaking of reasons, then, there is the fact that my father isn't here, and the fact that the guy my mother married is here, and the fact that my sister is feeble-minded in a hospital, and the fact that I can't really talk with my brother, and the fact that I have a lot of friends but no true friend. That's all so, but those aren't reasons. They seem to be more like triggers."

Sachiko tried putting into words the things she had been thinking about.

"Triggers?"

"That trigger my cold spells."

"You seem to be a very sensitive person. You said second year of junior high school, didn't you. Can you please explain these things a little more?"

"Mm, well … I tried thinking how it would be if my father was here. Mother would be a good mother, my sister would be a good sister, my brother would be a good brother, my friends would be good friends… Now if all of a sudden things like that happened to me, how would it be? I've tried thinking. Even at that, for sure I think I'd probably still feel cold. When I say 'trigger,' what I mean is that because I don't have a whole lot of advantages in my life, I get this feeling of being cold sooner than other people.

"Cold, loneliness—yes, that's it."

"Whether I have advantages or not, in either case I feel cold, and so it's something I've become aware of, and so there is nothing else but to die."

When Sachiko broke off her words, this time even the other party was silent. Straining to hear the other person's voice, Sachiko hunched over the phone. As she did so, the indistinct street noises still surrounded her, but for some reason she had the unmistakable sensation that she was steadily moving farther from a place with which she felt no connection. She imagined she was standing in an unknown place which was expanding from his end of the phone line to her.

"And then?" the voice urged after a while.

The previous phone call was also like this, thought Sachiko. The other party never relaxed its hold on her even during her silences, and then invariably there would be further inquiry. Considering that she felt there was no other option than death, it surely made sense for him to inquire carefully. Thus the kindly voice.

"Why are you asking?" Again Sachiko became a little combative.

"I want to listen to what you have to say. I want to listen tomorrow, too, and the day after tomorrow, and every day after that until you get to where you do not want to die."

Truly, it was a kindly voice.

"Oh. Really? So … Anyway, what shall I say?" And saying this, Sachiko felt inclined to talk about her problem.

"It was really crazy, but … A certain something just popped into my head.

At a time when I was so cold I just couldn't help myself. It's just one thing. And after I tried doing the thing I'd never done before, I thought I'd die."

"And what was that?" The voice did not relax its hold on Sachiko. It was not as if the voice had her in its clutches; rather it was as if his eyes were continuously fixed upon her.

"It was sex."

"What?" The voice was filled with surprise.

"I stood on the street and looked for a man."

"Oh, I see. And then?" His tone of surprise instantly vanished and the voice again gently urged her on.

"Because I was so cold, I was thinking surely it would probably warm me up. And so anyone would do. I wonder if that was something bad. The person I talked with when I called before said absolutely don't die, anything is better than dying, and so whatever I've done I've done as an excuse in order not to die. I was making a special effort not to die."

"A special effort … Yes, I see."

"But, y'know, it didn't turn out very well for me. The man told me I'm still only a child and that's why I was feeling so bad, he said. If I was a woman of thirty then I might sob, he said, though I wondered what would be the point of sobbing. But I really did still feel so cold. Because I'm still a child, that's why I didn't feel good yet, he said. The man said that any number of times. He said it to console me."

By this time Sachiko had raised her voice to a shout without even realizing it.

"What happened then?" asked the voice, also loudly.

"I got cold. Real cold."

"If we keep talking like this and you don't start feeling cold, let's talk the entire evening. I'll be right here the whole time until you start dozing off."

"Right here?"

"Yes, right here."

"That's odd. You say 'right here,' but in fact you're not here at all."

"Please rest assured I am here."

"Like a father or somebody."

"Your father?"

"No, Daddy died long ago."

"Are you at home alone now?"

"Yeah. It's only when no one is here that I can telephone like this."

"You're really a very strong person." The voice, too, changed from its gentleness to one more forceful.

"Um … What I was talking about just now, the man gave me some money. So I bought some sweets and ate them. Then it occurred to me to visit my sister in the hospital and offer her some snacks and money. But I … well … it's really crazy."

"What then? You can tell me anything."

"I said it didn't turn out very well for me, though the man really went out of his way to comfort me, and up to then I'd never known such a kind and consoling person, and so, feeling sort of dizzy, I went out again looking for another man. Yesterday evening."

"Wasn't there some alternative to that?" A note of sternness crept into his voice.

"Alternative?"

"Making a new friend, for example … yes, a male friend."

"Absolutely not. There's no such thing as a friend. In the end everyone is just thinking only of himself. That's all very clear to me."

"Yes. And then?"

"I wonder if you can really understand the things I felt. If it was a friend, I would always, always have to be concerned about that person's feelings, wouldn't I. And that person too would always have every one of my feelings on his mind, wouldn't he. Just like doing business. Because it's like selling off and then restocking the feelings. But it was completely different with the man on the street. For myself though, the sex wasn't good at all, but thanks to sex and being together with that man it got to be—how should I put it—very chummy for me. Because I'd never become chummy like that with anyone before, I was awfully happy. And for both of us, there wasn't a bit of that selling off and restocking the feelings like when you're doing business. And that man, afterwards he invited me out for dinner. This was the first time I'd ever had a relationship without that kind of doing business. For myself though, sex and stuff like that are no big deal, but if you are having sex, you ought to be able to laugh and talk…"

"You no longer want to die, do you. And that's good. Very good."

"But I do," said Sachiko stubbornly.

"What seems to be the matter?" The voice followed along with every twist and turn of Sachiko's emotions.

"There is something. Um ..." Sachiko hesitated. Yet she herself up to this moment had never really considered the matter.

"What is it?"

"Yeah, I'm really very sensitive."

"What is it you want to say?"

"If you thought this was a lie, I'd be horrified."

"A lie? What do you mean, a lie."

"That man's, um, kindness." A silence pervaded the space, and on that account Sachiko got the feeling that the voice, up to then kindly, was retreating.

"Please say something," said Sachiko loudly.

"Once one starts searching beneath the surface of things, there's no end to it, and although in fact there may be nothing beneath the surface, one still keeps searching. And if it keeps going like that, then it's getting to be like a sin, and so ..."

"Yes, yes," Sachiko broke in, though she did not altogether comprehend what was being said. She shifted the conversation back to the earlier topic.

"What I was saying a minute ago, y'know, yesterday also on the street I was looking for a man. From about 10 o'clock until 11 o'clock I was in downtown Shinjuku just standing around. Even though night had come, the temperature hadn't gone down in the least and it was awfully hot, and although I was constantly wiping away my sweat with a hanky, it seemed each drop of sweat was instantly freezing. Because I felt so cold. Around me lots of people were passing by like waves. On and on like waves rolling past. Even though there were so many people, I was thinking there wasn't a single person who cared about me. With all of these people, it wouldn't be at all unusual that at least one person might act kindly toward me, would it. It was so unusual—standing in downtown Shinjuku late at night with great crowds of people passing by. Before, I'd never gone alone at such a time to such a place. Because if I wasn't at home I'd get a scolding. But right now my mother and stepfather are on a trip in Southeast Asia. They've got plenty of money and eat greasy, spicy food, and they'll probably return home stinking of greasy, spicy food. I stood on the street corner and watched people go by. A number of people did approach me, but they were just teasing. Since I'm still just a kid, they weren't thinking that I might actually be looking for a man. The previous time I also just barely managed to find one. I had no other way than to just start walking around. I went walking up and down, up and down the streets, one just like another. After about an hour, I had the feeling that a person who had brushed by had stopped just behind me, and so I turned and looked back. The man was thin and so light that he seemed to be floating there. He was a young person, I thought, but when he approached me, he didn't seem so young after all. And all the while we were walking together, I had the feeling he was light like the wind. Though the man said absolutely nothing, I started walking along with him. After a long while he asked me what I was doing so late at night. Looking for a man, I answered. And then the man let out a loud raspy laugh. Hey then, tag along with me, he said, talking like a teenager himself. We walked for more than half an hour, ending up not at a hotel but at some filthy one-room apartment. It's not my apartment, but I can sleep over here any time I want, the man said. It didn't seem to me it would make me feel any better at all if I slept with that man, and so when I told him that, the man let out another loud raspy laugh. After that he just began pulling out all kinds of stuff as if he owned the place and started entertaining me. We played cards, ate some fruit, listened to music. I asked him several times if it was okay to do this in someone else's apartment, but he said don't worry about it, don't worry about it. You've been so kind to me, won't you please tell me your name, I asked him when I was about to leave. I take the name of Free Man, he said, teasing me. Even if you knew my name you wouldn't know me as a person and what's more you wouldn't have any way to find me, is what he said. And so then he took me outside and again we walked together for a long while, and suddenly he disappeared into a dark alley. Then today, I searched frantically for that apartment, but there was no way I could find it. And so, I got even colder than I'd been before. Free Man, or whatever his name is, was like an empty shell, and by clutching that empty shell I was thrown into a world of freezing cold."

Eight

MURAYAMA KAORI ROSE TO HER FEET when the nurse came to inform the patients that it was time for their work session.

Again today the late summer sun shone unabated. Beginning in the morning the locusts continued their buzzing in the pine woods, and Takeda Miyo was whining for the sound to stop. Flopped down on the rumpled white futon, she ate some sweets at every pause in her crying, and so since morning she had demolished all of three large bagsful. Having received an Off-Grounds Permit, she'd bought sweets the previous day with the money her younger sister Sachiko had given her and the bags were heaped up by her pillow. She was nibbling her way through them one after the other. The cabinet in the corner of the room where Miyo kept her personal effects was the place to store her candy, the nurse had said, but Miyo did not comply.

For her, you know, the act of crying and the act of eating are one and the same, which is why she keeps the candy close by her pillow—so Murayama Kaori intended to remark to the nurse, but wondered if she had said it or not. Sometimes she just couldn't tell whether she had actually said something or had just said it in her mind.

She'll cry with an inexhaustible supply of tears, Kaori was thinking, because of her loathing of those locusts, and yet it's not actually the locusts which are objectionable; rather there's a frightful energy inside her, an energy that makes her cry and makes her snack on sweets—one and the same thing; which is perfectly understandable because, whenever that begins to happen to me, I too encounter an inexhaustible supply of something.

When Kaori stood up and stretched herself, Uji Kyōko, who despite the heat was as usual all wrapped up in her quilt, suddenly rose to her feet. Up to this point Kaori had not looked directly at Kyōko. Now Kaori looked back at her, and Kyōko followed Kaori's movements with an unfocused and indifferent gaze. The two of them, one after the other, went out of the room. Since entering the hospital in early summer Miyo had been weeping continuously and she frequently did not appear for the patients' daily afternoon work session.

Pallid-faced patients began emerging from their rooms—rooms like classrooms squeezed together one after the other in a line along the corridor.

"You're in good spirits and looking pretty these days," greeted a patient from another room as she threaded her way past Kaori in the narrow corridor.

"Really? Looking pretty?" Kaori smiled.

The day following her latest seizure after a long interval, Kaori had begun conscientiously applying a thick layer of makeup every morning. Even at night she went to bed without removing her makeup. She herself was only dimly aware of the reason for it.

Kaori walked with Kyōko along a connecting passageway to the workroom. Other patients were walking along, both ahead of and behind them. Since coming to the hospital she had much improved, and so it was possible for her to show kind feelings toward those around her. Yet since her seizure the other day, people were again keeping her at a distance. They seemed like mere objects or something. The sound of so many slippers flopping along the concrete corridor struck her ear strangely. Those plastic slippers had become wet with the sweat from the soles of their wearers' bare feet, and she clearly felt the stickiness. Yet she had no feeling for any of these people as such; rather, she felt only the movement of their feet as dismembered physical objects. She knew it was the fault of the continual doses of powerful medications administered since the day of her seizure. Her mind was vague, as though she had become feeble-minded. Everything seemed fuzzy to her, like the hot sky as it broadened out on either side of the corridor. Nonetheless, whatever one might say about it, it was thanks to the medicine that her seizures had not recurred except for that one the other day.

"The medicine, yes the medicine … If I don't keep a tight grip on the medicine, I'll drop it. Keeping a grip on the medicine is like keeping a grip on the limb of a tree. A single limb, jutting out into the midst of empty space. And if I lose my grip, well then …"

"Well then—and what might that be?" casually asked Kyōko, who, walking a step ahead of Kaori, fell back abreast of her.

"The inexhaustible; infinity." Kaori had nothing more to say than that about the things she was feeling.

"I am entirely familiar with the matter even if you hadn't told me. I found out one day but nonetheless whenever I speak about it people say I've gone crazy. I've said so any number of times, and so people have put me in this mental hospital. But it's good here, really. Nobody says anything. Here I am forgiven," said Kyōko looking straight ahead, not glancing at Kaori.

"Forgiven?"

"Yes, forgiven."

Kyōko, tall and long-legged, walked along with long slow strides.

"Aren't you afraid of falling into the middle of that 'inexhaustible' something? I don't know quite how to put it, but after all it was there from before you were born and it will still be there after you die—that place of inexhaustibility …"

Kyōko remained sullen and unresponsive.

"Well, as for me, I remember exactly when it all began. Three years ago in summer—yes, it was just as hot as now. I was living in my hometown."

As Kaori started talking in this vein, she herself thought it most odd. The contents of her remarks, it seemed, were like those of another person's fate and were not in the least painful for her.

"Well, I was already married, then my husband fell deeply in love with my younger sister. So there were times when I raised quite a ruckus about it with my husband. I screamed at him like some howling animal. Three or four bouts of screaming. Even so, I felt that still wasn't enough, and so there was a fifth and a sixth bout. Then, gradually the feeling would return that it still wasn't enough and it came to where there was nothing but continual screaming. I'd cry for ten minutes, no, thirty minutes. That said, unaccountably there was something inside me—just where it's too vague to say, but in my very depths you might say—and somewhere in those depths I had the feeling that a membrane or something had ruptured and that I was getting mired head first in a slimy dark womb-like place. And even though it was a womb, it was a womb that went on forever, a womb without end. I understood that I was slipping head first into such a place. It was frightening. It was terribly frightening whenever it occurred …"

As they were nearing the workroom, Kaori stopped talking.

"And if I hadn't had the medicine," she added as a final remark, "what in heaven's name do you think would have become of me?"

Just then Kyōko caught Kaori's arm and, glancing hastily about, quickly drew her into a side passageway of the workroom and on into the back of the building. Kaori, surprised, wondered if it wasn't one of those frenzied seizures which she once in a while observed among the patients.

Kyōko came to a halt at the rear wall and loosened her grip. "I want you to hear what I have to say," she said.

Staring at her, Kaori felt that perhaps due to her own confession just now, a human-like quality was returning to her. The afternoon sun was blazing directly against the outside wall and radiating its heat inward, making the room extremely warm.

"Something happened last year," said Kyōko. "I was standing on the train platform. I was right in the middle of a job. I was standing there with a big company envelope clasped to my chest. I'd been given an errand to do outside. Because I had only a high school education, I was often sent out just to run errands. But though I had only a high school education, by nature, really, I had something like intuition with the power to understand everything. Eminent professors and such who have read books by the dozens and are possessed of great knowledge—well, I always knew the same things by intuition. Anyway, I was standing on the train platform, standing right at the edge. About a foot from the edge there's a white line painted along the platform, right? and they say it's dangerous to stand closer to the edge than that white line, well that line, you know, runs all the way to the far end of the platform, and beyond that are the tracks and people are not supposed to step onto the tracks, and so the freshly painted, crisp white line running all the way to the far end was something I was fixated on. And as I was doing that, without warning I felt something like dizziness, though not anything overwhelming, but still I had the feeling that something transparent was passing like a wave before my eyes, and, oh, if at just such a time the train should come, wouldn't that be dangerous, I was thinking. The announcement began: train arriving on track number such-and-such bound for so-and-so, passengers waiting to board please stand back of the white line, came the voice booming over the P.A. system. And then that feeling of danger overpowered me, and above the white line I was looking at which stretched all the way to the far end, something came fluttering down and enveloped me. I'd better watch out, I said to myself. How would it be, I thought, if at this very moment I stepped across the white line, a moment after which everything would be differentiated into plus and minus. On the plus side, if I held my feet firmly in check I would avoid a terrible accident. But if I was just a little careless, I would go to the minus side. The feeling that I was standing at such a juncture seized me, and I could see the train coming into the station. And as I was thinking about these things, I got the feeling of being purposely swallowed up in the danger, and before I knew what had happened, I'd fallen onto the tracks. It's not that I just fell accidentally or absentmindedly—I fell fully aware of what I was doing, which is mysterious, isn't it. The events immediately following I don't remember at all. But as a matter of fact, there wasn't any danger to my life, though it seems I did hit my head awfully hard. Because I had that seizure, or should I say, thanks to having that seizure, such accidents happen from time to time. Just now I said, 'thanks to that,' didn't I. I really do think so."

Uji Kyōko chattered on for an unusually long time and, having reached the end of her chatter, she again sank into silence. Then she spun around and with her back to Kaori, leaned her head against the hot wall and stood motionless.

"Kyōko, Kyōko," said Kaori, shaking her. "Are you going to just leave me here? It simply won't do not to have my medicine," she cried out.

It simply won't do not to have my medicine. I want something to hold on to. Something firm, sturdy, immovable; something like a steel beam. In order not to fall into the midst of that inexhaustible.

Kyōko, still leaning her head against the wall with the shadow of her eyelashes falling over her bloodless cheeks, held her eyes shut as tightly as a bird asleep. She gave the appearance of being in an altogether different world. All that seemed to remain human of her was the odor of her hair, warmed by the direct rays of the sun.

The work superintendent emerged from the workroom and took Kaori by the hand. She'd probably heard the loud voices. As she was being led away by the hand, Kaori motioned toward Kyōko with her eyes, but the work superintendent paid no attention and quickly returned to the workroom.

"My medicine, my medicine," said Kaori.

"What were you talking about? You shouldn't talk about things that get you excited," said the superintendent with a stern voice.

Entering the workroom, Kaori slumped face down on the table. Around her the patients were at their work, gruff breathing the only sound, but immediately a hush fell over them because of Kaori's strange behavior, and then there was nothing to be heard at all.

Sensing that an unusually long time had passed, Kaori finally raised her head, and saw laid out on the table before her the embroidery she always did during her work time. She picked up the frame and, resuming her work of the day before, began inserting her needle. It seemed the nurse had given her an injection, or was she confusing that impression with a previous occasion when the nurse had indeed done so—she just didn't know. Everything was so extremely fuzzy, and around her the patients doing their sewing or knitting or embroidery all seemed very far away, so the nurse must have given her an injection.

Kaori was embroidering yellow thread, one stitch at a time, into the sunflower part of a table doily she had been working on before. But her own hand had become blurry and her feelings toward the sunflower had completely died.

Whenever she was thus bent over her embroidery, it was her own inner self which she was somehow confronting. When, a moment ago there had been that flare-up, she felt that some thing like molten lava had flowed out and now was sinking ever downward. That thing, when it became apparent, was similar to a life lived to excess, and as such was threatening to her, but now, having lost her vitality, she was reverting to her old self. As for the stage where the drama of her life was playing itself out, the glitter that could recharge a life lived to excess had disappeared, had completely dried up, and in the void inside her something like a painting could be seen hanging.

Kaori was thus able to fix her gaze on that painting. She grasped every detail in it, but its frightening aspect had disappeared. Murayama Kaori was married; she was now Sanada Kaori, and her husband was Sanada Misao. They had married late. Her younger sister Michiko had married young, but being very particular in the matter herself, her own marriage was much delayed. Although Michiko had had a large number of suitors, for some reason or other she ended up choosing this rather unremarkable man, Nobe Keitarō. Perhaps because of her early marriage and exasperation at having been made captive by so unremarkable a husband, Michiko began fishing for more attractive men. When Keitarō was transferred to a city some distance away and she did not accompany him, there was a period in their lives of traveling back and forth, and so Sanada Kaori invited her sister to her own newlywed home. Kaori's husband, Misao, had aspired to be a painter, but, unable to put food on the table with that, he worked as a graphic designer. That often took him out of town on business, and there were many times when he did not return home until late at night. Sanada Kaori invited Michiko to stay when Michiko's own husband was away, and so the invitation was meant to divert the loneliness they both felt. It was Kaori's nature always to feel lonely if she was not with someone. Being like that herself, she thought others must be like that too. How much more so, then, she thought, given that they were sisters by blood. Nonetheless, Michiko hardly spoke at all to Kaori when she was at the Sanada home. After Michiko had pretty much moved in, Sanada Misao seemed to spend nearly every day when he was home in his studio working on his painting. When the three were together at mealtime, Michiko and Misao chatted away. Michiko was unfamiliar with painting; rather, it was Kaori who took painting as the subject of conversation. But when Michiko and Misao did start to talk, whatever the subject, Kaori could hardly get a word in edgewise, so closely interwoven was the thread of the conversation. Kaori suddenly noticed this one day. My sister is not satisfied with her own husband, Kaori said to herself, so she may try to charm away another person's husband, indeed is charming one away right now, she thought. Once that occurred to Kaori, Michiko's entire behavior could thusly be explained. Yes, that was it: Sanada Misao was a remarkable man. Although there were plenty of other men elsewhere, for her younger sister to steal another person's husband, especially if he were of "remarkable" character, it would be all the spicier. Kaori was now positive about this. She was observing it all, and Michiko just let her observe all she wanted. Kaori started assiduously applying her make-up every day. Her own features were far the more attractive than Michiko's. Kaori's were finely chiseled, and were enhanced by make-up. There were even those who had encouraged her to become an actress. Misao was now saying he would willingly give up his graphic design work, and that he had arrived at the decision to devote himself to his true calling. He also understood, he said, that he was being impelled forward by the source of creativity. When Kaori asked what he meant by "source," he answered that the source became active under erotic stimulation, and when she asked if that referred to marriage, he replied bruskly that it was not that category of thing. When he and Michiko happened to be together, they would begin talking animatedly. Even when Michiko returned from an evening stroll and saw lights on in the studio late at night, she might slip in and chat on and on. Looking at the two of them was like looking at a good game of catch as they tossed their words back and forth without a break. Kaori, even though able to force her sister out, seemed immobilized by fright of her, and was unable to put an end to this ménage à trois. One day, Kaori questioned her husband about it. She did not receive a clear-cut answer. She pressed him a second time, and, after enduring the situation for fully two or three months, her pent-up emotions inevitably erupted. She began shouting. In a voice even she thought bestial, she kept shouting. When that recurred, her innermost self unexpectedly opened up like a ruptured womb, and the womb broadened and deepened interminably, and into the slimy gloom she went tumbling head first. It was terrifying, simply terrifying. Yet she would still come to a halt at the same old place, and at that place every day she screamed at her husband and she loathed her sister. Both love and loathing drew extra life from the well of that psychological depression into which she was sinking, and so she was getting to the point she could no longer control herself as she used to. It was terrifying. Simply terrifying. Even more than losing her sense of self, she feared becoming her real self.

Kaori kept her head steadily bent over her embroidery frame, and sensed it might happen again. Because she had been given an injection she was trying to persuade herself: You're okay, you're okay; you have to think you'll get well by yourself or you won't get well at all; please do your best; please summon your strength to rise up. The remarks which she had heard from her doctor were ringing in her head.

You're okay, you're okay, Kaori.

Kaori, talking to herself, tried hard not to look downcast. Then, looking away from the room where everyone was working in stony silence, she gazed outside. In the narrow exercise yard where the sun was brightly shining, Uji Kyōko, bathed in splashes of light, could be seen walking back and forth. Tall of stature and long of limb, she walked with strides. Her face was lifted ever so slightly upward. Perhaps due to the strong rays of the sun, her whole body appeared to be transparent.

Nine

"MICHIKO, WE HARDLY KNOW EACH OTHER, and yet you went to bed with me just now without any hesitation? Why?"

The hollowness of the flesh-against-flesh friction with a woman whom he felt still to be rather a stranger left an unnatural feeling on every part of his body. Beyond that, however, there was an unnatural feeling about this woman's very substance.

"Why? That's just the way I am," replied Nobe Michiko in a languorous tone.

It was exactly the same voice he had heard on the telephone, thought Takuzō. Being with her for the first time today, he had an unexpected feeling about the way she expressed herself, which seemed to hint at something altogether different—strong views, reasoned thinking—from what he had felt over the phone. But now in the gloomy dimness, listening only to her voice, it was indeed the voice he'd heard over the phone.

"I see you as a very strong-willed person, but when you talk like that, it just doesn't seem to be you. I'd like to know the reason, and I'd like to know that in order to know you."

Takuzō persisted. He'd been like that when he'd first talked with her on the phone, too, but now he was seized by the fervor of wanting to know this woman. It was a fervor which seemed to presage an awakening of love.

"Reason?"

"Yes, reason."

"Because I'm in love."

"Huh? You mean, in what we've just done?"

Surprised, Michiko laughed enchantingly, but it instantly dissolved into the dimness of the room.

"I hadn't planned on saying that, but now that I have said it, I don't mind," said Michiko.

Takuzō was rather taken aback.

"We had that date at the coffee shop," she continued, "and then we were out walking, right? When we turned off the busy main street into a side street, the red signs of the love hotels floated up into the night sky and caught my eye. It may have been on account of those signs."

"There's any number of such hotels. There are dozens of them in this neighborhood alone."

Takuzō thought Michiko's reactions very curious, and so, his interest much aroused, he tried to unravel those reactions.

"Yes, and precisely because there's any number of them …," said Michiko, abruptly propping herself up on an elbow.

She arched her body, supple as a swan's, to gather up the clothes she'd let fall to the floor—a movement which riveted Takuzō's gaze. Yet that movement, even her figure, gave him no feeling of intimacy; rather, lurking in his mind was the unnaturalness of being together in bed with such a woman.

Michiko got out of bed, and before Takuzō could ask if she wanted to return home, she slipped into her sheer one-piece dress without even putting on underclothing, went to the table and poked through Takuzō's clothing.

"I'd like a cigarette," she said, and took the liberty of helping herself to one of his.

When she struck the match, the face that floated up in the light of the flame was surprisingly unfamiliar to him.

"Well then, let me explain," she said with a laugh, as she stood there holding her cigarette. Different from before, this laugh was forced.

"When we'd got past those signs, I felt a great relief. But after we'd had a drink and went out walking, we ran into those signs again. Even after getting past them, a whole lot of places we might have gone into presented themselves.

It was a signal to my body. And so I had to respond to it. It seemed to be a matter of duty."

Michiko, standing there holding a cigarette, seemed more to be standing there holding a weapon.

"A great relief. Matter of duty," said Takuzō, picking out phrases without having much understood them.

"At first it was, yes, duty. Because even if I had gone back home, it still would have been okay. It's always like that with me."

Michiko puffed away at her cigarette. And she just kept standing there.

"Always like that?" said Takuzō, wondering suspiciously, whatever does this woman really do?

"But once I've passed beyond the obligation, I feel wonderfully opened up."

Michiko crushed out her cigarette and jumped back into bed.

She seemed suddenly to have become another person. Then she explained why. A while ago, she said, it seemed like ritual, but with the second time I really go wild. Even the cigarette was like that, because normally I don't smoke, but when I go wild, smoking and drinking and talking get all rolled up together. Beneath the dress her naked body was velvety smooth, and the dress clung closely. She preferred having something on, she said. Being nude with a lover was like a sport, and wearing clothes was sexier than not. Really, this woman had gone utterly wild, and Takuzō, dispassionately viewing the situation, was greatly buoyed. It was rare that dispassion and arousal existed in such direct proportion.

Eventually Michiko lapsed into a death-like state. Takuzō continued to feel quite keenly that she was a stranger. After all, a woman about whom he knew absolutely nothing had unexpectedly entered his sphere. This woman, who presumably would be altogether impossible to meet in so vast a city as Tokyo, was now with him simply because of his misdialed phone call a few days previous, indeed was now with him in as close a relation as two people can have. Thus, it was as if he himself had somehow decisively chosen this woman as his companion. Had it not been for that misdialed phone call he almost certainly would not be having this encounter with her. But even now, without knowing her address, and with only her telephone number to go by, he had almost no connection with her at all. And should the telephone number slip his mind, she would be a woman impossible to locate. But no, on second thought, because her telephone number was so similar to the LifeLine number, he would probably not forget it.

Nobe Michiko began mumbling.

"Didn't I just say so? That there's no way of knowing where the evil tidings are coming from or going to, and even though it's only a crank chain letter, it's not the letter as such but the energy that sends the letter from one unknown place to another, and when that passes through me, I have the feeling of cowering before the devil, and it gets so I have absolutely no idea what I should do, and at that moment, you know, like a moment ago when those red hotel signs appeared everywhere beckoning us, I was already feeling cowed, and it got so I hadn't the slightest idea what I should do."

Takuzō listened intently to these mumblings. They were expressions to which he had never given any thought, and so it would take some effort to interpret their meaning. And even if he did make the effort, he still might not be able to understand her.

"But, you said a while ago that it was your duty to head toward the red-light hotels. Why did you say it was duty?"

"Because that's the way it felt to me."

"That just doesn't make sense. Can't you explain it a bit more for me?"

"Well … In order for me to become my real self, there's a boundary that I have to cross over. And for me, to cross over right on the spot like that, well, it's like duty, you know …"

Takuzō once again listened intently, because if he failed to catch even one word, it seemed he would completely fail to understand her. And yet he was also aware that even if he did catch everything she said, he still might not understand.

On the other hand, Takuzō was thinking that although he had been saying he would offer his views on the subject of discipline, he had not yet said one word about it.

Yes, there was indeed that discipline of his. But when he made up his mind to give practical effect to it, he was completely frustrated, and so his will to carry through with his discipline came completely to naught.

"May I speak to you about the discipline I try to practice in my life?" asked Takuzō, broaching the matter.

Still he was terribly hesitant. He felt there was one particular issue he simply could not put into words, yet if he did not speak of it, he probably would not be able to speak in truth about anything at all. As for other matters, they were of a kind that anybody would know about. If someone looking at certain actions of his and someone else looking at other actions of his were to put all their observations together, they would simply be the facts of his life for the last ten years or so.

"Ah, it's the discipline of becoming naked!" exclaimed Michiko, with a squirm vigorous enough to make the bed shake.

Takuzō sensed a slight change in her tone of voice. She seemed suddenly to have disrobed herself of that languorous voice of a moment ago when she was chattering about herself, and had now dressed herself in another voice. He'd had an unexpected feeling about her voice when she was chatting in the coffee shop during their first meeting, a voice appropriate to a stern look or strict logic.

"'Discipline' is the word I use for it, but in fact it goes beyond that term. It's the story of the real flesh-and-blood me."

"Flesh and blood" being an overly graphic expression that might evoke repugnance, Takuzō quickly elaborated.

"The question is, can corporeal man remold himself?" He thought this phraseology almost grandiloquent.

"That's not something that can be remolded, is it?" said Michiko, taking him by surprise.

"Huh?" he responded.

There was no reply.

Although he sensed a moment ago that he had come to be in a very close personal relation with this woman despite her being an utter stranger, he now had the impression that the woman had unexpectedly withdrawn to a distance.

"Remolding is impossible, you say? How is it you know that?"

Takuzō seemed to speak somewhat more earnestly, because he himself had recently come to consider that remolding was an impossibility.

"I'm sorry," she said. It was exactly as if some sweet little girl had said I'm sorry.

But Takuzō did not sense her to be a sweet little girl, and again he was bewildered.

During a lapse in the conversation Takuzō tried to concentrate his thoughts, hardly taking a breath as he faced the woman stretched out in bed beside him. This woman confused him.

"Well then, discipline?" Michiko urged. It was a continuation of the tone of voice of the woman who had said I'm sorry. What's more, she turned over in bed to face her lover, and struck a deferential attitude as she listened to his story.

"Discipline is that which …" said Takuzō, hesitating again.

Would he ever talk about that single special matter?

"You know, when I was a sophomore in college," he began, pushing aside the topic he was determined to talk about, "I was going out with two different girls at the same time—I'll call them Miss A and Miss B."

"You were like that, too? All the boys do that," said Michiko with a smile. It seemed to be a cynical smile.

"What do you mean by 'all the boys do that'?" Takuzō patiently allowed the conversation of a moment ago to run along in zigzags.

"I mean, your talk about going out with girls in the past. It seems one might say that if you did not puff yourself up with that, there would be nothing at all to puff yourself up with. Anyway, what about those two girls? Don't disappoint me."

"No, no, it's not that at all."

Takuzō fell silent.

And yet if he did not talk about even those two girls he could not talk about the totality of what was on his mind. The girls themselves were of scant importance, but they were linked to that single special matter.

Takuzō recalled the circumstances of more than a decade previous.

Miss A: Mr. Sawamura, you are quite the Don Juan—I realized that from the very beginning. I'm very attracted to that kind of person. You are very good the way you treat women—not frivolous but not overly serious either, somehow like a pinprick whose tingle just kind of spreads all over. Yes, that's the way it is. Having a relationship with you will be a little pinprick, which for me will leave an unforgettable tingle.

Miss B: Mr. Sawamura, you are a serious person. It seems you have a lot of women friends, but at bottom you are serious to a fault. I understand that perfectly, because we're always very much in tune with each other. Although there are men who are good listeners on a superficial level, you aren't that way at all, and when you and I get into a conversation, it's serious like when two gears mesh, and so I'd travel to the ends of the earth with you.

There was no reason for me to scoff at the different views of these two women. Rather, I was very much impressed by their insights. What Miss A said described my character very fairly and what Miss B said was also right on target. Both Miss A and Miss B each in her own way went on to expropriate from me the man of her dreams, whereas for me, their expropriation did not in any way diminish me, and my true self would eventually emerge. Just as one's bodily functions operate quite naturally, so too will my true self emerge quite naturally. Certainly I was partly like the man described by Miss A, and no doubt I was also partly like the man described by Miss B. A person acts the way others expect him to act. When I say acting, I don't mean simply performing a role in some contrived theatrical production; I mean, rather, conforming to someone else's model to form one's character. Acting is in essence just that. People lacking the capacity to achieve self-fulfillment are people who act according to others' expectations, or, to put it more forcefully, who act out falsehoods. As for acting according to the model of others' expectations, generally speaking an individual can achieve self-fulfillment only if he is not trying to follow somebody else's model. I was exasperated by the contradictory views of A and B—was I the playboy type or the serious type—and got quite wrapped up in those models. I am neither A nor B, but those models certainly did stimulate my thinking and I did get quite involved in them.

"Yes, I understand," said Michiko.

"You really do understand me then?" replied Takuzō, and again felt Michiko silently coming very close to him. Not in a corporeal sense, but by providing shared feelings.

"And so …" Takuzō groped within himself for the next words of his confession.

"At that time you must have sensed yourself to be some flaccid, unemotional person, didn't you," said Michiko.

"Yes. Yes, I did."

Takuzō came to feel he was being supported by her.

The thought flashed through his mind that maybe when she had gotten herself into a sexy mood, she was in fact not understanding, but Takuzō was focused on continuing with his confession.

"My mother committed suicide."

Finally he'd said what had to be said.

"What!" exclaimed Michiko, her voice leaping like a fish leaping out of water.

"It's impossible to talk about it in just a word or two."

And as he was saying that, he was groping in his mind as to what he might say to express the entire circumstances.

I've been concentrating all my energies on getting to the state where I can now talk about that time. When Mother was bedridden with her illness, she had such a forlorn and pallid face.

No … Mother … Yes, that's it—let me begin by saying what kind of person Mother was to me. I've never talked with anyone about these kinds of things before, and so from here on what I say will probably be extremely subjective.

When I was about three or four, there was a particular scene which repeated itself night after night. Whether it was every night or not I can't really be sure, but ever since then I do seem to have gotten into the habit of recollecting it as every night. Every evening I was made to sleep all alone in my own little bed in a room just for me. Sometimes lying awake at night I'd feel suffocated in a gloom that extended everywhere, I don't know how far or how deep. Of course this description is my present day description, and though a word like "gloom" wasn't even known to me then, I now use the word gloom to express something indescribable, and I would cry out. Lumping anxiety and fright together, I would cry out. Of course, both anxiety and fright are also words that I use in the present.

But then without fail somewhere in the midst of the gloom something like the rustling of wind would arise and slowly come nearer, followed by the sound of a door opening, and then finally something like a pleasant spring breeze would envelope me. I knew, or rather I should say I sensed, it was Mother. And just at the moment of that perception, the huge, dark, heavy thing which had been suffocating me would vanish into thin air, and I would become light as a feather and fall into a deep slumber.

Even after having gotten past that stage of my life, that scene has always remained a part of me. Or, put differently, in my thoughts about Mother that scene has always been included. Sometimes consciously, sometimes unconsciously. For me that scene has been something like the very bedrock of Mother's character.

A pleasant spring breeze—that's a rather commonplace way of putting it; nonetheless when a person enjoys peace of mind with another, that is something, I think, which should be a commonplace. Mother was a unique person who never hurt me, and a unique person who comforted me when I returned home after being hurt outside. Takuzō dear, she would say, it's all right, it's all right; it's nothing to be concerned about. And so, just as when I was a child and that huge, black, heavy thing that was suffocating me seemed to vanish into thin air, so too everything that I was worried about would somehow vanish in an instant. Even after becoming a junior-high school student, and a high school student, too.

Having said that, however, I was not a particularly loyal son. When I was away from home, I always got along quite well riding roughshod over the very world on which Mother depended.

However, I was so stimulated by Miss A and Miss B that it was getting out of control—a matter on which I said I was then concentrating all my energies. That was only one of the incidents. And yet, whatever I may have been involved with when I was outside the home, such matters were entirely separate from my connection with Mother's life. Ever since my childhood, she was always the same and never, absolutely never, changed in character, and when I came home she was always there waiting for my return.

Yes, I used the phrase "waiting for my return," but where else in this world could there actually be a person who, more than my mother, would wait for my return? Of course there would be no reason for her to sit patiently with eyes glued to the entranceway waiting for me. She would be busy with one chore or another, but the moment I came home, whatever Mother's appearance may have been as she went about her chores, I discovered that I was being awaited. I'd soon forget about it, but every time I returned I would again discover I was being awaited. Regardless of when or where I'd been or what I'd been doing, when I returned I was awaited, which, when you stop to think of it, is really amazing. Of course back then I didn't feel it was amazing or anything. That's because I was used to it.

So, getting back to the subject I was talking about a moment ago, when Mother was sick in bed with a helpless expression on her pallid face, it was for me something altogether unfamiliar. The mother whom I knew so well was totally changed. Exactly when she started changing, regrettably I hadn't noticed because I was all wrapped up in my relations with A and B. Eventually I did notice, however, and, thinking back on it, Mother's appearance had already been deteriorating for a rather long time before I even became aware of it. Her pancreas or kidneys or some other organ—it wasn't quite clear to me—was diseased, she said. For some reason or other Father seemed indifferent toward her illness, though my sisters were apprehensive.

Takuzō dear, I can't sleep well; I hate to trouble you, but would you please buy some sleeping pills for me? But don't tell anyone about it.

That's what she said to me one day from her sickbed.

Mother appeared in my room like a spring breeze as I lay sleepless; I could feel myself getting lighter and lighter as I fell into a slumber: such visions as these floated up into my childhood thoughts. Of course the actual situation was quite the reverse. The things my mother wished for I would certainly try to get for her, I thought. And yet, her condition was worsening and could no longer be disguised by those old scenes.

There was no way at all that the sleeping pills would be freely sold to me. I asked a friend familiar with that line of work to tell me of pharmacies where it might be possible to get my hands on the pills, but because no pharmacy would sell a large amount at one time, I could purchase only thirty pills at a time.

Takuzō dear, excuse me, but I've already finished up the pills; please buy some more for me. I try not to take a pill every day, so that dosage lasted over one month.

That's what Mother said again. It was the same as the previous time, too, but there was no one at home except myself to go out and buy them.

And so it was that, with Mother relying on me, I went six or seven times to purchase the medication. I was awfully careless about it. I was so emotionally divided over A and B, and so exasperated at being unable to reconcile my two conflicting selves that I did not speak with anyone at all in the family as to why Mother was sick in bed. I was not particularly attentive as to why Father was unconcerned about her illness, or why my sisters were so oddly anxious about it.

When the accumulation of pills I had purchased reached two hundred, Mother committed suicide.

Only later did I learn that she was not sick in the slightest, but had lost all her strength and taken to bed because of Father's affair with another woman.

At that time, when I learned the truth, I felt that someone had delivered a powerful blow to my head. It was, however, a somehow clarifying blow. I was dumbstruck by its clarity.

No one knew that it was I who purchased the sleeping pills. There was no reason for Mother to be in bed all day, and so everybody just assumed she had taken the trouble herself to buy them and save them up.

How often did I contemplate the circumstances! However many times I thought of it, I continued to think the whole thing simply defied explanation. It depressed me to contemplate whether there might not have been something else in this world that I could have done. And on top of that, the thought suddenly pierced me like the passing reflection of a glinting blade: was it not possible that Mother was waiting for me to stop buying the pills when sooner or later I became aware of her intentions to commit suicide? During those seven times I went back and forth carrying pills for almost a whole year, perhaps she expected that somewhere around the fourth time or fifth time or sixth time I would become aware of her intentions. Yes, possibly so. Yes, when you come right down to it, that was possible.

What you said a while ago and which I then thought were utterly incomprehensible comments—that there's no way of knowing where those crank chain letters were coming from or going to, that it was not the letters as such but the force behind them that sent them from one haunt to another haunt. That passed right by me at the time, but I'm now coming to understand that such a thing is quite possible.

Takuzō started to get up, thinking to return home. It was already past two o'clock. But Michiko caught him by the arm. Because his mind had been so utterly absorbed in the years of his past, he now momentarily savored an unanticipated feeling that next to him there was a naked woman.

Having listened to his remarks with understanding, she signaled unmistakably that her sexuality was again welling up in her, an indescribable sexuality that was taking possession of her, and she began mumbling things that were for him difficult to understand. I'm the type, you know, who once having crossed over the boundary, opens up limitlessly and becomes one with myself … Her voice for the second time seemed to reflect the fragrance of her body.

Ten

NOBE MICHIKO CAUGHT THE PING-PONG BALL in her paddle and hit it back to Keitarō. As usual it didn't fly very smoothly. Keitarō's shots, to the contrary, described a gentle arc and sailed back easily. At summer's end and shortly after he had returned from America, the ping-pong table had been delivered and set up. Having been made his partner these past three Sundays, she had not improved since her high school days, even though she remembered some technique from having played a little back then. It was the same even during high school—however much she played she had never become proficient.

"You're playing real well, don't you think?" said Keitarō, watching her return the ball. He caught it and volleyed it back. Despite his long torso and plump physique, his effortless shots usually landed nicely right in the middle of the table or slightly off to one side.

"Not at all!"

Feeling she was becoming interested to some extent, Michiko kept on playing. When Keitarō had decided to set up a ping-pong table on this otherwise pointlessly large terrace, Michiko was thoroughly unenthusiastic, but now that she was actually playing, her mood had brightened. She had been unenthusiastic because she and her sister were both in Tokyo, so she was in no frame of mind for anything like sports. It was a frame of mind, however, about which

Keitarō certainly would not be concerned, so Michiko opened up, at least while she was playing. Yet "opened up" did not mean she felt free to exceed the limits of the world he imposed upon her.

"If you try it, you'll be able to do it. If you don't try it, you're just being lazy." Keitarō smiled indulgently at her across the ping-pong table, as he stood legs apart, bobbing a little now to the right, now to the left.

"What do you mean, 'lazy'?" she pouted, returning with a smart whack the ball that came flying at her.

"Hey!" yelled Keitarō, pursing his thick lips.

Michiko said nothing, but her pout changed into a beam.

"Pretty darn tricky, that shot."

The ball grazed the edge of the table. Keitarō, figuring it would miss the table, had to take a hasty defensive pose in order to make his return.

Michiko slammed the ball back with another whack. The technique was coming back to her.

"Tricky, tricky!" Keitarō again cried out.

"Why? This time the ball landed just where it's supposed to."

"Yes, but it's not just this time. You often hit shots like that, Michiko."

"Shots like that? What kind of shots?"

"I mean that kind," said Keitarō, parrying Michiko's shot.

"Finally I've gotten the knack," she laughed.

"Those kinds of shots aren't for games that are just for fun."

"Really, and what kinds of shots are those?"

"The ones that are too strong."

"Too strong?"

"And besides that, they don't come straight. They curve on the way over."

Michiko, taken aback by his objections, began hitting more conventional return shots so Keitarō would stop complaining.

The ball continued to sail back and forth.

"Anything's okay with me," mumbled Michiko.

From the terrace, visibility was usually fairly good. For two days when typhoon winds had been blowing, there had been an autumnlike clarity, but on this day a leaden pall was forming in the sky. Though not particularly so in the morning, by afternoon the skies had become thick and murky, and it had turned chilly to boot.

The ball continued shuttling back and forth. From Keitarō invariably came a smooth arc-like lob, while from Michiko went shots of unskilled flight. However much she played she still did not improve, though sometimes she could win a game. Although she could manage every time to parry and return, her boundlessly self-confident opponent never stopped his attack.

"What a bore," mumbled Michiko. Getting irritated, she slammed the ball with an audible grunt.

"Hey, there you go again!" exclaimed Keitarō.

Michiko slammed a succession of shots.

"You're hitting shots impossible for me to receive, aren't you!"

Even so Keitarō parried and returned the ball, the dexterity of his playing belying his physical appearance.

She kept it up silently.

Michiko abstractly recalled playing ping-pong during her high school years when someone had said the same thing: You're hitting shots impossible for me to receive.

"If I'm to get serious about it, then this is the way it's done," said Michiko laughing again.

"You're very inconsistent. Your playing right now is completely different from just a little while ago. Damn, I've had it."

Even while uttering this protest, however, Keitarō did not give any appearance of being dissatisfied.

"Once I start hitting the ball this way, I just keep on hitting it. It gets so I just can't stop hitting it."

As Michiko was saying this she got the feeling she was somehow spewing forth something she couldn't keep under control.

It was the same feeling as being sexually excited.

Wondering thus, her affair with Sawamura Takuzō came to mind, and then the previous one with Sanada Misao. But with Keitarō, it was not a matter of sexual excitement. That's because he was her husband. That's because he existed within the bounds of family.

"I've had it, I've really had it," said Keitarō, tossing his paddle onto the ping-pong table. Then he stretched himself, and went inside.

Michiko, leaning against the ping-pong table, was left blankly standing there by herself.

Only when I was hitting the ball so hard did I really feel alive, she murmurred.

"I've had it, I've really had it," he said, his voice hanging in the air of the terrace. Keitarō had the good sense to call it quits. From beyond, where the heavens seemed to be wrapped in smoky obscurity, a pale sun was shining through. But the chill remained. Such unsettled weather. Since having moved to this city, she had not been particularly favored with refreshing days. The hot summer had lasted too long, and after that it suddenly turned cold. One sensed the weather had leapfrogged over autumn right into winter. People were saying this year's weather was quite out of the ordinary. When stories like this appeared in the papers, Keitarō reported each and every one of them to her.

He read the newspaper from beginning to end, and because he talked about what he had read, even Michiko, who hardly ever read a newspaper, naturally heard of just about everything. Even now, from the terrace off the bedroom, Michiko could see Keitarō sitting in the adjacent living room with the newspaper spread out before him. It had become his habit always to skim through three or four different newspapers every day. He subscribed to only one newspaper at home, but he would buy another on the way to the office to read on the train, finishing up during work breaks those parts he didn't get to, and on the way home he'd buy an evening edition to read. Today being Sunday, he had gone out in the morning to the newsstand at the train station, partly for the stroll, partly to buy some newspapers.

Michiko thought it odd that anyone could read newspapers like that, but people did it anyway. It was a mystery, Keitarō would say, that a person would not actively read the newspaper.

Think about it, he said. There are so many things going on around us. So if someone tries to get along in life without knowing anything about those things, how does he think he can do it? Because we exist in human society, to be outside human society for even a single day is beyond the realm of possibility.

With Michiko remaining silent, Keitarō continued in the same vein.

During the course of a day, if something should occur that I don't know about, my gears wouldn't be meshing with society's gears. In the final analysis one simply cannot live effectively if one doesn't read the newspaper.

So as a result, Michiko mused, it was probably in order to avoid anxiety in his life that Keitarō read the newspapers. That fact, plus his insatiable involvement in the outside world, was probably what formed his inner and outer selves.

Michiko left the terrace and went inside.

"Any interesting news?" she asked Keitarō, who was reading the paper.

She had no reason to want to hear any, but she had to mouth the appropriate lines as a matter of duty. Indeed: this thing called life was an accumulation of such duties, and if one didn't perform them, it would seem that one was suddenly protruding beyond the prescribed limits.

"I must have mentioned it this morning," he replied, barely raising his bushy eyebrows from the newspaper. "An article about a man who rescued a mother and her children trying to commit suicide by setting their own house on fire."

"Yes." Michiko recalled her feelings at the time she had heard the story.

"Look, the newspaper even has a picture of the man."

Keitarō spread the newspaper out on the table and tapped the spot with his fist.

Michiko came near and peered. It was a rather large photograph. Probably taken at the police substation directly after his rescue of two infants along with their mother from the fire, it caught the elated expression on the man's face. The admiration for such conduct as revealed in both the photograph and the news report fairly saturated the page, and it was obvious that the action had the support and approval of all the people in the background.

Michiko now felt herself compelled to say what she had not given voice to when she'd heard that story in the morning.

"What that person did was praiseworthy, you say. Why was it praiseworthy? Is it a praiseworthy man who pulls from the flames someone who wants to die and would have died?"

Michiko knew that her comment would not please Keitarō.

Something like a vacuum opened up between the two.

"Try putting yourself in the shoes of the person who would have died. Thinking that she already had had quite enough of this world, and thinking that such a world was utterly unendurable, she'd resolved to kill herself. Even coming to such a resolve could not have been easy. Moreover, even having resolved to die, beyond that there is the implementation, also not an easy thing. From resolution to implementation, it must have seemed there were a thousand years to live. Then, finally, the woman is enveloped in flames, and although she supposed she would die, because of someone's generous act, the next thing she knows she hadn't died at all. Could the man who rescued her imagine how she had felt? Could the newspaper imagine that? And what do you yourself imagine?"

Michiko looked at Keitarō.

"Well, well!" he said, letting out a laugh.

No particular opinion was expressed in the laugh. It was not that Keitarō was a man who did not hold opinions. However, whether in frontal attack or in the counterattack which Michiko was now apparently waging, he always left himself some room for maneuver.

Sanada Misao had been quick to take up Michiko's conversational style. Sawamura Takuzō would also quickly take it up. Whenever Michiko engaged in dangerous talk, there was a type of man in whom such talk kindled inordinate interest and who became very much engaged in the conversation. In such cases Michiko herself would plunge into increasingly dangerous talk, and her listener would flame up and the conversation itself would became charged with sexual magnetism and connect itself directly to sex.

"Shall I make tea?" asked Michiko, going into the kitchen from the living room. She got hot water and the tea things ready and returned to Keitarō's side.

"That's the easy way of doing it, but it tastes better if the tea is steeped in the pot," said Keitarō, glancing at the teabags.

"Yes, that's right," said Michiko. And she visualized herself preparing tea at home without teabags, selecting ingredients with great care and taking time to make their meals, cleaning every nook and cranny of their apartment, and constantly tidying up the drawers of snow-white underclothes, towels, and sheets. How such a life might be a very good thing. And yet how very tiresome it might be.

"When I was in the States on business this time, I became aware, rather belatedly, of a delicious way of making tea. I was invited once to a home in a New York suburb and they served excellent black tea for me. I was reminded of it just now," said Keitarō, politely taking in two hands the saucer and tea bowl which Michiko offered him.

"That's the way it is with Japanese tea, too. Even with the same leaves," said Michiko, noisily sipping her tea, "how hot the water is can make a difference."

"Water heated to sixty degrees centigrade seems best. In the case of green tea, anyway."

"And even the tea bowls themselves seem to make a difference, too. What kind of ware it is, how thick or thin it is."

"New tea bowls are just no good, in my view. But we have to get used to using them."

"And if you're not settled down and relaxed, the tea won't taste good, they say."

How tiresome! mumbled Michiko to herself.

Keitarō returned the conversation from green tea to black tea and recalled how on his way back from the U.S. he had stopped off at the company branch in Germany, where he was served vile-tasting black tea. He chatted away quite merrily. His mind seemed to run exclusively to things foreign, and he sometimes mixed English into his conversation. For a Japanese, he was quite proficient in English. In a company with many talented employees, immediately after being transferred to the main office he was sent on business to the United States, which showed how highly valued his language abilities were. Of course he had other abilities as well. Michiko knew this was a facet of Keitarō which was apparently quite exceptional. This was not, however, a facet which fired her imagination.

"Did you find out where Kaori lives?" asked Keitarō quite out of the blue.

Michiko looked at him, startled. "No," she said flatly.

What startled her was not that she thought Keitarō was criticizing her. He knew nothing of Kaori's mental illness and of course knew nothing of its causes. In any event, someone else's criticism had nothing to do with her feelings.

"She's in Tokyo, isn't she," he said as he got to his feet and switched the radio on to light music.

From this nonchalant action alone it was clear that Kaori's mental illness was a matter about which Keitarō knew nothing. And yet, in Michiko's heart the recollection of her sister collided painfully with the light music.

"I've tried looking everywhere," she replied for the moment.

"Tried looking? And you haven't even found her address?" Keitarō looked up at her as he tapped off the ashes of his cigarette into the ashtray. Whenever he cast a stern look like that, two dark furrows appeared on his brow.

"Yes, that's right, but … Well, she did say she wanted to go into the theater.

And she also said she was going to Tokyo to attend acting school. Even before she ran away from home she'd said that."

Michiko's sister had indeed said that back when she had gotten divorced and run away from home. Nevertheless, about a year later Michiko learned confidentially from a close friend of Kaori about the mental hospital situation.

The sound of the music became trying for Michiko. With her sister's affairs now the topic of conversation, she was made to listen to, of all things, this merry music.

"Did you inquire at the acting schools?"

"No."

"Well then, that's not like having looked everywhere, is it?" asked Keitarō, though without reproach.

"There's a lot of those acting schools."

"If you had checked them one by one, that probably would've done it. It's no big deal. Really, Michiko, you shouldn't be so lackadaisical."

"I tried looking in the phonebook."

"The phonebook?"

"Well, I'm not acquainted with anybody in Tokyo, so I can't very well make personal inquiries."

Michiko recalled her feelings when she had looked up the number for Riverview Mental Hospital in the phonebook.

"It was overwhelming," she said.

"What was overwhelming?"

"All those numbers in the Tokyo phonebook."

"Well, this is the capital."

There seemed to be a note of satisfaction in his voice when Keitarō uttered the word "capital."

"It's so huge. There are too many listings. Way too many listings. I got lost in them."

"Michiko, that's because you're so lackadaisical," he said, repeating his earlier phrase.

"That's not it at all. It's just that I have a distaste for practical affairs. And so the distaste is the reason for my inability. That's all it is."

"Okay. I'll find it for you," said Keitarō, getting to his feet.

"Huh? Are you going out?"

"No, I'm getting the phonebook."

And with that, Keitarō went to the shelf and took down the three volumes listing residential phone numbers and the two volumes listing business numbers.

Michiko was thinking about the flood of print when she had looked up Riverside Mental Hospital—the multitude of numbers, owners, addresses—when suddenly she recalled the number 264-4343, which so resembled her home phone.

How extremely distressful it was to live one's life.

Keitarō leafed through the pages with his thick fingers, muttering all the while.

"Not knowing the address of one's own relative—it's just not right! If the addresses of my friends and relatives and associates were not precisely recorded in my address book, I just wouldn't feel comfortable."

Eleven

HIS MOTHER'S SUICIDE CAME TO TAKUZŌ as a terrible blow.

Then he recalled that incident of long ago. It had occurred in a depression, a depression lower, one might think, than any other on earth, where homes of the impoverished were packed closely together. It was in fact more of a lowland than other districts, lower even than the water level in the drainage ditch running into the area. Such was the impression that had obstinately fixed itself in his mind. There, at a place where sunlight seemed only dimly to penetrate, he who had never been struck even once before by anyone was time and again pummeled by the owner of the stationery store with the strength of concentrated anger. Certain aspects of his character with which he felt he had hitherto been blessed fell away at a single blow, leaving him standing there stark naked, as it were, in that place which was a depression lower than any on earth. His entire body was pierced by feelings seemingly painful, seemingly cheerful. His astonishment that he, who had forever been praised by others, could be so despised and left defenseless, even trampled under foot, was instantly surpassed by his astonishment of having immediately reached his destination—to be psychologically stark naked.

Yes, he craved to become just like that. Suffering abuse from every last person, in the end he himself wished for the so-called humiliation of being ignored. He denied himself and he wanted to be denied.

During that period he had dreams like this one—

Whenever he stooped over, a huge nail was being pounded into his back. Even though it was "huge," it was a hugeness invisible to the eye. There seemed to be a person who was pounding the nail with a hammer, but the person also was invisible. The pain was terrible, unbearable. Still stooped over, he turned back to look, and the face of the person who was hammering the nail was faintly visible. Then a wisp of cloud was lifted away and the face became a little clearer. It was the anguished face of his mother. Oh! he cried, full of dread, and when again he stooped over, that nail was hammered klang-klang further into his back. The action was repeated over and over in a slow refrain. And blending in with it, a voice could be heard: Takuzō, dear; I've been waiting for you all this time to pay me some attention, and so it was that I gave you hints, didn't I; but for a fourth time and a fifth time and a sixth time, you didn't understand, did you; and you didn't notice even on the seventh time; and so by then I had no other choice but to perish. Takuzō, dear Takuzō.

Utterly dispirited, he lost all energy in one clean sweep because of this dream.

So it was, perhaps. And yet, whether in truth it was so or not, there was no way of knowing.

The words of his mother repeatedly came back to him when she received the medicine: Takuzō, dear, recently it has probably been exceedingly troublesome for you to procure those sleeping pills. It would have been fine even if you hadn't overly inconvenienced yourself for my sake, because it seemed that I was able to get some sleep, though the sleeping pills really have helped. Don't keep on inconveniencing yourself, don't keep on …

That was the way she had put it, which could be taken as a hint or, of course, not as a hint. Every single word a person utters conveys his inner self, but apprehending the meaning of that inner self is like trying to grasp a cloud. Contemplating this, he realized just how thickheaded a man can be in his relations with his fellow man. Particularly during that time, besides delivering sleeping pills to his mother, he was devoting so much attention to those women, Miss A and Miss B. How thickheaded indeed a man can become in his relations with his fellow man when he is devoting himself to other matters!

Paralleling these musings, he firmed up a resolution of trying to subject himself to humiliation. Yes, that was the only way: as the quintessential "man who had everything," he would consciously cast off the many luxuries with which he was personally encumbered. He would make what might be called transient and trivial things the foundation of his life.

During the period before graduation he distilled his plan to just a single unique item: a discipline of self-remolding by means of self-denial. To call the undertaking a mere "discipline" seemed inappropriate for a man in such distress as himself. But since he would have found it objectionable that something so serious might be tinged with self-pity, he settled on this dryly dispassionate term, "discipline."

Long ago at age eleven, because of the humiliations he had endured, he suddenly realized what experience had already shown to be so—that discipline was the living keystone of his being. He would habituate himself to that way of life, and because he had accomplished it at that time, he would surely habituate himself to it now, such was his resolve.

Takuzō had been in direct conflict with his father for some weeks because he adamantly refused to take the pre-graduation employment examinations. Sometimes a faint ember from his burnt-out dream of working in a prestigious firm would flash across his mind, but when he resolved to leave home even that vestige of self-esteem completely died out.

Withal, matters regarding his mother came up intermittently, and they pained him. The thought that agitated his heart yet more was the contrast between the pale and forlorn face of his mother now bedridden awaiting death, and previously when she had always appeared as an incomparable gentle spring breeze. That contrast was like being mantled in a blurry halo, akin to the halation effect in photography, such that even if he tried to look directly at her, there were things which could not be seen. Instead, something like awe flickered before the eye, and he hastily averted his gaze. And so, such peaceful recollections as these rushed over him.

Whenever, for example, he'd catch a cold, his mother would prepare for him some hot medicinal drink, two or three doses of which would always cure him. Once when he was on a school trip he caught a cold. The woman teacher was very attentive in looking after him and had him take some medicine but he just didn't improve. His cold progressed to a high fever and he felt miserable the whole trip. What really made the difference? Now he understood: it was, simply, that he had made his mother into a paragon.

And yet, what person was this mother who was deteriorating as death approached? Repeatedly his thoughts would turn in that direction, but he would suddenly divert them. He forced himself to recall his mother's face, like a gentle zephyr wafting toward him. When she smiled, something graceful floated upon that oval face with its bright clear eyes.

He had lost something important through his own thoughtlessness. Even so, leaving aside the undeniable fact that he had delivered sleeping pills to her, everything was so ambiguous. Maybe the ambiguity was a good thing, he decided.

I won't think about it; it's something I should not think about. His principle of discipline required he sever his entire past, both the good and the bad, which clung to him.

Thereafter he made discipline his normal practice.

He severed many extravagances from his life, and no longer expected anything from anyone, indeed expected nothing even from himself. He carried with him only the contours, the visible physical contours, of his own existence. Long ago, there was a certain place which appeared as a depression in the surrounding landscape, a place where sunlight should have bathed all in its rays but shone there only dimly, the very place where he had dreamed of being pummeled by a giant hammer. He now identified with those people and that place.

Even so, the feeling of keen pathos instantly evaporated and everything became abstractly bright.

At first it was most bewildering. It was something, he thought, which might have occurred to anyone, but he wanted above all to see for himself if he was capable of sheer physical labor. Despite his resolve to test himself with physical labor, however, he suddenly gave up the experiment due to unforeseen circumstances.

He stayed the night in a flophouse. In the middle of the night he was awakened by a tingling sensation in every pore of his body. The taste of the cheap saké he had drunk too much of after work remained strong in his mouth, and his head was pounding. After that, whenever he started to doze off he would be awakened by the same sensation as before. His whole body was weary, and he had no energy to get up, but whenever he began to drop off to sleep the same sensation would once again rush through his whole body. Suddenly he got up and took off the clothes he had been sleeping in, and rubbed his hands over his chest, abdomen, and shoulders. Nothing felt particularly out of the ordinary. He thought it was probably just an illusion due to his intoxication, but when he lay down, his eye caught countless black dots crawling around on the sheet. Because only a faint light shone from a lamp at the doorway, he couldn't see clearly, but they seemed to be bedbugs. He immediately crushed those black dots. The movement of his fingers produced innumerable dark traces of blood on the sheet. Feeling relieved, he lay down and instantly was sound asleep. Yet once again the same sensation arose, and this time he awoke with a jump, practically tore the bedding from him, and when he fixed his gaze on the sheet, it was fairly covered with black dots, but once aware they had been discovered, they darted off and escaped to their hiding places. Within an instant they had disappeared. And while he had been taking off his clothes shortly before, the same phenomenon of escaping bedbugs had occurred, because he had crushed only those few which had not darted off to safety fast enough. He sat there shuddering in the gloom, keeping his eyes on the sheet, but drowsiness forced him irresistibly into sleep. Minutes passed and as before he jumped up and saw unmistakably a profusion of insects creeping on top of the sheet. It was not only their numbers that appalled him, but that in spite of being so tiny, they all disappeared from sight simultaneously. It seemed that they possessed a common intelligence. After that, he began to wonder absentmindedly where, within that instant, they had disappeared. Surely into the futon, he assumed; so, taking only the coverlet, he crept into another, vacant room where once again he fell into a deep well of slumber. But it was the same as the old room. Now when he jumped up, the bugs seemed to swarm underneath where he had been sleeping, and black dots, as if tinged with evil, were swarming on top of the tatami he was lying on. Throughout the night he thus suffered these attacks, countless times changing his sleeping position or turning over in his sleep, until finally he greeted the dawn, exhausted.

Despite this, the men who emerged from their rooms exchanged only good-morning greetings with one another and not one of them brought up the subject of bedbugs. They were people each and every one who slept while being invested by hundreds of bugs. As for sleeping here every night, if not troubled with nightmares then they would surely be troubled by other things in their down-and-out lives. Yet in spite of that, the fact that every night there were indeed men who regularly lodged here seemed somehow to be a phenomenon which exceeded his own powers of imagination.

The beginning of his period of discipline could only be called a tale of failure.

He had been working part-time for quite a while as a deliveryman for a small department store. Whistling merrily, he enjoyed driving around. He felt light-hearted, and the atmosphere of the neighborhoods through which he maneuvered his little delivery van was also cheerful. Getting nowhere in his relations with Miss A and Miss B, however, he began wondering if he wasn't thereby simply dissipating himself. So he started paying more attention. Like himself, people generally acquire in differing degrees a great excess of things, by means of which they dissipate themselves, so he was thinking. Their fussing over such things was the cause of their dissipation. Never before, it seemed, had he gone so far as to consider such matters.

Was that not the fault of those empty, hollow things which made him feel tense both inside and out? Even though the pain of the circumstances surrounding his mother's suicide did not disappear, the pain had, curiously enough, receded into the distance. Even when it seemed he was getting around to recollecting those circumstances, he was able to ignore them.

Nor was he even doing much reading. In the evenings he was tired and slept soundly. He did not develop any entangling connections with other people. He merely transported himself around as if he were just some physical object. He felt that people simply make trouble for themselves, and a person encumbered with an excess of possessions causes himself a flood of troubles.

Although he began with an irresistible urge to deny his very existence, he now sensed that he could live while still affirming stark nakedness.

Besides that department store job, he had also waited table in a restaurant, peddled wares on commission as a door-to-door salesman, and so forth, but those latter two he soon quit. Dishwashing at a cheap eatery and typesetting at a printing shop lasted quite a while. His present work as deliveryman and cashier at the little department store suited his temperament better.

Ten years had gone by in a twinkling. But this year he felt less sanguine about his discipline.

The circumstances were these. He had planned to discipline himself as a person, but the result, he thought, was that he had not passed beyond discipline as a mere concept. That occurred to him when recently in the middle of the night, lying still in his room, he had the undeniable sensation of returning to his primordial self. Something from inside himself was telling him so. At a time when the homes in the neighborhood were all asleep and not a soul was about, he felt that the person within him had unexpectedly emerged, animal-like.

A person encumbered with too many possessions is flooded with troubles he has caused for himself—a fact he had previously considered. Surely he had rid himself of those things which he ought to have been rid of. Nonetheless, it did indeed seem that the contents of his inner self existed unchanged. He understood that something like a hibernating beast, matched to his own breathing, was breathing impurely within.

Mulling over in his mind what he had just been telling Michiko, Takuzō roamed the late night streets. The scent of her hair, even as she had wearied listening to all of this, accompanied him everywhere along his walk. This was now their second meeting.

I'd be so happy if you could understand me, Takuzō had said outright, and he could still hear his voice as he left the hotel room.

I'd be so happy if you could understand me, were the words that had issued from his mouth, and, indeed, he was aware that he did ardently hope that someone in this world—even just one person—would understand him.

I understand, I really do understand; that's the way people are, Michiko had said, lying on her back puffing a cigarette. From time to time she would raise her arm, cigarette still held between her fingers, and lazily describe a circle in the air, an action she kept repeating. In the dark it seemed to be a flaming red dot moving about. The color of that fire seemed to have been ignited from her own flesh.

When I talk with you I know you really do understand everything I say. But you haven't experienced such things yourself, so how can you possibly understand so well? Do you truly understand?

In saying he'd be so happy to be understood, Takuzō was actually diluting his own feelings. Up to now, when talking with a woman, he had never felt certain that his words were really being absorbed by her.

People say I'm smart, but that's not at all the case, Michiko had said.

No, you're very intelligent.

As for me, she went on, however difficult the conversation might be, I understand it. But rather than with my mind I seem to understand with my body. It seems that my body is joined together with my mind.

Can you expand on that a little more for me? asked Takuzō.

When someone says something, it immediately passes through my brain and enters my body and it's there that I understand it. Speech which I wouldn't understand as long as it stayed in my head I force into my body with all my might. So I have the feeling that in the recesses of my body something is there to help me—I'm quite sure of that.

Really, I don't understand the way you've put that, or rather, it's difficult for me to understand. That's because among my men friends it's never that way.

As Takuzō said this, he placed his hand on Michiko's head. Surprisingly cold, he thought, probably because it was moist with perspiration. If it was as she had just said, that was because her essence did not reside here in her head, he thought, caressing her.

Even though I understand it, I can't help it, said Michiko, her tone of voice suddenly turning languorous.

Why can't you help it? Takuzō was getting insistent. Frustrated by her indifference, he felt like throttling her.

That's just the way it is, she said. Even if I understand a person's concerns, they would still be that person's concerns, and if they were my own concerns, they would still be mine only, wouldn't they? I simply can't help it.

Walking the night streets back to his lodgings, he reflected on this. The woman had not uttered a single word about her own concerns. It had been that way on the previous occasion and now on this occasion, too. The woman had revealed virtually nothing about her own past and present, while he, for his part, had laid bare an enormous concern. Was it not as if his very substance had been completely plundered by this woman?

For the first time since having met her, a momentary feeling resembling hatred gushed in a torrent within him, a feeling swallowed up in a foul-smelling river.

Takuzō felt that his very being had begun swimming in that river. Hibernating for an interval of some ten years, he had accumulated ten years of physical stamina, and he had become far stronger than he had been before. Now only that part of him which had been stripped by discipline of useless things was becoming his single strength. His situation was like that of the holy man in quest of knowledge for numberless years who encounters a harlot. And so it was perhaps that he himself was somehow practicing a holy discipline.

Why, then, did this river smell so foul? Because of his encounter with this woman he had the premonition something was opening up, yet possibly opening up to something dark and destructive.

The woman seemed to be both selfish and selfless, both lively and lifeless. Considered intellectually, she assumed deep hues of corporeality; considered physically, her mind turned keen as a scalpel. The two opposites intermixed chaotically.

Takuzō's inner self was swept along in a raging river as he tramped the night streets. From the subway station he walked the distance to his lodgings as usual by tracing the route of the bus. Only the sound of his footfalls could be heard.

I'll chance it! he muttered aloud.

A cat, apparently startled by the voice, looked his way and scampered off.

He seemed to have walked right past his lodging house. The gate lamp was switched off, leaving the place in complete darkness. On the narrow walkway from the gate to the entrance a shadow moved. Takuzō stood stock still. The thoughts that had roiled his mind as he had been walking along likewise came to a stop. The shadow suddenly emerged from the darkness. There was a faint fragrance of perfume.

"What on earth, is that you?" exclaimed Takuzō.

"I came about nine and was standing here for almost thirty minutes. Then I went back home for a while, and since about eleven o'clock I've been standing here now for another hour," said Muro Sawako.

"But why? Don't you always just make yourself at home and go inside to wait?" said Takuzō, thinking it all quite strange.

"'Why,' you ask?" she said with a touch of laughter. With only a dim light penetrating from the entrance, he could not make out her expression.

"You must be cold. All of a sudden the weather has become like winter."

Takuzō turned and started toward the entrance. Although he thought Sawako would of course follow along, she did not. He looked back.

"Well, I suppose I should be going now …," she said.

Her round white face appeared to be floating in the darkness. Doubting that impression, Takuzō peered more closely. The thought inexplicably occurred to him that she seemed particularly light of weight because she seemed to have the capacity to make herself light.

"You must be cold," he repeated.

"No, not a bit," said Sawako. Then she added, "I'm not cold or anything. I think I once told you I'm a 'cheerful redcap.'"

"Well then ...," he said, making no attempt to hold her back. It did occur to him, however, that up until now she had never used perfume.

Twelve

THIS METROPOLIS, CHOKED IN DRY WHITE DUST throughout the prolonged and excessive heat of summer, was today exhibiting a landscape of scraps of newspaper and bits of plastic blown about by dark gusts vaguely cool on a day not yet autumnal. When she had first moved here and not at all knowing her way around, she kept having the sensation that, like some enormous skin, the great throngs of people in this vast metropolis were pressing against her. Coarse-skinned, goose-fleshed throngs.

What do you do every day? Sawamura Takuzō had asked.

Do? I don't do anything. There is nothing to do, had been Nobe Michiko's reply.

What a wonderful life, said Takuzō with a slight smile. His smile did not produce any real dimple, but there was a place on his cheeks that did indent a little, a feature captured perfectly by the adjective "charming".

It is not wonderful though, not at all.

Women your age don't usually say "there is nothing to do."

Then, let's just say that it's wonderful for other people like that.

You always try to contradict whatever a person says.

There is nothing to do, she repeated, and that's the truth.

But they say that all women have too many things they want to do and not enough time to do them in.

And so that's why I'm saying such people have a wonderful life.

That being the case, what do you really do? Certainly it can't be that you do nothing at all.

Michiko wondered how it would be if Takuzō pumped her about her husband's affairs.

I have a wife's work to do.

Since you have a household, you have a future.

A future? she queried.

Yes.

Michiko wondered if he was inquiring as to whether or not she planned to continue her married life.

Only the present exists for me, she said.

So you never think in terms of wanting to do this or do that, or wanting to become this or become that? Are you happy, he asked?

All is tedium, everything is meaningless—other than meeting my lover. That's the reason for living.

You certainly do care for me marvelously.

Although Michiko was speaking her heart, she wondered if her companion hadn't taken it as a joke. Again, Takuzō's cheeks indented as he smiled.

Michiko strained her ears to hear the station announcement. Because she had been reliving the conversation of the other day, she thought she might have passed her station, though in fact it seemed she was two or three stops before Yashio station. Edgewood Hospital in Yashio City. This was her third visit there.

Yes, now I remember. It must have been that day I had the conversation with Takuzō. No, maybe it was a different day. By now their meetings amounted to five, but since it was Takuzō who chose the places where they met, they had met at a different place each of the five times. Their meeting spots were not at coffee shops like the first time. Each time he found a different cocktail lounge for them. Whether such a conversation took place on that day or on another she couldn't quite remember, for on every occasion their routine had been the same round of cocktail lounge, hotel, and bar, or else cocktail lounge, bar, and hotel, without doing anything extra like seeing a play or movie or taking a stroll in the park, but just spending all their time in their own hermetically sealed secret world.

One day as Michiko was going into a cocktail lounge for one of their rendezvous, she suddenly looked back. Just then, on the street she had been hurrying along, the round, light-complexioned face of a short woman was peering out from the shadow of a parked truck. In spite of her chubby, pleasant-looking face, there was nonetheless something special in it as their eyes met, a face, Michiko thought, that she had seen before somewhere. It was not that the woman was merely looking at Michiko—she was walking in her direction. It was clear to Michiko that the woman realized she had been spotted, so she continued to walk along, acting as if she had not been peering at all. When Michiko went into the cocktail lounge, only three large wooden tables, burnished by age and long years of use, were set up and from the rearmost table Takuzō waved his hand. Instantly Michiko remembered quite clearly that special something which had revealed itself in the woman's eyes. They were the eyes of her sister. Her sister had looked at Michiko with just such a fixed stare. No, it was not merely that, Michiko further recalled. When she had met Takuzō in their first coffee shop rendezvous, she saw a woman across the way who seemed to be waiting at the bus stop there or, judging from the way she was standing, not waiting at all but rather staring in Michiko's direction. Those two woman closely resembled each other. As Michiko's association of recollections continued, another came to mind as the train now rumbled into Yashio station. After their first meeting, as she was walking along with Takuzō on the way to a bar, she felt she was being observed by someone mixed in with the throng of pedestrians, and she sensed that that someone was very much like her sister.

The announcement of arrival at her station sounded, and Michiko stepped out onto the platform.

As she did so, yet another recollection occurred. At that first coffee shop, she had inquired, Are you single? When Takuzō had replied, Yes of course, she declared, That being the case, I'm relieved to know it.

Having gotten off at Yashio station, she started walking toward Edgewood Hospital.

Now she understood why she had felt relieved. If he were a married man, his wife might be driven to insanity, and that would be troubling. But if she did not become insane, his affair with another woman probably would amount to no more than an ordinary occurrence in the normal course of life. Michiko was made aware of the degree to which one had to balance one's own desires with the sacrifice of someone else to mental illness.

At the end of the road that stretched out before her, a pine woods came into view. The hospital was located just before the woods off to one side.

She had first come here in the midst of that frypan-like late summer heat. Then the second and, so she had thought, the last time she had come was the day before Keitarō's return from abroad. Today, however, she had indeed come a third time. On the second occasion she had not actually gone into the hospital but only wandered around outside, then returned home. Today again she had no plan to go inside.

The pine woods drew closer. The trees stood tall with needles grown dense—a woods, somehow, of imposing melancholy. They were unlike the pines typical of her hometown, which were more delicate, shinier, drier. But then the color of the soil here was singularly black. Had not the trees soaked up the earth's color, such that black had become admixed with the green of the needles to become thickly somber?

Without turning in toward the main gate of the hospital, she kept walking, and followed a path leading into the pine woods. This took her around to the rear of the hospital.

During her second trip here she had circled the hospital three times. It was the last days of summer then and, walking about without either parasol or sunhat, she had become bathed in perspiration. Because there was no path running along the hospital's property wall, she'd had to walk quite a distance to complete a single round.

Today of course it was not hot, but she seemed nonetheless to be sweating profusely. Her very innards were panting with heat. There was the faint odor of pine resin. On hot days the odor was thick and adhered to the body, which in turn exuded the odor. Since the beginning of her relationship with Takuzō, her desires had been fermenting.

Craning her neck she looked toward the hospital. Beyond the closely spaced trees, there was a high concrete wall and beyond the wall a vacant lot or open space or something—she couldn't tell what—and well beyond that she could make out the second floor of an old two-story wood structure, much like a grade school or a T.B. convalescence home. It was some distance away, so she couldn't be sure, but she could make out something like grating fitted against all the windows. Beyond the grating she thought she could see shadows crowded together. Were they people, or was it nothing more than reflections off the windowpanes?

She wondered if her sister could see the pine woods from her room. Would her sister recall the pine woods near their childhood home? Could insane people have pleasant recollections?

There is nothing more nightmarish than an insane person. If it were a perfect stranger, then one could heave a sigh of relief. But that it should be a person sharing the same blood, a constant companion since childhood, raised the fear that the insanity might infect her blood too.

Emerging from the woods, she saw a number of shabby homes standing here and there separated by planted fields, and in the black soil characteristic of the area scallions and radishes were sprouting. Their white stalks stood out vividly against the color of the soil. When she made her way onto the dirt road, she was very far indeed from the hospital, having actually wandered into a side road, so she turned back in the direction of the hospital's main gate. Everything was the same as on the previous occasion. The road seemed to run parallel to the bare concrete wall, within which there were people's voices. Michiko stopped and listened intently. After that, she emerged in front of the main gate and with quickened pace passed by. Coming out onto the wide paved road extending directly from the station, she again approached the pine woods, and went onto the same road as just a while ago.

It was not summer but it seemed like summer, because, like saké, there were things making her head buzz and swirl.

Being alive was not interesting in the slightest. It had been so since her childhood. For most people zealous adherence to the rules that shape this world anchored their lives, but for Michiko all this could be thought of as so much dross. There was, however, one thing that was not like this.

And that was, in this hospital there resided someone who was punishing Michiko by having become insane. She tried to imagine the figure of her sister perhaps pacing back and forth within her barred room, her gaze fixed, saying all along, I won't forgive you, I simply will not forgive you. Although Michiko could not see it with her own eyes, she was aware that she herself was similarly surrounded by grates, pacing back and forth.

One's desires are limitless, and once having started there is no stopping them.

She passed through the pine woods and walked by nondescript homes and fields. At a considerable distance from the hospital she turned right, retracing the path. She followed along the high concrete wall and again emerged in front of the main entrance. She had twice circled the hospital. With quickened pace she went past the main entrance and from there came out onto the wide paved road. Should I circle around once more, she wondered, hesitated, then at last, feeling she had broken a spell, headed toward the station.

She boarded the train and thought to herself, Well, what shall I do?

By the time she had arrived back at Shinjuku station, it was already dusk. Lights were burning, but they had not yet become a vivid illumination, having only a pale dimness which oozed through the membrane that was the interval between day and night. From the other side of the shopping district, desires seemed to be oozing forth. Thereupon her whole body was seized by the feeling that she wanted to be together with her lover.

The thought occurred to her to return to the bar she had previously visited with Takuzō and look around. She had no expectation she might actually bump into him but, impelled by that hot current of ardor, the bar simply became the destination of her walk. Compared with this limitless ardor, she thought, one individual man seemed a mere trifle.

Michiko descended into the downstairs bar. She cast her eyes about the room, still largely deserted. Naturally Takuzō was not there. Feeling slightly disappointed, she realized she did after all have some expectation.

She sat down at the counter, ordered a scotch and water, and took a sip.

After a time, someone burst into the place like a gust of wind. He had come running down the stairs and pushed the door open with a bang. Michiko looked around, but of course it was not Takuzō. The man who had come in sat down at the counter beside Michiko. He too ordered a scotch and water and began drinking steadily.

The man perched on his barstool like a bird, giving Michiko the impression that he was light as a feather. Slight of build with a small face and keen of hearing, he somehow seemed different from the ordinary run of men. Her curiosity piqued, Michiko looked at his profile.

Then, quite unexpectedly, the man began talking.

"It's really and truly an amazing thing, don't you think? This enormous and complicated incident, this thing filling up the newspapers every single day, this thing happening right before our very eyes. Really! Here we are, one hundred and twenty million people like silkworms spinning our cocoons. But unfortunately, there isn't any silk. It's just people spinning out incidents. Something spins out of the mouths of just about everybody. That's what I think, so won't you please just take a look at this enormous and complicated incident. It's simply appalling! And what's so appalling about it? It's because you can see the mouths of people at the bottom of society opening and closing, yakity-yak. Furiously opening and closing their mouths. If there were no mouths, there'd be no incidents either. Talking animals. If there weren't any talking, the world would probably come to look a whole lot different."

His small eyes glanced quickly in Michiko's direction. But rather than looking at Michiko the woman, it was more like simply turning his eyes toward a conversational partner.

"Is that something you affirm or deny," he asked.

Michiko felt inclined to join him in conversation. The gentleman did not seem to be aware of her as a woman, and so that current of ardor she had felt a moment ago did not flow in his direction.

"Well then, Ma'am. To affirm or deny—is that something that can be decided by me? Supposing I do decide. Even so, that decision would have nothing to do with how things exist. It's just like the ebb and flow of the tide."

This did not seem to be a man simply spouting drunken nonsense, Michiko thought, so she asked, "What sort of work do you do, sir?"

Without replying, the man laughed a loud, raspy laugh. Along with the cigarette smoke of the customers who were now gradually filling the bar, the sound of that raspy laugh, like the wingbeat of a bird ascending, rose up toward the low ceiling.

Thirteen

264-4343. THAT WAS THE NUMBER TAKEDA SACHIKO DIALED.

"Hello?" came the voice at the other end.

"This is LifeLine, isn't it," said Sachiko with a sigh of relief, for it was a man's voice.

"I'm the person who called before," she began. "I'm the person who said I'm so cold, terribly cold and there's nothing that can be done about it so I want to die. Actually, I phoned yesterday too. But because I got a woman, somehow or other I just couldn't talk about my problems very well. I told her it was easier for me to talk to a man, and so the woman—she wasn't put out at all—was kind enough to tell me that if I called today, a man would answer. I was surprised she wasn't offended. Well, since she was a woman, you know, I thought for sure she would take offense. Are you the person I talked with the last time? I can't see your face, so I can't tell. And I think your voice also seems different from the voice last time. Anyway, whoever it is that's okay with me. Just so long as it is someone kind enough to listen."

"If a person prefers to speak with a man, then a man will take the call, and if the person prefers to speak with a woman, then a woman will take the call. Because the important thing is to meet the needs of the caller. But whether it's a man or woman who takes the call, both will equally listen to what you have to say."

"Yes, I understand that. My father died when I was just a child, so I hardly knew him. When it's a man's voice I guess it makes me think of the father I never knew. When it's a woman's voice I just think of the unpleasant voices of the many women I've known. And so I just get to where I can't talk. I suppose that's not right, huh? I suppose that's selfishness on my part."

"No, no," replied the voice, full of kindness.

"Well then, it's okay?" Hearing his voice, Sachiko could feel herself softening.

"So then, you must have met with another painful experience."

The question struck her at the very core.

"Another painful experience? No, it's not just that. It's always, always a painful experience."

By this point in their phone conversation, Sachiko realized just how enormous the thing was that she had bottled up within herself.

"I see. Let's talk about it, then. Not just one person considering it, but the two of us considering it together. If we do it that way, something may come to us."

The voice was kind, yet at the same time firm.

"I'm fourteen years old and in second year of junior high school."

Sachiko repeated what she had said on the previous occasion, for it was not at all clear to her that the person she was talking to was the same as the person before. Indeed, the voice had become abstracted: it was unquestionably a male voice, but it was stripped down to the basic characteristics of maleness.

"You said, 'I'm so cold, terribly cold.'"

"Yes, I am so cold, terribly cold and there's nothing that can be done about it and so I'm always thinking I want to die. Um, I'm sorry to say it, but I actually came close to dying," said Sachiko in a burst of courage.

"Close to dying?"

It was not as if he were interrogating her; it was rather that he was repeating her words in agreement with her.

"About a week ago I tried to commit suicide, but I wasn't able to."

"Oh, you poor soul."

"Huh? What did you say?"

"I said, 'Oh, you poor soul.'"

"Really? Well, I can't believe that another person would be so kind as to think that about me."

"I'm always ready to listen carefully. I have been listening carefully to what you are thinking. Based on my own thinking I listen to what you are thinking."

"Yes, yes," she said agreeably, but for Sachiko the words were merely words and did not echo in her heart. Her greatest hope for today was to have someone listen to her situation. So she went on.

"Day after day I've been searching for a particular man. I've been walking back and forth looking for him in the busiest section of Shinjuku where I'd met him once before. He's not what you'd call my boyfriend; he's more of a big brother. And the reason why is because I don't particularly think of him as the opposite sex. Also probably because he doesn't treat me like a woman. It'd be funny to treat me like a woman. After all, I'm still just fourteen. But I discovered that by selling my body, I can come close to being a grown-up. I think I have become remarkably like an adult. In the space of only about two months. That's not just on account of my body, though. It's because I've gotten involved in relations between one person and another in a way that up to now I hadn't known about. It's really amazing that by just selling my body I can get close to a person. When I say person, I mean just men. Why is it that an avenue opens up to me just with regard to men?"

"That's the most easily understood form of love," said the voice, almost in a whisper.

Somehow even those words didn't really make sense to Sachiko, and so she rushed on.

"I was looking for a particular man I'd met just once. Even though I say 'just once,' it was just once for every man. In the crowds of Shinjuku, it's unthinkable I might bump into the same person a second time. But as for the person I was looking for, I wanted for sure to meet him a second time. Perhaps that's because I didn't regard him as being particularly masculine. As for myself, I want him as a human being, not just as a man, to become close to me. But as for the people I can be intimate with, of course they are of the opposite sex."

"You're just fourteen years old, you said. Oh, how you must be suffering."

"Suffering? Well, for me, that's all I have."

Her voice broke off for a moment, but she knew that the person on the other end of the line was waiting for her.

"Please listen, please keep on listening," she called out to the waiting voice.

"So what did you do then?" came the voice, conforming to Sachiko's change in feeling.

"I gradually got tired. The person I was looking for seemed to have faded out of existence. So for a time it got really cold for me. It's something I'm very familiar with."

"And then?" he urged.

As long as her listener was there, Sachiko felt she was being supported.

"What was that period of time like?" asked the voice again, for Sachiko remained silent.

"Why do you keep asking?"

Why was her listener ever so attentive to her, who felt within herself nothing other than cold?

"Because you said you were so cold, terribly cold. I can't do anything about the cold you feel, but at least I can listen to you talk about the cold."

"I've already lost all connection both with people and with things. It was better when I was struggling with being hateful and angry. Because then I was connected with the people I was hating and angry with. But even that has disappeared, and I've fallen all alone into a cold, cold place. It's like the whole world was immersed in icy water. And I am squatting right in the middle of the water."

"And yet here you are talking with me like this. You had the idea of dialing me up and talking with me."

His voice was like a beacon.

"Yes, that's true." Sachiko was now crying.

"So, you were thinking of dying; and what did you do about it?"

"Because I seemed to be in the middle of icy water, I wondered if it wouldn't be a good thing if I really did go into icy water, so I went to the ocean. For the entire evening I sat on the beach. But I came to realize that it was really frightful. Though I'd thought it would be no big deal to wade into the water, when I actually looked right at it, the night sea was really scary. I had no idea it could be so vast and so deep. Those murky black waves, just like ink, came crashing in. Dying is such a struggle with fear. I just couldn't do it. Just couldn't."

"Why do you think you were so afraid?"

Sachiko shook her head back and forth. Then, suddenly aware that she was invisible to her questioner, she added, "I was just afraid, that's all. It was just instinct."

"Yes, because you are still living. Because you are a life."

"Me, a life?"

"Because you're brimming with life."

"Brimming?" Sachiko tried to figure out what he meant.

"Please always keep this fact in mind."

"No, no; whatever life is, I don't understand it," she cried out to the invisible voice. "Really, I just want to die."

Fourteen

~

EVER SINCE MOVING TO THIS UNFAMILIAR metropolis Nobe Michiko more and more felt she was drifting atop a wave. Of course nowhere was there any such thing as the blue ocean. But its waves rolled uninterruptedly to the outermost reaches of the city, and they pushed her this way and that. These were not waves of water; they seemed more like waves of wind. Countless waves were forever rising up, and because for Michiko there was no fixed direction, she was time and again pushed along willy-nilly. In this manner she drifted about God knows where. And so she had been drifting until now. Her parents having died early, she and her sister, Kaori, were entrusted to their aunt for their upbringing, and so from the beginning there was no real foundation. Because their aunt's family was very well off, there had never been any material hardships, and yet they had constantly lived within a context of only a thin blood relation. Since Kaori, Michiko's only close relation, had severed the bond between them by becoming insane, there was nothing left of their relationship. That did not particularly perturb Michiko, however. Even supposing she had sought a bond in her marriage, that would not in the slightest have connected her with the family. Michiko was just drifting through life.

She had had no family in the past and seemingly none now. Even though her existence had been planted in the soil of family, it apparently had not taken root. Whatever the reasons for that might have been, one was as good as another.

Lying face up on the bed, Michiko began talking.

"There happened to be an article in the newspaper recently about a man pulling to safety a woman and her children trying to commit suicide by setting their house on fire. Did you read about it?"

"I probably read it," said Takuzō. "Because things like that have been going on all the time recently."

"Even if it were just another 'thing,' as you say, isn't that kind of rescue pretty unusual?" Michiko was now reviving a question she had previously put to Keitarō. "What do you think about what that man did?"

"It's of no particular interest to me," he said outright. Though of no interest to him, to show his interest in Michiko herself, Takuzō amenably shifted his position, turning toward her. Bending his elbow, he propped his head up on the palm of his hand.

Michiko was aware that as a living man he avoided talk of suicide. Nonetheless, she disregarded the thought and continued with her story.

"Although it was said to have been a wonderful thing that he did, I disagree. Totally disagree. How can it be a wonderful thing to rescue from a fire a person who wanted to die and was in the process of dying? More than just disagreeing, I shudder. Everybody's trying to cover over danger. Like the article's emphasis on the man who carried out the rescue. Danger is taboo. The truth is always like that."

As Michiko was speaking, she got the feeling that she was dredging up Takuzō's taboo.

Whenever Michiko talked soothing talk but then ended up rubbing someone's fur the wrong way, she found it a pleasant sensation, indeed a very sexy sensation.

"To let people kill themselves who want to kill themselves, as you say, is rather simplistic thinking," said Takuzō, reaching out and resting his hand on Michiko's neck. His long fingers seemed somehow sinuous.

"I know what you're trying to say." Michiko felt that the place where his hand was in contact with her had suddenly become hot like burning charcoal. She couldn't distinguish whether it was his hand or her neck that was hot.

"So what is it I'm trying to say?" he said in an arrogant tone, quite contrary to the gentle stroking of her neck.

"Rather than my saying it, wouldn't it be better if you spoke for yourself?" returned Michiko in the same tone of voice.

The living past, which Takuzō was avoiding, stood between them like a ghost.

"You're being mean, you know." And he squeezed hard on her neck.

"I am not," she said with a laugh. "It's not quite that." And with her cheery voice a hot wave suddenly billowed from her mouth. Her feelings were again on the rise. It was not the consequence of his hand caressing her neck, but rather the consequence of their verbal exchange.

"You're teasing me, and so that's why I'm saying it. It's not simplistic to say that a person who wants to die should just die. Even if the person who wants to die is let to die, there is a part of him inside which does not want to die. Or rather, probably does not want to."

"Hmm, well then, like most people you also think that the example in the newspaper of the man who rescued them ought after all to be thought of as a splendid thing," she said, purposely twisting his words.

"No," he said gravely.

"Yes. When a man who wants to die is let to die," she continued, "some chance passer-by would detect the particular part of the man which says I wish not to die. The passer-by would be quite able to see right through him. It stands to reason, then, that the newspaper praised the act."

Michiko was searching him out. She had the feeling that she was strongly giving off a scent something like the resin of that pine forest in summer.

"Good heavens, do you actually want to die?" said Takuzō, now shifting to the offensive.

"No," replied Michiko, shaking her head back and forth. His hand upon her neck seemed like a weight bearing down on her.

"That being the case, if I asked you if you wanted to live, when all is said and done you'd probably say no."

Michiko glanced at him, saying nothing.

"Just now your eyes were green."

"I realize that. Wasn't there a movie called 'Cat on a Hot Tin Roof'? Me, I'm always just like that."

"Well that's not how I see it. That's not the way I feel about it."

"That being so, you think you'd like to die? Have you ever thought you'd like to die?"

"Why have you from the first been so concerned about death?"

"Why, you ask? Well, it simply goes against the grain," said Michiko, pleased to be in her own territory.

"I don't think I want to die."

Takuzō covered her eyes with his hand, and so a hot darkness came over her.

"Really?"

"I'd choose humiliation over death."

"It's that discipline of yours. You're tough."

"When I'm looking at you, it seems to me that you're eager for death."

Michiko laughed, and the laugh rippled through her body. The phrase, "eager for death," aroused her, gave her goose bumps. Speaking about death was taboo, and taboos are sexual. Even without any overt violation of that taboo, anything revolving around such speech was itself sexual.

"You're someone who doesn't like to talk about herself."

"I do, actually," she said, "and since a little while ago I've been overdoing it."

"It hasn't been anything more than ordinary chit-chat. Everything important has been left out".

The two of them drew close. By now they had been in the room for about two hours, and again they were becoming intimate.

"Well," he said, "I don't think you're trying very hard to get to know about me."

"I suppose you're right."

"I don't understand what you are hoping for." Takuzō's voice was filling with something strong, resembling anger.

"Here, just being here together is perfect, or rather something close to perfect."

"You don't believe that, do you, neither yourself nor your partner."

"Partner?"

Yes, probably so. The man she loves probably plays only one role, Michiko was thinking. This was certainly the man she loved, but by means of this man it probably was only her own appetites that she was waiting for. Borne along by her appetites, from her innermost being a dreadful woman would be revealed. A woman how many times more secretive than the everyday self, a crazed woman one might say, naked, greedy, frenzied, accumulating the excess of her energy into her body like a single-minded killer, a woman who was a stranger but a woman whom she knew from before birth, though when she inquires, "who are you," the woman seems to answer, "I am you, there is no one else save

I alone." That kind of woman had now come out into the open. The truth is I am in love with this woman, but in order to meet this woman it is necessary to associate with the man I love. From the beginning, such a woman nibbled the bait of dangerous talk, and thus dazzling sexual excitement arose, instant by instant closing in to become a union with me. Takuzō's body was wonderfully soft, though not carnally; rather his graceful carriage was like that, softness and nimbleness melting together as a harmonious whole, becoming an elusive existence, strangely fading away. As for Michiko, it was only the cruel feelings arising from the depths of the dreadful woman that were concentrating in her. Responding to that concentration, the woman was drawing closer, fitting herself perfectly to the contours of my body. The zigzagging that occurred before becoming united would be prolonged indefinitely. To that extent it seemed just like the anguish that repeats itself before a person dies. Isn't it just an imitation of death? Isn't it just a gimmick the same as death? That woman would be only too happy to be anguished, and so the man would be surprised, and in his surprise would completely abandon himself to that woman. That woman would moment by moment draw closer, dancing round and round, and in the end would suddenly attach herself to me. At that time I brushed against something close to perfection, and to that extent the I who had given life to the false self felt the self which was not false, and I felt that it was precisely this time that I was united with myself, and then that woman instantly dies.

Indeed: I have not died, but that woman has died. It is as if some eerie creature, gasping for air, were being pushed upward by hydraulic pressure from the sea floor, and immediately upon surfacing would surely die, some thing which one could not say was an existence, rather some thing one might call a phantom or illusion, yet notwithstanding it had life. I am always summoning that woman and for that purpose I do not refuse her anything. Once I become intimate with that woman, surmounting all obstacles without regard to sacrifice, I summon that woman. In everyday life I have already assumed that woman's nature, and have become naked, greedy, frenzied. Nonetheless people do not pay much attention to my transformation, for it is something that is within myself.

"What a face you're making—what are you thinking, I'd like to know." It was Takuzō's voice.

"I really should get up," she said, lifting her eyes up to Takuzō who was standing there, and realized that some little time had elapsed since he had moved his body away from hers.

"I'd like to snatch your thoughts away from you. I'm always thinking that, and that's what I'm thinking right now. Be so kind as not to forget that." Takuzō spoke with intensity, but also with composure and the gap between the two hinted of arrogance.

"They can't be snatched away, because they're inside me," replied Michiko, still languidly sprawled across the bed.

"Quite so; I was asking the impossible. That's because I seem to be a mortal who always likes what is impossible."

Yes. Even his discipline was like that, and this man seemed to be grappling with something invisible, thought Michiko. To carry out such discipline was no trifling matter. Even if there were real flesh-and-blood individuals who think, "Let me remake myself," would there be anyone who even after ten years actually accomplished it?

Yet as for myself, thought Michiko, reconsidering, I've gotten too cozy with that invisible woman. Now, while Takuzō is in the bathroom, I have not gotten up, and that woman's aftertaste is still in my mouth. Even if I say she's dead, she'll come back to life at any time. I know I'm restraining her from coming overly close to me. I can summon her as many times as I want.

So musing, her thoughts once again went to Takuzō's discipline. There was no denying that this man who had been cultivating discipline for the past ten years was a man with enormous latent power. From here on how might such power be exercised?

Takuzō came out of the bathroom fully dressed, but Michiko was still stretched out on the bed. Looking up at him, she thought him particularly tall.

"Sometimes you're very fickle in the way you pay attention to me," he said with a laugh. As a person who from childhood had continuously been praised, he had an easy laugh. At the same time, it was a laugh which, akin to that dimple-like indentation on his cheek, also seemed somehow to include an allure suggesting decadence.

"No, honest; you're really very handsome," she insisted.

Standing firmly between herself and Takuzō was that woman's apparition, which seemed to shine upon him an incomparably virile radiance. Sitting down on the sofa, crossing his legs, pulling out a cigarette, striking a match—

the suppleness of this whole series of actions somehow gave the impression of clothing him in near perfection, perhaps because Michiko saw in it something which neared the perfection which endowed that woman.

She had once talked with a man about that woman within her. Without hesitation the man had said, You're a narcissist. Actually I am not that type of a person at all, she thought. Surely it is only women who draw life from the regions of darkness. It occurred to Michiko that when a man witnesses that which exceeds his own understanding, he seems to attach the term "narcissism."

They left the hotel and as the two of them were walking, that woman, though fading away, still followed. Was it gratitude toward that woman which now filled Michiko, or was it gratitude toward Takuzō? Although she wasn't able to differentiate, gratitude was gratitude. It was strange that such a word, related to virtue as it was, could fall from her lips. Because that woman—naked, greedy, frenzied—would not hesitate to destroy everything for her own sake. Because she vehemently hated to see her own plans blocked. Thus Michiko felt that something akin to violence was developing inside her. Even if she tried to stop it, it could not be stopped. They continued meeting on average about once every five days, but it would be even better if they continued to meet everyday.

"I have to call home," said Michiko, the thought having occurred to her. "I wonder if there's public telephone around."

"It's a little chilly, but let's have a beer. It would be pleasant to sit down and enjoy a glass, then make your call." And so Takuzō headed off to a beer hall he knew.

Night in the big city with its crush of people walking so meaninglessly held no interest for her now; rather, because she was looking through the embers of the fire gushing forth from her inner self, night in the big city seemed a mere ripple within the great ocean of life.

Despite the cold, the beer hall was packed. The reeking throngs pressed up against her body, and their breath fanned the embers within her. And so, she had the feeling that again a small flame was rising up which soon, as if smothering her, would envelope her in a raging pillar of fire. For that reason Michiko could think that the man accompanying her was a peerless lover.

"I've got to make that phone call," said Michiko, rising from her seat.

If it had been anything else, Takuzō would have inquired to the last detail, but in the case of her husband he did not inquire at all. It occurred to Michiko that some time or other she might herself try bringing up the subject.

She dialed the number. It kept on ringing. Keitarō had not yet returned. When he met with foreigners who came to the company, it often happened that he was with them until late in the evening. That apparently was the schedule for today. Since, after all, it had now gotten to be nearly twelve o'clock, Michiko felt she owed it to him to let him know her whereabouts. If she did not do so, she had the feeling that from here on she might at any time find herself gradually slipping morally downhill. Her head reeled as the darkness of life lay gaping before her.

"Not in," she said, returning to her seat. She omitted the subject of the sentence, and Takuzō did not inquire.

"I do have a husband. Did you know that?" asked Michiko, jokingly broaching the subject. Sometime or other she might herself try bringing up the subject, she had thought, and she felt now was the time for it.

"You feel within yourself some contradiction—is that what you're saying?" said Takuzō coldly, though, to the contrary a mole on his nostril revealed genuine emotion by turning all the darker.

Although Michiko's brother-in-law had been very much aware of Keitarō, Takuzō never even mentioned him. Michiko took this to mean that he was simply unconcerned. Perhaps it was because Keitarō was a completely unknown entity that Takuzō's imagination was not exercised.

"Not really. Why? Because from the beginning there have been contradictions inside me. Falsehood and truth have been mixed together. Would it be a good thing if falsehoods were simply eliminated—no, it's not that sort of thing at all."

Quite so: if falsehood were completely eliminated, there would remain nothing but sexual climax.

"I've said it so often, haven't I?—that I can't grasp the real you. If asked why I can't, it's because I want to understand you completely, but to the extent anyone tries to understand completely it just gets lost in a fog. And so in the final analysis, the fact of your having a husband is trivial in comparison with my own utter inability to understand you."

Takuzō's remarks seemed on the surface to strain logic, though there did seem to be some truth in what he was saying.

Because she was in no mood to talk about her private self, Michiko said nothing beyond that, and kept on drinking.

"I'll try telephoning once more."

Michiko got up. If Keitarō had not returned, she would like to continue what she was doing. But if she did phone home and no one answered, she of course would still not know if Keitarō would return later tonight. And if by chance he did not return, she would like to be together with Takuzō the entire night.

The ground was crumbling under foot, and she had the feeling that she had embarked on a descent with no end in sight.

She dialed the number. After ringing five times, the connection tone sounded and Keitarō answered.

"It's Michiko." She was a little disappointed, for she had hoped her own absence from home might be offset by his, too. Glancing back at their table, she could see Takuzō looking straight at her, though the dense haze of cigarette smoke blanketing the beer hall likely dimmed his view.

"Having a good time?" said Keitarō. It was a teasing tone of voice.

"I'll be back home soon." Michiko spoke to him in her customary voice.

"Maybe you've got a boyfriend or something? You've been staying out awfully late these days, haven't you?" It was the same teasing tone.

"It's getting unsafe out now," said Michiko truthfully.

"Really now, that's not like you at all."

Michiko, much flustered, was unable to reply.

"Bring your friend back here to entertain."

"He's a boyfriend," said Michiko.

"That's okay, that's okay."

He must either be drunk, thought Michiko, or playacting the father.

"Well then, I'll be back soon."

"Hey, hold on a bit," said Keitarō.

"It's a payphone; I'll be cut off."

"Put in six ten-yen coins."

Michiko deposited all the ten-yen coins she had in her purse. There were only three of them.

"What is it?" She thought for a moment that she might be cross-examined. But she might not necessarily feel bad about that. In any event, she often felt that in her everyday life she was somehow inflicting terrible harm. It was not the point that someone was harmed, but rather, if she could bring herself to recognize it, the feeling that she herself was responsible for bringing harm to things in the world around her.

"It's an acting school!" exclaimed Keitarō, leaving Michiko in mute amazement.

"What's this all about? There's no rush, is there? Tell me when I get back."

"Actually, I've only just learned about it, and so, anxious to talk with you about it, I came straight back home, but you weren't here. When you do get here, I'll probably already be right in the midst of a heavy snore."

His voice came across sluggish, but with a spring to it.

"I think we've got a clue. It seems that Kaori for a while was in some theatrical troupe, a very small troupe whose name I'd never even heard of before. That much is clear to me. But even if it's only that, still it's an important discovery. The other day when I checked the classified section of the phonebook for theater companies, well, wasn't I dismayed! Because there were so many listings—not just 500, but 700 or even 800. What I wanted to find out, of course, was the name of her acting school. But any and every thing related to the theater is arranged under 'theater companies,' and just when I was getting to feel it was useless to search for her particular acting school buried among the hundreds of entries, I decided that, however daunting, I'd give it a try. And so I'll keep looking. By the way, the information about Kaori's situation which I've gotten thus far comes from a colleague knowledgeable about the theater, who referred me to a news reporter …"

The public phone disconnected. Michiko was now forced to recall that her existence had caused harm to things in her own living world, and had inflicted one wound onto the world. That wound was her sister.

Ruminating on these matters, Michiko returned to her seat.

"I don't want to go back home," she said.

"What was it? Something that was said to you?" inquired Takuzō, avoiding use of the word "husband." Whether he was really concerned or not was quite unclear.

"No, it's nothing. Really, a very fine person," she replied. A very fine person—yes, that's the way it was. Whereas in contrast, Takuzō, a rather proud, quick-witted, and, furthermore, wholeheartedly passionate man—a lover worthy of the name—had invaded her heart, and affection was growing intoxicatingly strong.

"And so, speaking of your pursuit of discipline, that's all you're going to do with it then?" she said, feeling that she too in her own outward appearance as a lover was swathed in the rosy haze of a love affair.

"Because I have met you, it's clear that my course of discipline has reached completion. Or, rather than completion, let's just say that I'm through with it. Nothing is ever fully accomplished."

Possibly because he declared bringing an end to this discipline, his skin flushed a bit, and his face took on a livelier expression.

"And now that your regimen of discipline is over, how will you conduct yourself?" she asked.

Michiko reflected on the strength she thought she saw in him a moment ago. Because of that apparently immense inner strength, she was attracted to the man. And his strength balanced her own.

"What do you mean, how will I conduct myself?"

"How you'll use that inner strength of yours," she said.

Fifteen

ENCLOSED BY WHITE WALLS AND WHITE CEILING, Murayama Kaori was sitting on her white-covered futon. She had for some time been staring dully out the window. There was nothing before her eyes but white walls and white ceiling pressing in upon a white void—that was all. Were her delusions not projected onto the screen of that white void, there would be nothing but utter whiteness, and one might well think that as long as she was facing that white void, she would herself become utter whiteness.

Outside the window, however, there was color and there was movement. If only there were no bars over the window, the eye might wander freely, but the bars sliced the view vertically. Moreover, because it had gotten cold the window was kept shut, and since the lower half was frosted glass, it was only through the window's small upper portion that one could actually look out. Nonetheless, there was indeed color and movement beyond, and so Murayama Kaori consoled herself by looking out. The window faced a courtyard cum exercise ground, where at the edge stood an enormous zelkova tree whose branches were visible, and she could make out the leaves which, sensitive to the cold, had of a sudden turned yellow. White fleecy clouds one after another skittered across the sky beyond her window.

Aside from just dully staring out the window, Kaori was unconsciously listening to the endlessly repetitive mutterings of Takeda Miyo, sitting on the adjacent bedding.

"Me, how did this ever happen to me—ever since I was a child my shoes have given me so much trouble, they really did trouble me, and no matter what shoes I put on they never fit well, and when new shoes were bought for me and I started wearing them never once did I not get blisters, and even when the blisters healed and I'd gotten used to the shoes my feet would still always hurt, and I thought it must be the particular shape of the shoe or the give of the leather or something but when all is said and done even with another pair of shoes it was always always the same thing, so how did this ever happen to me that whenever I wore shoes my feet would hurt, and always whenever I was walking around, I'd think how life was so difficult, with my feet hurting life was difficult, and yet every single day I had to wear shoes, didn't I, and it was like that when I was in grade school and like that when I was in junior high school and when I was in high school, and after that even when I went to dressmaking school it was the same, and although it wasn't so bad in the morning by midday without fail my feet would start to hurt, and walking along I had the feeling that I always had to keep it to myself and couldn't tell anyone else about my sufferings, but you know what, I couldn't tell anyone because it was no big deal to anyone else, yet if I told someone I had a stomach ache she'd say 'Oh, you poor thing' and look after me, wouldn't she, and if I went to see the doctor he'd give me some medicine which for sure would make me well, and if I had a toothache or a hand or foot injury, then yes I'd certainly get treated, and yet when my feet hurt from wearing shoes then there's nobody to fix the problem, and when my feet do hurt, whoever I tell he'll just say 'Hmm,' and even when I take my shoes off and show him my feet, he'll say 'Yes they've gotten a little red but it's nothing to be concerned about,' and though they hurt but didn't hurt enough to make me scream still on account of that I felt it was difficult to go on living, and so that's the way it was, and day after day after day when I put on my shoes to go to school there was never a day when the shoes weren't painful, yes the shoes were very painful for me."

For a long while now, Takeda Miyo had been muttering time after time about the same thing.

Of the three roommates, Kaori's bedding was laid out in the middle, while

Miyo's was next to the door and Uji Kyōko's by the window. This day the three of them were seated on their white futons, yet each facing a different direction so that their lines of sight did not meet.

"I've gotten very much better. I haven't had another attack," said Kaori to herself. There was nothing she could do about Miyo's annoying complaint, so she pushed back with thoughts about her own improvememt.

"How did this ever happen to me, my shoes have given me so much trouble..." And Takeda Miyo went on with her complaining.

"You're probably better because of the advice I gave you," said Uji Kyōko suddenly, still facing away.

"Huh? Are you talking to me?" said Kaori, looking at the back of Kyōko's small head of disheveled chestnut-colored hair.

"I did give you advice, didn't I?" insisted Kyōko.

"Oh, yes, I remember now," said Kaori. "You did mention it before. And did you get that advice from someone else?"

"No, I did not."

So curt was Kyōko's reply that Kaori had no inclination to continue the conversation, but what Kyōko said reminded her of things she herself had done.

At first, Kaori pretended to be ignorant of the image of them flocking together, one tagging along close behind the other. Maintaining that ignorance required considerable effort. If they were out in the open she could close her eyes and that would be the end of it, but this was inside the mind. However, she persisted in the pretense of ignorance. And then, like a swimmer plowing through the water with both arms churning, she plowed right through the image of that closely bunched flock and swam somewhere into outer space. That's what Kyōko had said. Swimming until you push right through and away, away, brushing aside with both arms the insubstiantial dross of the world and continuing like an airplane finally emerging through a sea of clouds—then you emerge into the blue yonder. Kaori had not yet emerged into what Kyōko called the blue yonder. But even doing the imagining certainly made her feel better than doing nothing at all. When brushing aside the clouds and swimming on through, there somehow comes a clearer sense of direction because one is still earnestly thinking about the unseen blue yonder.

"... for sure my feet would start hurting," Miyo continued, "and always I'd feel like I was walking along enduring a hardship I couldn't tell anyone about and, you know, I couldn't tell anyone because no one thought it was really worth talking about anyway ..."

Murayama Kaori again looked out the window. In the sky that was visible through the unfrosted portion of the glass, one patch of clouds after another scudded past. By the looks of it, the sky had the color of an apparently cold day. Not until the first of November would the steam be turned on in the room, and because cloudy days were particularly cold, bedding had been left spread out on the tatami floor instead of the usual floor cushions. Uji Kyōko was seated at the head of her futon facing the wall, Takeda Miyo was seated toward the center of the room half on and half off her bedding, while Murayama Kaori, whose view took in Uji Kyōko's back, sat facing the window. Three people, yes, but doing nothing, scarcely even moving.

Very hard to bear, these two years, Kaori was reflecting. If she tried not to let memories one after another enter her head, they would not enter, and that was good. She was able to sort out the dozens of mental pictures she had drawn of the numerous scenes in her past life—another sign that she was getting better. Her outrageous screaming at Sanada Misao brought on her first seizure, after which there were messy complications about divorce, and then she'd had another seizure. However, that all came to an end when she ran off to Tokyo, enrolled in an acting school—her heart's desire—and was completely free. She had in mind that if she became an actress she could look back in triumph over her sister, but perhaps because they were separated by so great a distance her sister's affairs somehow had gotten very hazy. Never quite able to perform in real plays, she simply did not rise above student status, though for one of her course assignments she did read roles for a number of plays. On one occasion she was assigned the role of a jealous woman. When she was performing it, she was unexpectedly overcome with the feeling that she herself was falling into the mind of the woman, and she had another seizure.

"What a queer thing, that," thought Kaori.

"What's so queer?" asked Kyōko.

Kaori became aware that she had spoken out loud.

"I mean, I really hated that woman. Really, really hated. As for me, I understand that mankind's strongest emotion is hatred. Hatred of the opposite sex is not the important thing. It's hatred toward one's own sex, hatred to the extent that it completely destroys both body and mind. Because I came to harbor an extreme hatred toward a particular woman, I came to understand well before then that I hated women in general. I do hate that particular woman. Oh, dear, I'm sorry—because you're a woman, too. But you'll forgive me. Now then, listen. After I began to hate that woman, I became aware of the fact that my hatred for women of the entire world came by chance to be concentrated in hatred of that particular woman. To harbor such hatred toward one woman is something hard to conceive of. Doubtless I was hating women in general without being aware of it—a general hatred which went pouring into that particular woman. As for the reason I hate women in general, it's really quite simple. No doubt when I was born I already harbored such hatred, so it was born with me, I think. Before my birth, hatred belonged to no one in particular, but when I was born it became mine and it lodged within me—that's how I feel. That's why I'm able to speak this way. When I hate that woman, the women of the entire world, as conveyed through me, hate that woman. Period. It's hard to believe that I could bear so much hatred toward just one woman. What we call love, you see, is not like that. When I love a certain man, I do not at all think that the women of the entire world, conveyed through me, love that man. Love is one to one. But with hatred, even if it seems to have nothing to do with me, still I feel I'm a party to it. Hatred is the most powerful among the emotions. Powerful isn't quite the right word for it, though. How should I phrase it—it's something that's not really part of me, but because it increases within me, it gets beyond my control and becomes something that overtakes me, and then it destroys me."

She had never before made such assertions as these. She herself was usually not even aware when her thinking took her this far. However, when Kaori did spontaneously put her thoughts into words, even she considered, well that's just the way it is.

"'Something that's not really part of me', indeed," said Kyōko chiming in. She remained at the head of her tatami facing the wall even as she was speaking.

"Yes, really; that's so," said Kaori, recollecting the circumstances of nearly two years previous, a recollection which now no longer induced more seizures. Perhaps by chance it was thanks to Kyōko's being here.

"You do feel that you were quite involved in that 'something that's not really part of you.' Just a little bit more. A little bit more, passing through there—it would be good if you could cross through there," said Kyōko. She spoke neither forcefully nor encouragingly; her voice seemed abstracted.

"Cross through?" asked Kaori in return.

"That's what I said. Brushing aside the insubstantial dross of the world."

"Oh, you're talking about emerging toward the blue yonder."

"Yes, yes."

"But, I don't understand that yet."

"You'll certainly understand sometime."

"How do you know that?"

There was no response. Kyōko was sitting with the white blanket covering her lap. She was extremely thin, so her baggy wool sweater seemed to slip from her shoulders. She continued to face the wall.

"I sometimes go into the blue yonder," said Kyōko, mumbling on.

"Oh?" Kaori stared at her rigid, unmoving back.

"I went into the blue yonder again just a moment ago. Although I am here, it often seems as though suddenly I am not here. At such times I've gone."

"Gone? To do what?"

"God."

"Huh?"

"I meet God."

"Huh?"

Kyōko sat silently.

"Huh?"

Again, no response. Kaori ceased to inquire. "You really are crazy," she said.

"Me, how did this ever happen to me, since I was a child my shoes have given me trouble, my shoes have really given me trouble ..."

Takeda Miyo as always was repeating herself.

Kaori had become completely depressed. Both the person sitting on her left and the person sitting on her right were insane. And with the window barred by a security grill, she could escape only into the corridor, but even so she would end up meeting just the same kind of people.

Because I am just such a person myself, she muttered.

For me this is quite a comfortable place. Because being insane is permitted, or so Kyōko had once remarked. Yes, I should take better advantage of the opportunities and talk more with Kyōko, about that blue yonder.

Sixteen

~

IN THE MORNING SUNSHINE SAWAMURA TAKUZŌ was walking to Muro Sawako's apartment. Because his own day off rarely coincided with hers, they seldom met during the day. The tax accountant office where she worked was closed Sundays, while his day off at the department store was quite unpredictable. Nonetheless, on her free days Sawako would from time to time come to his store to put in an appearance. There she would do some shopping and chat with him a while, then return home, and that was all. She was ever mindful that her presence cause him no inconvenience. Because a visit from Takuzō was rare, it was Sawako who frequently visited him. This would be only the fourth time that Takuzō had gone to her apartment. However, today he and Okada Heisuke had been specially invited to lunch and he had accepted the invitation. Up to now, of course, this had never happened.

Nobe Michiko was still firmly lodged in Takuzō's heart. He nevertheless had no reason to feel that Sawako presented any obstacle. He liked her open-mindedness.

Sawako's apartment was not overly far away. By bus it was four stops, but a shortcut through a residential section put it within easy walking distance. Today Takuzō felt he'd like to take the leisurely walk.

He liked walking when he felt frustrated with Michiko.

But it was not clear even to him what exactly was frustrating. Perhaps it was because of her deeply private feelings which he, however much he tried, was unable to grasp. How things became that way, he just couldn't say. For example, when she had said, "Oh, you're wonderful," naturally he very happily accepted the remark, but examining the remark closely, he felt a huge nebulous expanse lay behind it, and the remark came somehow to be disingenuous. However, even supposing he had grabbed her by the hair and yelled, "Tell me the truth," he understood that she probably could not have made any remark but that one. Just as she might keep her distance from him by the way she expressed a blunt remark, so too she kept her distance from him by the way she expressed a complimentary remark. Indeed, with any particular remark at all that she might make, she distanced herself from him. That's because he examined them one by one. Trying to understand her was like trying to grab an eel: the harder he tried the more it would evade his grip and slip right back into the sea whence it had come, a sulfurous sea turbid and roiling.

How many times had he recently intended to telephone her, his finger poised above the dial only to withdraw it a moment later—something that was happening again and again. If he were to telephone during the day, he knew for a certainty she would answer. And if he did dial 462-4343 and always got through to her, how wonderful that their hearts would be in direct contact with each other. As he was thinking about such matters with the telephone receiver in hand, another telephone number in fact crossed his mind. 264-4343—LifeLine. More than dialing LifeLine, however, calling her number now would seem to be of greater urgency.

How good it would be, thought Takuzō as he turned into the street leading to Sawako's apartment, if he could call her and have a direct connection to her heart.

The street, running slightly uphill toward her apartment, seemed more like a narrow alley such that a single car trying to pass through would fill its entire width. A public housing complex of five four-story concrete structures could be seen on the left. He always took this route, which passed in back of the buildings where the inky dirt on the rear walls of the apartments was exposed. Of the five buildings Sawako's apartment occupied the one at the far edge, and Takuzo always decided to enter from here. As he turned into a gently winding lane, Sawako came into view, her hand raised in greeting. At first he didn't recognize her, because she was cradling an infant in her arms and a toddler was following along at her side.

"Even though you must be busy with preparations, you're actually babysitting?" queried Takuzō, now recognizing the familiar round face.

"The meal's already completely done. I got up early this morning, went shopping, and got everything all ready. So I'm not tired at all," said Sawako. She did not go into the building, but kept standing at the edge of the lane. As always, her hair was done up to perfection.

I suppose Okada's not here yet?"

"No, not yet," replied Sawako, somehow wearing an unusually pleasant expression.

"You're in frequent contact with him, then," said Takuzō.

"If you'd move a little more to the side ... otherwise if a car comes along it won't be able to get through." Sawako tugged at his sleeve pulling him toward her, so the two of them were standing side by side at the edge of the lane.

With the mention of cars, Takuzō looked up the sloping lane but no cars were in sight; he saw only a young couple who, apparently thinking Sunday morning a good time for a stroll, were out walking with their children.

"How did you get in contact with Okada?" inquired Takuzō again. Because Okada so often was not at home, even if Takuzō thought of getting in touch with him, there was very little likelihood that he would be able to so.

"Remember that bar you took me to once? I went there and left a message for Mr. Okada about today's luncheon."

Sawako, still wearing that pleasant-looking expression as she stood beside Takuzō looking up at him, now froze like one posing for a photograph, as she unconsciously turned toward the approaching young couple and their children.

"Well then, that being the case, he's not necessarily coming?" said Takuzō, sniffing the milky smell of the child Sawako was cradling. The other child was squatting down scribbling on the pavement.

"No, I was told that Mr. Okada had received my message. I made a point of confirming that."

As the couple passed by in full view, Sawako's pleasant-looking expression turned near beatific.

Takuzō instantly felt that he and Sawako were being observed by that couple, who with their two children were strolling along the street by their apartment building. And then he suspected that Sawako had from the first apparently plotted that she and Takuzō be observed here in public.

"I don't particularly care for children, so …" The remark indicated his irritation with her, and he entered the building by himself.

While Sawako was walking the children back to their parents, Takuzō seated himself in the Japanese-style living room of her apartment and smoked a cigarette. Curtains, apparently hand-made by Sawako herself, were neatly gathered at either side of the window, and frilly pleats had been cleverly fashioned to hide the curtain rod. The cloth was of a pale yellow, like the first light of dawn, a shade which perfectly reflected the woman herself. Color expresses the character of the person who selects it, he thought, and gazing at the curtains he was reminded by contrast of the strong colors which Nobe Michiko wore. Takuzō's eye then fell to a large table apparently laden with food hidden from view by a cloth spread over it, and then wandered around to highly polished chiffoniers for Western and Japanese clothes, and to Kyoto dolls in a case placed atop the Japanese chiffonier, and to her hand-made basket of paper flowers, and finally to a cuckoo clock hanging on the opposite wall whose hands pointed to eighteen minutes after twelve. Everything was done to a nicety, not a speck of dust, nothing out of place. Reflecting once again, Takuzō wondered what kind of apartment Michiko lived in. After that, he looked overhead. The lampshade on the ceiling fixture differed from the other things. Though matching the color of the curtains and apparently recently purchased, it was a glossy enamel-like yellow.

"Sorry, I've kept you waiting," Sawako said, "but I got carried away chatting." And in she came to the accompaniment of the flip-flop of her sandals.

Not having waited particularly long, he hadn't even noticed, but now that she mentioned it, he had indeed been kept waiting for over ten minutes. The cuckoo clock was already pointing to twenty-five past.

"Did you return the borrowed children okay?" he asked.

"Borrowed children?" Sawako gave him a momentary blank stare.

With that reaction and his speculation about the contrived scene a few minutes ago, Takuzō realized what a careless comment he had blurted out.

"Well!" exclaimed Sawako with a pout. "What a good joke!" Whereupon she began laughing uncontrollably, and, going into the kitchen, she continued her laughter, raucous like the sounds of a zoo, her whole body shaking. It seemed she'd never stop. Her pale round face reddened deeply as she kept repeating "What a good joke," even though, despite trying her hardest to speak, she was just barely able to form the words, and spittle dribbled from the corners of her mouth. She wiped it away with the back of her hand, and as she took her hand away from her mouth, the saliva stretched out long after, and she just couldn't stop laughing—the first time in her life she had ever experienced such a strange phenomenon, she said, whereupon she was engulfed in yet another wave of laughter that left her gasping for breath.

Takuzō thought that she might be trying to cover up the jolt she felt due to his slip of the tongue, but to be rewarded with such unexpected laughter as this bewildered him. Realizing he had seen through her, was she trying to cover it up with laughter, he wondered. While that really didn't seem to be the case, there was indeed room for ambiguity. She herself seemed to be unconscious of his having detected any dissimulation. Although she was somehow aware of her unconsciousness of being seen through, she did not actually realize she was aware of it, and that was pretty much the same thing as being unconsciously aware. So she was probably laughing at that borderline. Thus pondering, he felt that within this woman who continued laughing, there was a vague, ill-defined marshy area stretching out in all directions. Holding her sides in laughter, writhing and contorted, she looked as though she were embracing such a marsh. She thus contrasted sharply with her perfectly arranged apartment and did not seem to be mistress of her own home. Suddenly Takuzō saw there the same qualities and confusion he felt toward Michiko. While he was still trying to figure out wherein lay the common qualities, for the two women were after all very different, Sawako had finally stopped laughing, and, mopping up her tears with a handkerchief, she walked straight back into the living room.

"What was so funny?" For a moment he felt something to be slightly wrong with her that wanted explanation, so he ventured the question.

"Because I laughed so hard, I've completely forgotten," she said, much to his disappointment.

And she really did have the look of having forgotten. But she also seemed not to have forgotten.

"You sure have got everything prepared!" Takuzō decided to stop paying attention to her laughing bout, and turned his eyes toward the table.

"Oh, that? I borrowed it from a neighbor. Whenever a lot of my friends come over, I always borrow it," she said, referring to the large square table. As for the large number of friends, she easily got on close terms with colleagues at work, acquaintances at her lessons, as well as the neighborhood children.

"Hey, take a peek!" So saying, she lifted the edge of the table covering. She had covered the food with plastic film, on top of which a carrying cloth was spread.

Takuzō's eye caught a glimpse of the jumble of colors and variety of dishes, then Sawako covered it all up again.

"That's a lot. I can hardly eat so much, and it will be the same with Okada. Anyway, I wonder if he's coming."

Takuzō had come today precisely because it had been a long time since he'd last seen Okada Heisuke.

"I've made a lot more. It's all sitting over there." Sawako nodded toward the kitchen, curtained off at the end of the dining room which, with its sliding paper doors removed, was connected to the living room. "There's enough even to invite another person," she said.

"Another person?" For some reason or other Takuzō had the feeling that Sawako seemed to be referring to Nobe Michiko.

At that, he looked hard at Sawako. But her expression turned foggy, as if she were feigning ignorance of his implication.

"That must be Okada," said Takuzō.

Feeling some discomfort, Takuzō spoke in the direction of the corridor where he could hear approaching footsteps. His discomfort, however, was a matter within himself alone, for Sawako simply did not know a thing of his relation with Michiko.

The footsteps were coming closer, then passed by. This was the first floor, and ranged along the concrete passageway there were about ten apartments, of which Sawako's was in the middle.

"Wrong," Sawako said simply, feeling that for some reason or other time was starting to hang heavy. Although she was in her own home, an uneasiness pervaded her manner, and not simply because the preparations were already complete with no further chores to do. Going over to the Japanese clothing chiffonier, she fiddled with the paper flowers on top of it.

"I wanted to invite another person, but …" she repeated.

"Whoever comes will be fine with me," said Takuzō. By which he meant, whatever she thinks would be enliven the party, let's do it.

"Okay," she said, and just as she said it there was an unexpected knock on the door.

"Am I at the right place? This is Okada," called out Okada Heisuke from the other side of the door.

"Mysterious fellow," chuckled Takuzō, getting to his feet. "Listening with pricked ears we heard footsteps but they were not his, and then when there were no footsteps that's just when he shows up."

Then suddenly, perhaps for but a few seconds, something like an oppressive emptiness, he thought, began fomenting between himself and Sawako, fixed on listening for Okada Heisuke's arrival.

"Come in, come on in!" she said cheerily, going over to open the door.

"I didn't think you'd be coming," said Takuzō, whose attention was arrested by Okada Heisuke's short stature, darting eyes, and filthy jacket; but given that he was able to get together with him after such a long time, his feelings at once softened and he extended his arm thinking to shake hands with him.

"No, nor did I think I'd be coming." Heisuke, without noticing the outstretched hand, just sat himself down cross-legged.

"Oops!" he exclaimed almost inaudibly. He seemed to have become aware of the big hole which opened up in the sock of the cross-legged foot on top, and for the purpose of concealing it he placed his hand over it, but apparently aware again that he could not very well continue that way forever, he recrossed his legs, now with the problem foot underneath.

With that series of maneuvers completed, Sawako, who had been looking on, gave out a laugh.

"Last night I was woken up any number of times during the middle of the night, and thanks to that I was able to come here," said Heisuke incongruously, and the next instant tamped tobacco into his pipe and began puffing away. The utter lack of concern for his appearance was completely inconsistent with his sophisticated pipe-smoking habit, but to an extent that inconsistency suited him perfectly.

"The housing complex where I was staying yesterday …" Heisuke began, but Takuzō cut him off.

"You don't stay in your own place; it seems you often stay in other people's apartments. How come?"

"No need to discuss that. It's simply a habit well suited to my temperament, that's why."

Heisuke motioned with his right hand to check Takuzō's objection. His little finger was twisted and shriveled—the result perhaps of some childhood injury.

"Today is the day for me to try to figure you out. Your real character." Takuzō really wanted to get to the bottom of this man.

"Okay now, take a look!" said Sawako, removing the table covering. With the carrying cloth in her right hand the plastic film in her left she waved them like flags.

"Wonderful—a full-dress show indeed!" exclaimed Heisuke, staring at the many dishes.

"First a little beer." And Sawako cheerfully bustled about pouring beer. Finishing that, she raised herself up on her knees and offered a hearty "Bottoms up!"

Her happy face, right in front of Takuzō, appeared large as though seen through a magnifying glass. That face was not looking at him, but was looking into blank space. He was reminded of the scene a while ago on the street. He felt Sawako somehow was really making an effort about something, but he just couldn't figure out why. After all, she could not possibly know Michiko.

Heisuke started talking.

"That housing complex where I was staying yesterday? Late at night there was a wild wooh-wooh sound like a lion or something, y'know, which woke me right up. It seemed to be coming from the neighboring building. The owner of the apartment where I spent the night was away on a trip, so he let me stay in his place. In the darkness I couldn't figure out what sort of sound it was, though I kept listening to it real closely. There was just that wooh-wooh you could hear. Of course it must have been a human voice, since there was certainly no reason for there to be any wild animal in such a place. One might think it was somebody sick or with an injury, groaning in pain. However that may be, the sound was nonetheless very much like an animal. Then it let out a really terrible shriek. I was listening closely and after a while in the darkness I seemed to become aware of some other cry being raised, and at the same time the regular wooh-wooh sound came to a stop. After that as I was dropping off to sleep, I was awakened by that cry again. So finally I got up and went out to the terrace to take a look. The sound seemed to be coming from the third floor of the building right across from me. But the windows over there were completely dark. Some people had come out onto the terrace next to mine. An elderly couple, it seemed. Since they too were looking in the direction of the noise, I asked them what on earth they thought it was. What was making the noise was a woman of fifty-five or -six suffering from encephalomalacia, they said—some kind of brain tissue degeneration, they explained. Until very recently she had been hospitalized, but since there was neither any prospect of recovery nor the money for an indefinite hospital stay, she was sent back to her son and daughter-in-law's place. So that was that. Confined to bed, it seems she was in circumstances requiring help at mealtime and with the toilet. On top of that, they said, all night long she'd moan just like an animal. On those occasions the son and his wife between the two of them would beat her into silence. Huh? Really? I said, all the while looking at the window of the building across the way. Then I noticed that in one of those dark windows the mother, who had become a virtual animal, and her son and her daughter-in-law had emerged into clear view. People were coming out onto other terraces as well, and some of them were even picking up pebbles from the flowerpots and throwing them at the neighboring building. Everybody was fed up. This was something that had been going on every night for over a week. I wondered if maybe even the person who'd lent me his apartment hadn't run off to escape the commotion. Because of the noise that went on throughout the entire night, I was kept wide awake, and even before it got light out, I left the place. After that I slept on a park bench until just a little while ago. So that explains it. If I hadn't had my sleep disturbed like that, I would have had a whole day's work ahead of me starting from early morning. And if that had been the case, I would not have been able to come here. By the way," holding up his emptied glass to Sawako, "might I have another beer?"

With mention of the mother who had become an animal, recollections of Takuzō's own deceased mother flitted across his mind. "Well then, now that you've told us such a story, what do you make of it?" he asked.

"Hmm, well, just groan. Ha-ha," replied Heisuke with a dry laugh.

"Tell me, won't you, how you explain the meaning of it all." Takuzō, frustrated by Heisuke's unfeeling reaction to the story, felt like grabbing him by the lapels.

"And if I do, so what?" Heisuke turned his small round eyes to Takuzō.

"If you don't, you must regard it simply as a trivial incident."

"But, after I do give you an explanation, nothing would be changed."

"Oh! Why are you so indifferent?" exclaimed Takuzō.

"Hey now, please help yourselves. You can talk while eating," said Sawako, breaking in.

"Explain, explain, explain—you might just as well ask me what the blazes we should do with this world of ours," said Heisuke.

"Trying to dam up something that is streaming out everywhere is just wishful thinking—that's what I think."

"And as for the story I just told, surely you don't plan to advance the old-fashioned arguments for social welfare or something, do you?" asked Heisuke.

"Of course not. Such policies can't change anything, can't change the nature of what we call mankind."

"If that's the case, what then do you say should be done?"

"I don't know," said Takuzō.

"So if you don't know, don't make explanations."

For a moment a vacuum fell between the two men.

"'Hmm, well, just groan to you. Ha-ha,'" said Takuzō, now his turn to laugh. Still, he couldn't figure out what his friend was really thinking.

"Well, now. This is sashimi from fish I bought this morning and prepared myself—squid and tuna and abalone. What do you think? Good as a pro, huh?" said Sawako, trying her best to assume the role of peacemaker.

"Whether denial or affirmation, I'll do neither; no I'll not do either," said Heisuke, as he vacantly took up a slice of sashimi.

"Looks delicious." Takuzō made a pleasant face and took a small dish of sashimi offered by Sawako. Then he said to Heisuke, "You just looked on, choosing to do nothing?"

"Indeed. I guess I didn't take it very seriously. Because nothing at all would have changed."

"I'm not that way," said Takuzō, finally moved to assert himself clearly.

"Everything's like the ebb and flow of the tide."

"How do you know?"

"Let's just say," replied Heisuke, "that it's because I've seen far too much. Or rather, it's actually because I've been shown far too much."

"Is that so. Oh, how I do respect you," said Takuzō. "In any event, I'm not that way.

"So what is it then?" Heisuke's small eyes suddenly burned with excitement.

Without even thinking, "I'm searching for it," Takuzō stated abruptly.

"For what?" And Heisuke's small eyes, burning with excitement, narrowed yet more.

"I don't know. I only know that it's something, some particular thing."

That phrase, "some particular thing," was visualized in Takuzō's mind as "some particular woman," but he quickly erased it from his mind. Nonetheless, he felt that some particular woman and some particular thing were in some way indefinably connected.

"Sorry, Sawako, it's become an argument that seems not to interest you," said Takuzō.

For a while now Takuzō had been drinking Japanese saké, and Heisuke whisky-and-water. When they had switched from beer Takuzō had not noticed.

"I've been listening. It's fine with me just to listen," said Sawako.

While serving the two men, Sawako indicated with a pleasant nod that all was well with her.

"I neither affirm nor deny, nor am I either pessimistic or optimistic. And because of that, extraordinary patience is required," said Heisuke, continuing his train of thought from a moment ago.

If it were Michiko rather than Sawako, thought Takuzō, she'd certainly join in the conversation.

"You're a drifter," said Takuzō, "and I'm a drifter, too. But in other respects we do seem to differ.

"As for me," said Heisuke, "first I study the external reality of a given situation and then I set about to study its underlying principle. But one never stops studying. Because things continue to go on as they do. Let's just say that I'm a person who has chosen the view that in life there is no fixed principle."

"Yes. I've noticed that about you. Myself, I've been searching for a fixed principle, I suppose. An absolute, so to speak. If I find it, it'll provide me a secure mooring. Until that time I'll probably just drift along."

"Try not to fall into a trap," said Heisuke.

"Why do you say that?"

"Nothing, just joking."

"Really? Just joking?"

"Advice from your elder," said Heisuke.

"So you are my more experienced elder?"

"Could you get accustomed to the freedom that someone like me has? Your tenacity is in some respects dangerous. Do be careful," Heisuke warned.

"Thank you. Since it's my tenacity, I feel quite safe. Even though it may seem dangerous."

"Then excuse me for speaking presumptuously," said Heisuke, getting to his feet, for it was time for him to return.

Sawako tried to restrain him, but he insisted and left.

"That was a good pipe he had. Very high-priced. I used to be a saleslady at a department store pipe counter, so I really know about such things," said Sawako.

"That guy's terribly careless with his money," remarked Takuzō, "sometimes riding high and sometimes destitute. Strangely inconsistent.

After Okada Heisuke left, an unusual nervous restlessness sprang up between Takuzō and Sawako. She went into the kitchen and seemed to be staying there forever. Takuzō, somewhat feeling the effect of the saké, kept on drinking as he pleased, without paying much attention to her.

The cuckoo clock struck two.

"Shall we go out for a walk? Saké at midday somehow makes me feel restless." He raised himself up on one knee trying to get to his feet.

"Takuzō...," Sawako began, half emerging through the curtain that separated off the kitchen. "Mr. Sawamura," she said, addressing him more formally.

Takuzō, who was sitting in the living room, sensed the presence of Sawako standing there, whose body was shielded, as it were, by the curtain. That curtain was the same as the window curtain—pale yellow in color.

"Um ... I ... I'd like to meet the woman you're so fond of."

Takuzō was dumbstruck. He remained utterly silent for a while. Then he said, "I'm fond of you."

Not uttering a word, Sawako slowly shook her head back and forth.

"It's true," he said. Yes, that was true, he thought. She was similar to that pale curtain, and he liked it. So thinking, however, he also thought of changing the topic of conversation.

"I know all about it." Standing there, Sawako looked very light-hearted. Or, rather, it seemed she was trying to look light-hearted.

Takuzō recalled that only just the other day he had had similar feelings about her.

"What is it you know?" he asked, wondering how she could know of Michiko's existence.

"There is no special agreed upon relationship between you and me. So I won't press you in the slightest for explanations. I'd also like to be on cordial terms with the other lady. And I'd like her to try some of the delicious food I make. That's all." And she smiled.

A smile which impressed a bewildered Takuzō as particularly peaceful. And was not that impression, it occurred to him, possibly the reflection of the pale yellow curtain that curled around her body? She pushed out only her face, while her body remained hidden by the curtain. Only her face was assertive, while her body as a whole, it seemed to him, lacked self-confidence. He had no idea how to reply.

"Don't make such a face. I'm not at all pressing you for answers," said Sawako, as if it were for her to do the comforting.

"It was around the end of September," she continued, "about the time when everyone was getting awfully sick and tired of the heat which seemed to be lasting forever, and I went to your apartment bringing along some sushi rolls, right? You were just getting ready to go out. You seemed to have some special purpose in going out and were in a big rush. So you were changing into a black shirt, which is not something for everyday wear. You've never been style-conscious, as you yourself have said. I urged you to drink a beer, and so you started sweating a lot after you'd already changed shirts. You pulled a hanky from your pocket and wiped away the sweat. Though it was a fresh hanky, after you'd wiped the sweat just that once, it's as if you'd said 'that hanky's no good any more,' and you casually tossed it into your dresser and pulled out another fresh hanky from the drawer. It was then that I understood what it was all about."

Sawako spoke without faltering. Was this, as it seemed to be, a well-rehearsed speech?

With mention of the black shirt, the fresh handkerchief, and so on, Takuzō's state of mind turned from dumbstruck to astonishment.

"After that, some days went by and then when summer seemed to immediately change into the cold of winter, I was near the gate to your rooming house at night and I was standing there waiting, right? When you returned it was after twelve. When you brushed by me in the darkness, there was a soapy smell coming from you. Soap used in a bath—yes, that's what it was ... That's one example of this sort of thing... And there are lots, lots more. That one was a trivial matter, but it was a clear signal."

Sawako's expression became slightly sad. "A trivial matter but a clear signal": it was that fact which seemed to sadden her.

Takuzō recalled having taken notice of Sawako's perfume that night. Was it that she had planned on trying to rival the other woman by using that scent?

In any event, Sawako, still smiling, continued talking.

"Don't worry at all about me. I wish for the happiness of everyone—that's what I live for. Of course I include my own happiness in that. I want to be on good terms with her. What a nice woman she must be! That's why you love her."

Stunned, Takuzō was at a loss for a reply. He was aware that Sawako was keeping a forced smile fixed on him.

"I'm going to take a little walk around the neighborhood," he said finally. "I'll be back soon. I guess I've had too much to drink at midday, and I'm feeling kind of funny from the effects of it."

Feeling stifled, Takuzō abruptly got to his feet.

"But I'll be back soon. After that I'll be here the whole time. Night, too," he reminded her, seeing the anxious expression that floated up upon Sawako's face.

"You're going out to telephone her, aren't you," she said very slowly.

"No, not at all. Why?" replied Takuzō, surprised.

"If you want to make a phone call, that's fine, I was thinking. There's all this left over from the meal," said Sawako again beaming.

No sooner had he left the apartment than Takuzō suddenly did feel very much like calling Michiko. He quickened his pace toward the public phone booth.

Seventeen

NOBE MICHIKO WAS SITTING LANGUIDLY ON THE SOFA, a vacant look on her face. With the heater running smoothly, she was wearing only a blouse over her chemise. One leg propped up on the sofa, the other drooping to the floor, her upper body listlessly leaning against the back of the sofa: for fully thirty minutes she had not moved from this position. Seated at a table by the window of their large living room was Keitarō, his back in her line of sight. Because the heater was not too effective in his study, he said, he had brought out a pile of economics magazines and spread them out on the table, where he had for some time been busily taking notes. Tomorrow morning, Monday, he had a conference.

Because their living room window faced another apartment building, from the place where Michiko was sitting she could not see the sky. If the window were open, the multitude of noises making up the rumbling of the city would invade their apartment, but now, thanks to the glass in the sturdy aluminum sash, not a sound was heard in the room. Yet even so, she still seemed to have a faint awareness of the muffled rumbling outside, and its vagueness intruded upon her lethargy. The only specific sounds occurred when Keitarō turned a page or set down his pen after scribbling some notes.

How unfortunate it is that we seem to know nothing of Kaori's current address. So Keitarō had remarked the day before yesterday when he had come home. Yet wasn't it so that Kaori had indeed attended acting school? Michiko had said.

Until Michiko had been informed by her sister's only close friend that Kaori had been institutionalized, she knew nothing about Kaori's circumstances in Tokyo. She had been a student at that acting school for about half a year, and then she suddenly just disappeared. Nobody there knew anything of her whereabouts.

Keitarō thought it most unfortunate that his efforts to locate her turned out to be futile. He was a man for whom determination was his very foundation. Whether at the company where he worked or in his marriage to Michiko, by persisting in his determination, he thought, his hopes were usually fulfilled. And he was determined to do better, ever better.

How might Keitarō react if he knew that Michiko's sister was in a mental hospital? If the names and addresses of relatives, acquaintances, and friends were not precisely recorded in his own address book he could not rest easy, he had said, so merely to record "Edgewood Mental Hospital" in his address book with no other detail could hardly be reconciled with all the other entries in his address book.

The telephone rang.

"Michiko, would you get it?" said Keitarō, without looking up from the table. Although Keitarō usually answered the phone when he was at home, his mind now seemed completely occupied with next day's conference.

Michiko went to the dining room and picked up the telephone sitting next to the china cupboard.

"Hello?" she said languidly.

"Mrs. Nobe? … Nobe Michiko?" An excited voice, apparently urgent, came across.

"Ah!" Her languor somehow changed instantly. She had the feeling that every sex cell in her body suddenly started jangling.

The voice faltered. A long delay. Yet there seemed to be no void.

Silence. From Michiko's side, too, no voice came forth.

By thus keeping her silence, she thought, was she not conveying her own desires to her caller via the telephone? I want to convey those desires, she thought. Indeed, she was convinced they were being conveyed.

"What are you doing now?" Takuzō's voice suddenly turned bland.

"Nothing at all," replied Michiko matter-of-factly, accommodating her own voice to the change in his.

A silence came between the two of them.

What must he be thinking, why did he suddenly change his tone of voice, Michiko asked herself, pressing her ear closer to the silence. Why was she so involved with this man? Why was she listening intently to his every change of voice?

If it were a man with whom she had no physical involvement, certainly it would not have become like this. Of course with Keitarō it wasn't like this. So then, for a partner with whom she had a strong physical connection, she really did seem to become a magnet. Every part of her partner was attracted to her like iron filings to a magnet. It was a feeling bordering on cruelty. Yet everything that came from the partner entered her body and became fuel.

"I can't even imagine what you are doing. I've tried to imagine it, but I just can't figure it out." Takuzō's voice, the first to break the silence, was again emotionally warm.

"This is a third-floor apartment in a high-rise. It's a three-bedroom. With a telephone installed in the kitchen-dining area. And outside the window, there's a really large terrace, the reason being that below this apartment the area of the first and second floors is given over entirely to the apartment building's utility rooms. Because our apartment is at the very end of the third floor, it was possible to build such an unusual terrace."

Knowing that Keitarō could hear, Michiko replied in this business-like fashion. All the while, she was looking out at the ping-pong table, which was set up on the broad terrace occupying the space outside the dining-kitchen area and bedroom. She said nothing about that. Now that she had become Keitarō's ping-pong partner, the picture of the two of them lobbing a friendly ping-pong ball back and forth and the picture of her involvement with Takuzō—how different were these two worlds!

"What I envision is only the building's structure. But what are you doing there? All of a sudden I was thinking I'd really like to know. Though I already know you well, I'd like to know you even better."

"I don't ask you, so why do you ask me?" asked Michiko.

"Why not? When I'm not with you, like today, you don't ask anything about what I'm doing," replied Takuzō.

"Yes, because people only care about themselves." Michiko, aware that Keitarō was right there, spoke as sparsely as possible.

"In some ways you and I are very different," he said.

"That's not so. We're very close."

"Close? What?"

"Yes, we're getting close," she repeated.

Michiko realized that the desires she felt were apparently not being conveyed via the telephone very effectively. The emotions expressed in his voice seemed anxious, as if he were looking for some sign of Michiko's closeness to him.

"Well, then, see you later. This kind of phone call just isn't like me. And why do I say this isn't like me? It's because I'm phoning on top of having had a lot to drink in the middle of the day."

And with that unusual speech—a cross between arrogance and confession—Takuzō hung up.

Michiko, still standing in the kitchen-dining area, was taken aback. The phone call just now had ignited a fire inside her.

She looked around for a cigarette, found one and lit up. Beyond the broad terrace outside the window was the brown wall of some building or other; she raised her eyes above it to the gloomy sky and the view gradually broadened out. Then she walked over to the window and opened it. From the direction of the National Line's Shinagawa station, where numerous trolley and train lines converged, a cacophony of noise suddenly arose; departures of trolleys and of trains with ten or more cars linked together rushed toward her in a terrible screech. The noise pierced her very body, she felt; the train cars grated her innards.

"Hey, hey!" came Keitarō's voice. "Has my wife become a tobacco addict?"

Michiko inhaled deeply and looked over her shoulder at him. She smiled broadly.

"You didn't know? I used to smoke once in a while before." Michiko looked at Keitarō who was now standing just between the dining-kitchen area and the living room.

"I noticed it only once."

He came in and sat down at the dining table. Then he too lit a cigarette.

"Noticed? When?"

During a two-year period when Keitarō had been transferred to a distant town, living separately but visiting back and forth, Michiko was already smoking. It was then that she was seeing Sanada Misao.

"No, I've noticed it twice," correcting himself.

What else might he know? thought Michiko, looking closely at him.

"Where?"

"I've forgotten. Hmm, where was it, now?" Keitarō, who really did seem to have forgotten, leaned an elbow on the table, chin propped in his palm.

"Keitarō?" A smile flitted across her face.

"What?" He turned his big, thick-lidded eyes toward her.

"That phone call just now—who do you think it was?"

"A friend, probably. A boyfriend, for all I know."

"If that person and I were close, what would you do?"

"Well then, hmm, that's a difficult question."

"Why difficult?"

"Because I've never thought about it, that's all."

"Why haven't you thought about it?"

"Because it's pointless." For a moment Keitarō's face turned very serious.

"Pointless …" With every cell in her body tingling from that phone call a minute ago, Michiko was trying to see how the word "pointless" could possibly apply. She tried saying "pointless" to the feeling of happiness when meeting with Takuzō and experiencing the near perfection of sexual climax.

"To say 'pointless' without even thinking about it seems strange. You ought to say 'pointless' only if you have thought about it." Michiko had a mind to get to the root of Keitarō's thinking.

"Quite so. Yes, of course I think about it. I think about it because I married whom I so wanted to marry—you. But even when I think about it, it still seems like a dream."

"Why?"

"It's not that; there's a more serious matter."

"And what's that?"

"I'm making you happy. I could make you even happier. That's the indisputable fact. Isn't that so? This life, the life that I'd hoped for …"

Keitarō, trying to indicate such a life, stretched his arms out wide as if to take in all that was around them.

Happiness, murmured Michiko to herself. Yes, she was being made happy by Keitarō. So it was with the other housewives living in this apartment building who reflected on their happiness. Indeed almost all women reflecting on their happiness were made happy by their husbands, just as happiness was provided to Michiko by the irreproachable Keitarō.

So it was, Michiko continued to muse. Keitarō seemed to be saying that fulfillment of his designated roles made him happy. For Michiko, however, the desired moment would arrive when, by casting off all her roles, she became what it is to be female. To become what is truly feminine, nay, to become what is truly living—did that mean brutal frankness, coarse vulgarity, and sheer greed? If so, then the word "happiness" at bottom seemed not to fit.

"Keitarō?" A smile again flitted across Michiko's face.

"I've really got to continue with my work," and he got to his feet.

"Where my sister's living … I know it now." Michiko abruptly resolved to speak about it. Indeed, she had long thought about broaching the matter to him. He was a man who unfailingly fulfilled his responsibilities, even though that mental hospital was a place for which he had no responsibility at all. Thus, she suddenly became aware that what must be called the unvarnished truth of her insane sister's life on the one hand, and the abyss of the life she was leading with another man on the other hand, were perhaps the same.

"Oh?" Keitarō abruptly leaned closer.

Because of that concrete gesture of interest, Michiko felt inclined to forget the matters she had just now been thinking about.

"She's in a mental hospital. She's insane."

Why she was insane, Michiko did not say.

"Not really!" Keitarō turned blank.

"It's a fact," said Michiko emphatically.

How would Keitaro, a man of drive, who ordered his life according to his responsibilities, straying from which, he insisted, was pointless, how would a man like him handle this situation involving his sister-in-law with whom he had no blood relationship?

Without saying a word, he went back to his table by the living-room window.

Michiko, standing between the living room and the dining-kitchen area, spoke to the back of Keitarō, now sitting at his table.

"Do you think I'm fibbing? I've never mentioned it because I wasn't sure about it. But since coming to Tokyo I've gone out there and verified it. I haven't actually met her, though."

Michiko was revealing the facts piecemeal. Actually the matter of her sister's divorce and disappearance from home occurred during the time when Keitarō had been transferred first to that distant town and then from there directly to Tokyo, so he had little opportunity to learn in any detail about these developments.

"In a mental hospital?" he said. Keitarō, though having just sat down, stood up and looked around at her.

"Yes, that's right," said Michiko nodding in assent.

"Let's go there, right now, Michiko; let's go." Standing with his back to the window, Keitarō's face, viewed against the light, appeared terribly dark.

"What are you saying? Let's go? But why?"

"It's not right not to help."

Michiko was dumbfounded.

"Because we are the only relatives she has."

"So … it's a duty?"

Without replying, Keitarō began preparing to leave.

As Michiko was making up her mind about whether to go with Keitarō to visit her sister, the two of them simply threw on overcoats over their at-home casual wear and went out.

"My sister, she lost her mind because of a disappointing love affair," said Michiko tersely as she tried to keep up with Keitarō's quick pace.

Along both sides of their building's long corridor, the apartments were lined up one after another just as in a hospital, and being a Sunday it seemed as if almost everyone had gone out on an excursion, for the place was empty. They took the elevator down, and on the ground-floor lobby three young housewives were standing about chatting. Some kids, their children apparently, had gone out into an open area beyond the entrance and were riding around on tricycles.

Downhill a hundred meters or so was a broad avenue leading to the station. The roar, dust, and fumes all of a sudden came blowing into them on a cold wind. Whenever the two of them walked there, because of all the noise and smell Michiko was able to catch only fragments of whatever the ever-voluble Keitarō was talking about, so she simply kept her silence. Today, however, he too had lapsed into silence. As they neared Shinagawa station, the noise and smell intensified, with the bells and P.A. speakers only adding to the cacophony. Differing from the colors of her hometown taxis, the ones lined up in front of the station here were glossy yellow and orange—colors that stabbed the eye.

People were pouring in and out of the station. Although it was not a commute day, indeed because it was a day off, everybody had apparently come outdoors simply to stroll about. Because so many train lines converged at Shinagawa, people being transported here and there all had to pass through this station. Below the pedestrian overpass many lines of track were imposingly ranged. The hubbub of people meeting and parting was palpable. Michiko and even Keitarō, who was walking alongside, seemed to be just drifting. The movement produced by the coming and going of countless trains and trolleys was the only indication of reality.

They boarded the National Line and, hanging onto the straps, stood there, eyes closed. When, from time to time, they opened their eyes, only building after building could be seen. Because most of what could be seen from the train were the buildings' blackened and smudgy backsides, billboard advertisements took on a curious vividness.

They stepped out at Shinjuku station and stood amidst the throng. How many times had she passed through here on her way to Edgewood Hospital in Yashio City? Michiko glanced around fleetingly, aware that she was searching for the figure of Sawamura Takuzō. The crowd, closely packed together, was the only thing that could be seen. Where might it have been—that public phone from which he had a moment ago called her? Where might he be right now? His existence seemed to have disappeared into the dust of the city. Once their secret relationship emerged from behind its locked doors, it would likely share its fate with this city's run down appearance, she thought.

They transferred to the private Odakyū Line. This was her fourth time.

What on earth might he be thinking? mused Michiko, glancing at Keitarō, seated next to her. Since leaving home the two of them had exchanged no meaningful remarks. His profile showed the impassive expression characteristic of one deep in thought.

"When we get there, what do we do then?" asked Michiko, trying to broach the subject.

"That's just what I'm thinking about," he pronounced, and again lapsed into silence. Such was his character that he never even hinted at a decision while still in the midst of formulating it.

Sitting with eyes closed, Michiko let her body rock back and forth with the motion of the train car. Was Keitarō thinking of rescuing her sister? How does one go about rescuing an insane person? How does a well-ordered person like Keitarō plan on trying to play a part with an insane person? Moreover, how would he deal with the situation if he had the opportunity of knowing the Michiko who protruded beyond the framework of the things that made up his happiness? Might he forcibly cut away that portion which protruded? Or would he, saying he forgave everything, embrace her, including that protruding part, within his own well-ordered life? No, no, that would never be, thought Michiko, pushing aside her own selfish fantasies.

After that her thoughts turned to Takuzō. That the two of them were so compatible—wasn't that because they both were greedy for what extended beyond orderliness?

Finally they got to Yashio station.

Side by side they started out, walking in the direction of the pine woods just ahead. How many times, she thought, had she passed along here as if on a pilgrimage. They turned right just before the pine woods. An unpaved lane of a hundred meters or so led to the main gate.

"I'm not going in." That thought suddenly occurred to Michiko. In the final analysis she was ambivalent about the meeting.

"Really? Michiko, if you're not ready for this, well then it's best you not see her."

Keitarō went by himself through the main gate.

Michiko called after him. "It's not Murayama Kaori! She calls herself Yamakusaki Kaori! If you don't say that to the reception clerk, you won't get to see her. She's here under that name."

Keitarō waved his hand as if to say, "I know, I know."

Michiko, if you're not ready for this … She repeated the remark to herself, a remark directed seemingly not to her but to some other woman.

Okay, whatever it is, it's okay, she said to herself, and slumped down by the side of the main gate.

Even though her sister might reveal absolutely everything without restraint to Keitarō, whatever it was, anything was okay.

While Michiko was waiting for him to come back out, her mind wandered. There were some matters which Michiko deeply wanted to discuss directly with her sister, who, however, sensing as much with a woman's intuition, would probably not allow it. Thus, rivaling, as it were, Michiko's search for answers, Kaori herself would probably have to find some other way of confronting those very same issues. Being insane was probably like that. Michiko, because she had the same blood in her, was in that respect closely connected with her sister, and in her heart she could hear the silent weeping of her sister who was trying not to be overwhelmed.

At length, hearing footsteps, she looked up. Keitarō had emerged from the entrance and was walking on the paved road straight toward the main gate. He seemed to be all worn out, judging from the droop of his shoulders. Michiko quickly pulled herself up.

"How was it?" she asked, tensed up.

"No," he seemed to be signaling as he approached shaking his hand back and forth.

"How did it go?" she asked again when Keitaro had gotten within a few paces of her.

"A wasted effort." Looking utterly disappointed, he came up to her and just stood there. Then, after a pause, "She was the same old Kaori whom I knew so well before. And yet, she said she didn't know me. Even though we'd met five times before this. When I said I was the husband of Nobe Michiko, she said she didn't know anybody by that name. She does know, of course, and she's not crazy now. But she keeps saying she doesn't know you."

"I see. Then there's nothing we can do about the situation," said Michiko.

Sharing the same blood, Michiko easily accepted Kaori's malevolence.

Eighteen

MURAYAMA KAORI LEFT THE RECEPTION ROOM, walked down the corridor, and returned to her room.

"Kyōko! Kyōko!" she called out to Uji Kyōko, who was standing at the window looking out. "I did what you told me—I said I didn't know."

Murayama Kaori went over to the window and stood next to her.

"I kept saying 'I don't know, I don't know.' That was the best thing for me to do. So, because I kept denying everything, things came out quite well. But if I had stopped talking like that even for a bit, that hatred would have come gushing out like an evil spirit. The hatred toward my sister … the hatred. Yes, I have many memories about my hatred for that woman, and it's only when I reveal it openly that I'm not considered insane. But some day hatred of that woman will surpass the hatred even I personally feel toward her. Eventually, however, hatred will somehow lose its substance. I myself will become insubstantial. Haven't I explained this to you before? Well, how shall I put it? When I fall into a deep depression, I feel like I've come to hate all women, or perhaps I should say, I've come to hate womankind. It's at such times that I'm considered insane. Do please try to understand me."

"Because you've gone that far," said Kyōko with sudden feeling, still looking out the window.

"'That far,' you say?" said Kaori, looking at Kyōko's chilly profile.

"You've sunk that far," said Kyōko. "But compared to the blue yonder, that is still a very, very shallow place. You mentioned evil spirits and how they haunt you wherever you are. And at that place, when you're worried sick, from there suddenly you are able to emerge yonder."

"Into the blue sky."

"Yes," said Kyōko.

"You say the blue sky exists within me. Really?"

"Yes," said Kyōko.

"I don't understand. However much time goes by, I'll never understand."

"One might say by way of analogy that an airplane can pass through a heavy cloud layer and emerge into the blue sky above it. Such a universe exists within me. It exists within you, too. Your inner being and my inner being are linked together. What we have in common is a place without limit, and at the very end of it all, there is God."

"Oh?"

"There is God," Kyōko affirmed.

"Oh?"

"I see God. Of course, when I say 'see,' I don't mean seeing with my eyes."

Murayama Kaori edged backward into the room. Still going backward, she quietly moved further into the room. Although each and every word was spoken with precision, Kaori could not but think that Uji Kyōko was insane. So musing, she had the sensation of bumping up against somebody and she let out a little squeal. That somebody also squealed. She had collided hard against Takeda Miyo, who had plopped herself down on the tatami in the very center of the room.

Miyo, sitting on her calves, seemed very much asleep. Just as she opened her eyes, quite like a mechanical doll that moved, she began chattering.

"Recently my younger sister, you know, from time to time has been bringing me money. Me, whenever I've got money, I spend it all on snacks. And whenever I buy snacks I eat them all up. Me, that's just the way I am. It's an eating disorder. The nurse told me, 'Miss Takeda, you've bought so-o-o many cookies and crackers again.' Because whenever I get an Off-Grounds Permit, I come back loaded down with snacks. Because I do nothing but sit around and eat all day, I've just gotten fatter and fatter. Me, since coming here I've put on ten kilos. When I'm not eating, I'm sleeping. And when I'm not sleeping, I'm eating. I've gotten to be such a fathead. My body feels plugged up with fat all the way to my brain. That's the feeling. Even when I try thinking, my brain just feels all plugged up with fat. I've gotten to be a real fathead."

Kaori turned away from these mutterings and went out of the room and walked to the end of the corridor. From the window there she could see the entrance to the hospital. Opening the window she gazed outside through the grill. No one was in sight, probably because already some time had elapsed since Keitarō had visited.

"Hello!" Kaori called out anyway, cupping her hands around her mouth like a megaphone.

Her call only increased the isolation she felt pressing in upon her. I don't know you, she had said, and she had driven those people away.

The clammy shadow of those people, it seemed, could still be seen clinging around the entrance. The people who come to this place to live are hardly human beings at all, so the fact that two human beings came particularly to visit her remained vivid in her mind.

"Hello!" she called again, this time more loudly.

It was not necessarily to those two people that she called out. But she simply had to call to someone. Until those people had come, she had not the slightest awareness of being isolated, but since they had in fact come, she realized there did indeed live here a person who had become very lonely—herself. Yet even if those people, hearing her call, had come back, she probably would again have said, I don't know you.

"Hello-o-o!" this time yelling at the top of her lungs.

The bell rang for mealtime, producing a vague movement in the corridor. She had become so accustomed to the scene when meals or chores started that she no longer gave it the slightest thought, but now, perhaps because the visit of those two people a while ago had made her look past her own human-like feelings, she was very much aware of the strangeness of the movement. From the countless rooms ranged on both sides of the corridor, people with slack-skinned faces were emerging sluggishly. There were some who walked to the dining hall with a quick pace, but in general the movement was like the vagueness of a cloud forming. Having utterly lost any purpose in life, they had become thoroughly insensible about even the evening meal.

Kaori also started out from the end of the corridor, catching up with the movement of the others. She had the feeling the women were walking right inside of her. She too, having lost all purpose in life, felt little interest in heading straight to the dining hall. Though she was hungry and actually did feel like eating, the space between herself and her destination was somehow very fuzzy.

When this fuzziness cleared, like a quickly lifting fog, she would be able to return to the functioning society of ordinary people, so her doctors were telling her. Kyōko, however, was just the opposite. Although the doctors said that it was commonplace for a mental illness to be cured when the patient emerged beyond it, Kyōko said that having slipped further into the illness and then having passed through it, she came to understand that she was in another world. "Illness is simply an alternate term for it," she said.

Still lost in the movement of the others, Kaori entered the dining hall. The dining hall itself was also filled with the same movement. Although people had formed a line in front of the kitchen service window, it hardly seemed to be a line at all. From the service window, trays filled with the evening meal were handed out and in turn received without expression or gesture, everyone somehow following one after the other.

With only a plate of stewed chicken with potato, a bit of wilted lettuce for a salad, and a big bowl of rice, Kaori took the tray and as always sat herself down at a table by the window farthest from the kitchen. The chair which she had decided upon was in the middle of a table for six and faced the wall. There were those who always sat in the same place, and those who didn't. When her own seat happened already to be occupied, Kaori would become very unsettled.

A number of people were watching the TV placed in one corner of the dining room. Some were standing, others sitting. Only one person was voicing any sensitive reaction to the television program, while the others watched in silence. Pressed by a nurse, two or three persons were being urged toward the kitchen serving window, but one among them returned to the television, sticking to the group like glue. All were watching seemingly without the slightest interest, but the knot of people around the TV set simply would not disperse for their evening meal.

Absently gazing yet again at the familiar scene, Kaori slowly ate her meal alone. From a while ago, in one corner of her mind loneliness had already started hurting.

Have you really forgotten me? I'm Nobe Keitarō. Since I've met you fully five times, it's really a shame that you've forgotten me. The first time when I was invited to the home where you and your sister were living, I was treated to a meal. You had a knack for making desserts, and because I was coming you'd baked a batch of cookies for me with lots of butter. Yes, and the second time I went you'd made coffee gelatin for me.

Thus had Nobe Keitarō warmly reminisced in the reception room.

No, I don't know you, Kaori had repeatedly said.

Actually, Michiko also has come here with me. First of all, though, I went to the reception desk just by myself and requested a meeting with you. Shall I ask Michiko to come in with me? I'd make every effort to get you to remember us.

No, I don't know anyone by the name of Michiko.

This man by the name of Nobe Keitarō, if indeed I had met him somewhere, sometime, I'd doubtless think him a trustworthy person on whom I could rely. Precisely because he is Michiko's husband, however, he has already become a person with whom I have no reason for getting close. That person has become, so to speak, contaminated by his association with Michiko. Although that is no fault of his, my feelings for him border on hatred.

How lonely it is, thought Kaori.

"What's lonely?" It was the voice of Kyōko, who was sitting across from Kaori looking straight at her.

"Terribly lonely, I think," said Kaori, taking a mouthful of potato. She had not intended to voice her thoughts, but had she perhaps really spoken aloud?

"Everybody's lonely. That's only to be expected."

Kaori could see that Kyōko was now becoming animated. Surely she had returned here from being in outer space, thought Kaori for no particular reason.

"Quite so. Everybody here is like that."

Kaori eyed the people around her. Had Kyōko read the thought that she had not actually given words to, she wondered. Increasingly she came to think so.

"The people who are here, as well as the people who are not here—all are like that. I wish you might understand why it's like that."

Kyōko briskly nibbled away at her lettuce, rather like a squirrel.

"I am lonely because I am hateful. I understand fully."

Kaori was thinking that she had turned away not only her sister but husband as well, indeed had turned away the very world in which her sister lived.

"All the same, you are indeed alive."

"Huh?"

"Don't you think it's miraculous that you are living right here and now?"

"Huh?"

"I mean, with the end of the world apparently coming to a place like this, even then you'll still be living. Good heavens, what kind of a thing would that be?"

Something like the power of Kyōko's words was injected into Kaori, who stared hard across the table directly at her.

"As for me," Kyōko continued, "that's what I've always thought, always. For as long as I can remember, I've done all kinds of things. I've done this and I've done that, and yet before I knew it, I had come to this kind of place. And when I consider why I am in such a place, I can't in the slightest figure it out. I can't find any reason for why I'm here right now. And yet in spite of it all, here I am right now. I'm living, I exist. I'm not dead; I'm living, I exist. Even after coming to this place, I've been existing. It's a mystery, isn't it. What do you think of this mystery?"

Nineteen

SAWAMURA TAKUZŌ HAD LEFT the department store where he worked part-time and was taking a bus to an auto shop; he was to pick up a van left there for repairs. Since leaving the store with instructions to run this errand, he had fallen, he knew not why, into a certain mood, the reason for which he now finally understood. All along the route new buildings were being constructed, old homes were being converted, pedestrian bridges were appearing here and there, the road was being widened, and the outward look of the houses was changing—all of which he had at first been unaware. The bus was now headed toward the repair shop, but a left turn off the main thoroughfare would take him into the neighborhood where he was born and raised. He looked at his wristwatch. It was eleven past three. He had said he would be back at the store by five. If he picked up the van and drove back, it would be about that time. All the same, that thoroughfare was heavy with traffic. One could hardly see the pavement for all the cars that were continually going up and down the street. But being very familiar with this neighborhood, he thought he could avoid the congestion on his return by taking side streets.

With that in mind, the thought of getting off the bus here and now abruptly occurred to him. And so, a moment later when the bus pulled up to the next stop, he put the thought into action. He then started walking.

Surely there must have been a shop selling clogs and sandals at the corner of the street that went off to the left. But since running away from home nearly a full decade ago, he had not once set foot in the neighborhood, so the details were, after all, quite hazy. Certain scenes revived from his childhood memories, however, were much the same as now, and this neighborhood in a sprawling and chaotic Tokyo was now breathing new life. That former clog shop in the same old structure now appeared to him through the warm cloud of memory to have become itself reinvigorated. But on the opposite corner of the street a large pastry shop had appeared, and as he looked at it, he could not remember what had been there before.

Passing through a section of small shops and houses lined up one after the other, Takuzō came to a slight rise in the road. From this vantage point large homes began coming into view. Standing at the intersection he now wondered from which street he should approach. The approach, he thought, seemed somehow to hold important meaning. Avoiding the street running in front of its main entrance, he decided to take a good look at his house from the road in back. For some time he just stood at the intersection, sweeping his eyes across the many houses he was seeing after a ten-year lapse. He had not been accustomed to walking along on this back road. The elementary school, that particular hollow area where he had been beaten, the convenient train station—all these places were on the other side of the street running in front of his home.

As he started walking, little by little the slope of the street became more pronounced. Homes came into view along the hilltop, each with its own unique stone wall, one ranged above the other, and as one continued up the hill the stone walls became higher. After walking for about ten minutes, his feelings since leaving the department store gradually intensified, and a lump formed in his throat. Here, excessively large homes were arrayed, and numbering among the grandest was the one in which he was born and raised where, nearly ten years previous, he had rejected the protective armor of his entire inheritance.

Takuzō, now a mere cast-off shell, as it were, of his former self, wended his way through these imposing and beautiful homes. He finally stood at the back of his own former home and gazed at the high stone wall and the hedgerow of podocarpus which surrounded it. Evergreens towering in the spacious yard beyond the hedgerow seem to have grown luxuriantly during those unseen intervening years, and they now obscured the outlines of roofs piled up in countless layers barely visible from the road. Here his father must be living with the woman whom he had remarried. His sisters had one after the other married and left home, or so he had heard secondhand. In such a huge house could there be only just his father and the woman?

"Ah!" exclaimed Takuzō aloud. Could that be the woman who caused his mother to commit suicide?

Mother, who deeply loved his father, committed suicide because his father loved another woman in another place, and that image of his mother, which hitherto he had tried not to bring to mind, now cut him to the very quick. He was much perplexed, and wondered why he was trying so earnestly to avoid thinking of the matter.

Stepping back a little to a spot that gave him a better view, he could make out the eaves and window of the room on the northeast corner of the second story. Storm shutters were pulled down over the window. In the old days, too, the window was usually shuttered, as the room was set aside for overnight guests. Below that was his childhood room. A small bed was placed in a corner of the six tatami-mat room.

As an infant he felt it was an absurdly large empty space, and when it was filled with darkness it joined with the darkness outside, and there was a vague, interminable gloom which engulfed the bed. In the dead of night wide awake, he instinctively shuddered in the darkness. Not knowing what it was all about, he experienced the deep fright of being alive. And so, he cried out. In the expanse of darkness everywhere, that cry brought forth something like the rustle of an awakening breeze. As the breeze slowly drew nearer, it became an incomparably gentle vernal zephyr coming to visit him. As it brushed against him, he became wonderfully light, and fell into a tranquil slumber.

Takuzō, dear, the only person in this world who really loves you is your mother; other people may say they love you but their love is intermixed with lies; the only truth is me, your mother. Such comments were constantly passed on by his mother. In actuality it was not that he heard them by ear, but rather that he probably felt them, and yet he had the impression there was no room to entertain even the slightest doubt.

"Yes, but," said Takuzō aloud, still standing there on the street corner.

He now recalled that immediately following his mother's suicide, whenever he might try thinking about it, he intentionally pushed such thoughts from his mind.

"Yes, but," he again said aloud.

Was is possible that the person whom he knew did not have the genuine feelings of a mother?

My mother loved the man who was my father, and that love was far stronger than the love toward their son. Tragically, because of that she chose death.

Takuzō started to walk away from the house. A little ahead, as he remembered it, was a garden plot next to a floral shop where he thought he might sit down to reflect. He proceeded about twenty paces, then stopped and looked back. Towering above the high stone wall stood his home, enshrouded in lofty evergreens, solemn and forbidding. He started walking, but the place where the floral shop used to be was completely leveled and paved over with concrete to become a pay parking lot. Resigning himself to it, he just kept walking.

The reality of that former time, when he was concentrating on delivering sleeping pills to his bed-ridden mother, had now been replaced by another reality which held him firmly in its grip.

Things which he thought he already understood he was still far from understanding.

Musing thus, he spotted a public telephone in front of a tobacco shop and headed toward it.

He phoned his store, leaving word that in the midst of his errand he started feeling somewhat unwell, forcing him to stop and rest, and he would probably be unable to drive the van back from the repair shop. Since starting his life of discipline, today was the first time he had slighted his work.

He replaced the receiver and, as if having made a firm decision, picked it up again and dialed 264-4343. "Damn! I've called LifeLine." He dialed again, this time 462-4343.

"Hello?" came the usual listless voice after repeated rings.

"What have you been doing?" asked Takuzō, repeating the greeting he used every time.

"Nothing," she said in that same tone of voice.

"A penny for your thoughts," he said.

No sooner did he hear her voice than Takuzō, who had always hoped so much to grasp her inmost thoughts, tired of his eagerness. It was not because he wanted to monopolize her, but rather that he wanted his love to reach her. If it were a matter of carnal love, he could easily reach her. But there was within him a love, an inexhaustible love, which he wanted, like an arrow shot directly toward its mark, to reach its destination. He was aware that prior to becoming acquainted with her, indeed since his very birth, there existed this love within him.

"And as for you, what are your thoughts? What are you thinking right now?"

"Um …," he stammered.

"Shall I tell you what I was thinking before the telephone rang?"

"It's all right now; I'd rather …" Takuzō hastened to return to the object of his telephoning her in the first place.

"Well as for me, I was thinking about you," she said, in a clearly sexual tone of voice.

"Really. I'm happy to hear that." That's what he said, but Takuzō had the feeling that whatever comment he might hear would in fact be unsatisfactory.

"Again, what have you been thinking? All of a sudden you fell silent." A slight moodiness now crept into her voice.

"Well, I wanted to ask you, as a woman …"

The buzzer sound indicated his three minutes was almost up.

"Sorry, but I don't have another 10-yen coin. I'll look around for a public phone that takes 100-yen coins. I'll call back right away," said Takuzō hurriedly, and hung up. Then, feeling like an unsophisticated teenager blinded with passion, he started out. Wasn't it bizarre that for a talk with Michiko he had dialed her up having only a single 10-yen coin on him?

He fished through his trouser pockets and found two 100-yen coins, and walked off impatiently. Realizing that he typically walked with long slow steps, he tried hard to quicken his pace. He had the feeling that, somehow like being inside a huge cloud, he wanted to get away fast. The cloud was steamy and clammy, broadening layer upon layer, vague and intangible, mysteriously winding toward him from beyond.

Descending the narrow and sinuous hillside street, he came out onto the main thoroughfare, which he had shortly before traversed by bus. It seemed unlikely that in this neighborhood with no train station or shopping area he would find a pay phone that accepted 100-yen coins. He recalled that the district post office was nearby, so he hurried off in that direction, certain he would find such a public phone there.

He finally found a small phone booth to squeeze into which, though facing the noisy main street, was glassed in and sheltered by a recently renovated concrete building, so it was quiet enough.

Takuzō dialed.

Once connected, instead of the usual "Hello," she answered, "It's me."

"What on earth is it with you? Something strange seems to be going on," said Michiko.

"As a matter of fact, there is something strange about me. It's rare that I get strange like this," he said.

"You're certainly not one to show weakness … So, what on earth is going on?" There was no languor in her voice; rather she spoke with another, edgy voice.

"May I inquire of you as a woman?"

"Please, go ahead."

"It's okay?"

"What is it that seems so important?"

Suppose you had a child and then fell in love with another man. If you were forced to choose one or the other which would you take?"

"Well!" and she laughed gaily.

Why are you laughing?"

"I've already decided."

"The man, I suppose. In that case, what about the child?"

Even before making this phone call Takuzō thought he already knew her answer to the question, but he wanted to ask anyway.

"Why can't you understand? When a woman is truly being woman, there is no other choice than the man," she said.

Takuzō figured she'd say as much. He was fascinated by exactly this kind of woman. And yet, now another stubborn matter seemed to be entangling him.

"And yet, because you have no children, in fact you cannot know, can you."

"No, that's not the case."

For some reason or other she spoke with dignity.

A long silence ensued.

With an effort Takuzō suffered through the wait.

"For some reason or other," she explained, "a long time ago I had already studied this thing called woman. Let me simply say that I have bared my heart and examined it. From there what has been continually welling up has been the impulse to seek men, and that's all there is to it. A woman's awakening is her awakening to that fact. Can you please understand? No, you can hardly understand, can you. Anyway, that's my opinion. Since coming to that understanding, I started closely watching all kinds of women. So, although the women who are aware of their womanhood are very few, I can see that every woman does possess at least a latent awareness. Most women are not aware of it, though, and they talk about other things. That's why I didn't have children. It would have been a hindrance to my finding men. So, if it had been left up to nature, I would have had children. When a woman is truly a woman, she will toss her children aside and look for a new man. A woman wants a man. For that purpose she will have no qualms about sacrificing her children. That's the truth about the flesh within me. But if by chance I happened to have a child, I should think he would be very precious to me. Even if at such a time I started to love a man, however, my desire would surely overshadow my whole world, and the child would disappear from view."

As he took in these extensive remarks spoken by an unusually talkative Michiko, Takuzō's attention wandered off to a different voice.

Takuzō dear, because I do understand that your father's feelings for me have grown so very distant, I thought I should take my life. Your father says that such was not the case, but the fact is that, as a woman, I understood everything. You were there for me precisely because your father existed. I'm so sorry, Takuzō, but that's the way it is with women. The times when I was so tender toward you were the times when I was loved by your father. I'm so sorry.

"Michiko?" said Takuzō at length. He was going to say something very uncomplimentary, but when he started to speak he spoke something else.

"You're a very honest person. What I mean by honest is ..."

Certainly Michiko was talking in a reasonable way, but scenes of physical love-making weaved in and out of a vivid reality. Passing beyond that, female sexuality then entices the male into a bloody abyss.

As for me there is only that. Beyond that, there seems to be nothingness. Yet it may just be that female sexuality is itself a nothing, which I probably can't do anything about. Or so Michiko had said at one time or another.

"But I'm different!" said Takuzō, dropping in another 100-yen coin as he shifted the receiver to his right hand.

There was no reply.

"I'm not a man with appetites alone."

He wanted, if he could, to announce to her his own aspirations. Her essential nature having become, so to speak, an archery target, he wanted, if he could, to loose in that direction an arrow laded with the power of love. To hit the mark perfectly, if he could.

I'm searching. So Takuzō had abruptly said the other day.

For what? Okada Heisuke had asked.

Dunno. Something; something unique. That's about all I know.

And just then, he thought, that particular woman came to mind, and that unique something and that particular woman somehow or other inexplicably converged.

"You say you're not a man solely of appetites? Yes; quite so. You're a man of remarkable discipline. The extent to which you balance the desires which you've let lie dormant with that discipline shows great strength. That's the reason I love you. When I'm in bed and my personality is changed, I derive strength from you."

Takuzō laughed awkwardly.

"Oh-oh, haven't we about used up your 100-yen coin?"

Michiko assumed a more practical tone of voice, then, flustered, spoke further.

"This evening I'll have occasion to make the acquaintance of a certain Muro Sawako. I received a phone call from her. She's good friends with you, she said. And because I also am good friends with you, she said she wanted to make friends with me too."

Michiko laughed. It was a generous laugh, though somehow flavored with a dash of peppery sarcasm.

"Is that so," said Takuzō. "She was saying the same thing to me too, though I didn't know that she'd be contacting you today. She insisted I tell her your phone number, and so I did, but if you had objected, it would have been okay with me to have refused her." He considered it all just tiresome pleasantry.

"No objection at all. Although it would be better that she not meet the likes of me."

"Huh? What do you mean?" asked Takuzō.

"What do I mean?" repeated Michiko, saying she would phone him afterwards the same evening and hoped he would be in his rooming house. And then she hung up. As for Muro Sawako, Michiko seemed not at all ill disposed toward her.

When Takuzō came out onto the main thoroughfare, he recalled his feelings when he had come away from these crowds not long before. Looking at his watch, he saw it was past five. In any event he would at least have to put in an appearance at his workplace. He took a bus to the train station, where he boarded a local headed for the store.

Throughout that interval he lost himself in thought. To see after some ten years the house where he had been born and raised, and to recall long-buried memories, especially those unforgettable memories of his mother. And Michiko's belittling remarks. Was it really that way or was it otherwise—thus he debated with himself. As for Michiko, he suddenly harbored an enmity toward her. And at the same time this evening's meeting between Michiko and Sawako flashed through his mind.

Since that day about two weeks ago when Okada Heisuke and he were drinking together at Sawako's apartment, he had not once seen her, although on the evening of that day he did let himself be badgered into staying the night in her apartment. Throughout the entire two years or so of their acquaintance, she had not shown even a fleeting romantic interest in him, but on that evening she tugged him by the hand, clinging to him, pestering him to stay the night. Just once, that's all, she had said.

I'll keep my word. Just once. That's how much I think you're important to me. Afterward certainly nothing will change between us, so you can put your mind at ease about that. It will be just as always. Nothing, absolutely nothing will change.

As Takuzō was idly recalling Sawako's remarks, the words she was speaking and the woman herself were now coinciding to a tee. Indeed, "that's the way she is" was the impression he had of her right up till now, a matter he recalled giving him peace of mind. That was altogether different from his feelings which were rushing toward Michiko, the inner meaning of whose remarks was, however much he contemplated them, elusive and vague. Even while sensing that he had unwittingly fallen into a trap by staying overnight with Sawako, he had fallen into that peace of mind.

Sawako, in Takuzō's embrace, asked with her honest and open heart, "What's her name?"

Even after their midday conversation in which this had never come up, visions of Michiko intruded.

As for me, I'm different from ordinary women. Don't get me wrong. Because ever since I was a child, I never quarreled with anybody. That was one of my talents, so my teachers at school told me. I don't think it was a talent, really; I just liked everyone.

Sawako kept talking, nestled in his arms. She seemed wonderfully happy; her face was pure rapture.

I'm so glad I'm going to make a new friend. And that person will surely be fond of me, too. Why? Because I like her so much.

Takuzō, who shortly before felt peace of mind opening up as Sawako's words and the woman herself coincided, now pricked up his ears upon hearing these strange words and unexpectedly sensed the inner meaning of her vague remarks. And then, it occurred to him, the more one analyzed the situation the more chaotic things became; indeed, during these nearly two years he had not analyzed Sawako at all, he mused.

"I don't understand women," said Takuzō to himself as he traced his way back to the store.

He felt the same way about his mother.

He had the feeling that he was getting caught up in a dreadful misunderstanding. After their night together, it was true, Sawako had made no demands on him. She had not come to visit nor had she telephoned. So, she really did seem in all sincerity to be carrying through with her promises of the other day.

Takuzō forced himself to switch his attention and recall the more important matters he had previously been considering. From the moment he was born, already within him there existed something like love. He felt that it was an immeasurably larger matter than all else. Spanning the nearly ten years of his disciplinary regimen, he realized he had been nourishing that love.

Although it was a love which had to be focused on just one woman, he really wondered if Michiko could be expected to accept such an abundance of love.

Returning to the store, he apologized for not having picked up the van, and on account of that he decided he should put in another two hours' work. While busying himself attaching price tags to merchandize, not his normal responsibility, suddenly the determination welled up within him to quit the job. Just before leaving for home, he informed the manager of his intention.

He ate his evening meal out, then returned to his lodgings and waited for Michiko's phone call. Something was beginning to happen to him. His regimen of discipline was losing all meaning for him; its significance had now passed. Although the refreshing tension, as if he were a Buddhist practitioner taking an icy bath, had continued for these ten years, now, however, a self existed which was like his original self, a self intending even more than previously to have good judgment, but he was facing a prospect different from his former one.

He thought he'd like to talk with Okada Heisuke. Not that he wanted to talk about his own affairs; he just felt like enjoying the fellow's strangely entertaining banter. Except that he didn't know his whereabouts. Heisuke had mentioned where he lived when they had first met at a bar a year or so previous, but it seems that he hadn't gone back there very often. Nor had Takuzō bothered about enquiring into the nature of his employment. For the purpose of plumbing the inner worlds of politics and business, however, one might suppose Heisuke had just the right kind of aggressive character and wiry build to glide through such turbid waters. In a dream one time, wasn't Heisuke carrying something light and squarish like a sheaf of manuscript paper such as newsmen use? Takuzō himself was also swimming agilely through the dregs of society, and occasionally would meet Heisuke face to face. Although they were much different in personality, they got along well.

Finally the telephone rang.

He picked up the receiver. It was not Michiko, but an acquaintance from his part-time work.

It was nothing important, and after a rambling conversation, he replaced the receiver.

Unexpectedly the scene of Michiko and Sawako meeting each other sprang vividly into his imagination. With only their facial expressions and gestures visible, however, the scene resembled an old silent-screen film. Contemplating the scene more carefully, something painful—though a pain he could not understand—gradually intensified.

Nobe Michiko is a very nice woman, and because I cannot possibly rival her, I bequeath you to her, Sawako would say, and the next day would not a beaming Sawako come visiting? Such a thought crossed Takuzō's mind, an egotistical thought, however, which he immediately brushed aside.

The telephone rang again.

It was Michiko. It was not her languid voice nor was it her tense voice, but it was a little bit different than usual. Takuzō tried to read her mind, but her voice was flat, devoid of emotion.

"Right now I'm calling from outside. It's so noisy around here it makes me jittery."

And indeed, as she spoke he could hear vague background hubbub, people talking, and so on.

"Where are you?" asked Takuzō instead of his customary inquiry, What are you doing?

"I'm close to home on my way back, and I'm at the station right now."

"And?" he urged her again, thinking that if she had returned home her husband would be there so she was phoning en route.

"And?" Michiko repeated his word and laughed. It was almost like teasing him.

"Quite an unobjectionable person, isn't she?" With no other recourse, Takuzō in this way broached the subject.

"She's too good; it's almost annoying," she parried.

"It seems she wants to be on good terms with you."

Without mentioning his own relation with Sawako, about which he had already given something akin to an explanation, he decided to continue the conversation. There was no reason to evade it, because, he thought, he and probably even Michiko alike both considered Sawako to be a woman of different status.

"I've accepted her invitation for next Sunday. She said she'd prepare a delicious meal for me. After that, she said she'd show me how to make paper flowers."

At that, Takuzō laughed aloud. Michiko, however, did not laugh, but continued talking.

"As for me, I happily accepted the invitation—she is a good person after all, and besides, because I'm so bored, it's a way to kill some time.

"Ah, that being the case, on my behalf please have a pleasant time with her, because you alone are enough for me."

“That would seem to be something contrary to her wishes. She hopes for the happiness of all people, she said. Up to now she has always been concerned with the happiness of all people, she told me.”

“Well then, I’ll gladly leave the matter to you,” said Takuzō, even himself thinking his manner of speech a bit light-hearted and so, on the point of hanging up, he felt almost duty-bound to say something more about Sawako, but, choking up with emotion he brought up another subject.

“I decided to quit my present part-time job. We agreed I’d leave after working one more week. Because I thought my disciplinary regimen required I bring things to a clear conclusion.”

“You must be kidding! And after that, then, you’ll enter a large company, and you’ll probably plan on marrying me, won’t you, and if that’s the case, it will be a great disappointment to you.”

In the background as she was speaking, one could hear a baby whining, which a moment later dissolved into the hubbub of the train station.

“No, it’s not that at all. Definitely, it’s not that.”

As if wreathed in a lunar halo, the picture of him entering a large company and marrying Michiko floated through Takuzō’s mind, though he was aware he had not thought seriously how he might wrest her from her husband. What he wanted was a union even more impossible, and because it was impossible, he had not even begun to consider how he might go about securing it. Saying nothing further about that, he abruptly inquired, “Why are you so concerned about me?”

“But … it’s exactly as I told you earlier today. Because when I’m in bed I become the real woman that is inside of me, and you have the power to accept me. Of course, it doesn’t necessarily have to be you, I suppose. So long as there is some man possessing such power.”

“The real woman?”

Takuzo savored the strange sensation of that phrase. Nameless, expressionless, inscrutable, an ordinary woman, but not the ordinary woman whom one might see just anywhere, but rather a woman whose layers one might peel off like layers of an onion and, peeling off countless layers, finally opening up to something fetuslike at the innermost core, where a woman shows her true self. Was this not perhaps the woman who has haunted myths from time immemorial?

"Oh, it's gotten terribly noisy around here. There's a group passing through that has apparently returned from a tour. Can you hear my voice? Can you hear me? You'd think it was a foreign country here. Though I've never yet been to a foreign country, Tokyo now seems like a foreign country. Standing here in the station anyway, that's what I think. Everybody's just madly jabbering away. Whatever language it is, I don't understand a word of it. Ah, finally the group has passed by. And? Continuing what you were saying a minute ago ..."

Twenty

TAKEDA SACHIKO DIALED 264-4343.

"Hello," the other party answered.

When she had called on previous occasions, if it was a Monday she knew a man would answer, and sure enough the other party was a man's voice.

"Hello," said Sachiko brightly, though it was dark within.

"Has something been troubling you again?" It seemed to be a somewhat smiling voice.

"Oh! You know who I am?" said Sachiko cheerfully, sensing from the party's tone of voice that he did indeed.

"Junior high, second year, fourteen years old, right? I don't know your name, though."

"Yes, yes." Tears came to Sachiko's eyes.

"I always remember when someone calls here even after just one phone call. A single phone call formed a bond between us."

Sachiko was speechless. It was somehow a strange thing to hear.

"I don't know your face, but I remember the voice. Each person's voice is different. Each person's thoughts are different, too."

Mouth agape, Sachiko couldn't utter a sound.

"Well then, has something happened? Today as well there must be something that you want me to listen to." His voice was consistent in its tranquil and unassertive gentleness.

"Lots has happened. Lots, so much it's like all bottled up inside of me."

"I see, I see," said the man.

"Can you please understand me?"

"If you want to tell me the whole story, then you have to start by calming down. Because it's so much for you …"

"So much?"

"So much that you seem somehow to have lost the ability to express yourself."

"But I really do like to have someone listen to me," said Sachiko. "And after somebody listens to one of my problems, I want to have someone listen to another. Then, little by little, I continue on...yeah, even little by little it goes on and adds up, but probably for sure it doesn't become the whole story, and yet because I'm not strong enough to keep everything bottled up inside me, I'd like you to listen even if it's just one part of the whole."

Sachiko said it all in a single breath. She had never before said such things to her school friends, nor to her mother or brother or sister, but now it just naturally poured forth. That was probably because she felt the other party understood everything.

Yes, yes, let's get it all out right away, all the changes in your life between the previous phone call and this one.

"Standing in the entertainment district of Shinjuku and searching for a man has become a routine for me. That began when my mother and stepfather went on a trip overseas, leaving me at home alone, but after they got back they found one reason or another to argue with each other, swearing at each other about everything. Because of that, Mother started paying less attention to my doings than before. If I came home late, she'd scream at me something terrible, but after screaming she'd forget all about my doings. And so I've begun just hanging around in the streets all the time. Of course I go to school. Although I don't study much, I'm really a very good student. But even that isn't anything to boast about. Because everything during this cold, cold time is grey. My only wish is to become close with someone.

I guess I've already told you about how, though I'd met him only once, there was someone I've always been on the lookout for. And yesterday I actually did meet up with him unexpectedly. Not in the entertainment district, but somewhere else, during the day. I thought I'd go to the park, so I walked there. It was drizzling out, so the streets were wet and I was too, which kind of calmed me down. Starting from the area where the park's concrete moat is, there wasn't a soul about, and lots of leaves that had fallen from the trees hanging over the moat were stuck to the wet footpath. Just then, that very same person came in through the park entranceway. He wasn't carrying an umbrella. He came walking right toward me kind of quickly. Both side pockets of his raincoat were bulging way out, and as he got closer I could see that they were newspapers. At first he didn't recognize me. That's because I was wearing my school uniform. So it was me who spoke out. I felt a relation with him more than just that he was of the opposite sex, but more like I had the closeness to him of something like a family relative. There was surprise in his small bean-like eyes, but more than that, the surprised expression on his face showed he knew me from before. Then he asked me, what are you doing? in a tone of voice as if I was somebody he bumped into and greeted all the time. I'm out for a walk, but what are you doing, I asked. I was reading newspapers, he said, and he patted both pockets full of all those newspapers. He'd probably spread them out to read in the park arboretum, or so it seemed to me by his appearance. Well then, let's get together again, he said, and he seemed about to pass right on by. But where, I immediately asked him,

We'll be able to meet, some time or other. Like this way, by accident.

That's so. I feel the same way as you do.

That's because I'm forever wandering the streets.

What sort of work do you do?

That I can't say. That's something I don't tell anyone.

But since you meet me only by accident, it would be okay if you told me.

Yes, of course. Because we're on good terms with one another.

He took out one of the newspapers stuffed in his pockets and thrust the front page right before my eyes. It was about the political scandal rocking the whole country now. I'm caught up in the middle of this maelstrom, he said.

Maelstrom? I said, not quite understanding.

He laughed his same old laugh. I kept talking with him, though I wasn't understanding much. Is that good or bad? I asked him.

Well now, what's good and what's bad is something I try not to think much about. When I was young, it was something I thought about, and it was something I simply could not understand.

At that point we parted company. How many minutes was it that I just stood there in a daze. I'd been searching for that person for such a long time, so why did I let him get away from me so soon? That thought really weighed on me. Then, something else occurred to me. Despite that I'd been searching so long for that person, another thought was gelling in my mind, and I began slipping in that direction. At first there wasn't anything good at all about this sex thing even though I was only trying to become close with someone, but recently I'm beginning to understand that the sensation is quite unusual. And so my grades in school have been steadily falling."

Twenty-One

NOBE MICHIKO, SEATED IN FRONT OF THE TABLE, watched blankly as Muro Sawako removed from a closet her accumulation of paraphernalia for making paper flowers. Not a tall woman, Sawako stood on tiptoes to get her hands around the large cardboard box as she wrestled it down from an upper shelf. Her muscles flexed under her light cream-colored blouse. Inside the closet could be glimpsed ten or so boxes of clothing the contents of each indicated by attached labels, then neatly piled bedding, and other necessities as well, all very efficiently arranged. As Sawako set the box on the table, with her head thrust right in Michiko's face, she expelled an unpleasant warm gust of breath. Michiko was perplexed: she couldn't tell whether Sawako's behavior was terribly careless or completely intentional, and was unsure how best to react. It would be simple to view her with animosity. But then how would she be able to face this woman who wanted to be on good terms?

Sawako then went into the kitchen where the sounds seemed to indicate preparations for tea.

After she had accepted Sawako's luncheon invitation, Michiko wanted to excuse herself from an awkward meal. Deciding, however, to let herself be entertained for just two or three hours in the afternoon, Michiko telephoned Sawako at her work place and changed the engagement to just tea at Sawako's apartment. It was not long previous that Michiko had noticed the same woman.

It had been Michiko's first meeting with Takuzō and they were sitting by the coffee shop window chatting and she could see her. Had the woman followed Takuzō or had she come with him to some place nearby? Standing at the sidewalk bus stop as if waiting for a bus, the woman was strangely peering their way. On another occasion, as Michiko was about to enter a café where she and Takuzō were to meet, upon looking back there again was that same woman peering from behind the shadow of a truck. Realizing she had been observed by Michiko and perhaps thinking that she should give the impression she was not staring but simply passing by, she abruptly started walking toward her. Michiko tried to match that woman against the woman who was now pressing her friendship upon her. Michiko then tried to determine what there was between those two Sawakos. Even Michiko's inclination to take advantage of Sawako's invitation was due to just such an interest in her. Why else would Michiko endure so inordinately long a session with a woman with whom she seemingly had absolutely nothing of mutual interest to talk about? She was not unaware that, if she were uninterested, she would probably feel spiteful during their meeting.

Although she was positive that it was Muro Sawako's eye she had caught as she looked back from the entrance of that café, Michiko acted as if she knew nothing. And for her part, Sawako also did not mention it.

"Now then, please help yourself."

Sawako came out from the kitchen bringing tea and cake, and sat down at the opposite side of the table.

"Oh, how attractive!" said Michiko.

Michiko's own apartment was altogether different from this one, which was neatly arranged though lacking in character, but such was her first impression and so she said as much.

"Really? Me? You think I'm attractive?" exclaimed Sawako girlishly. She blushed, drew her hand across her hair and rested it against her cheek—the typical reactions of a young lady showing embarrassment.

Michiko realized Sawako had misinterpreted her remark.

"Yes, I really do."

Despite the misunderstanding, Michiko wanted the conversation to move forward. She understood intuitively that her companion wanted to be admired as a woman.

"It would be a real pleasure for me to entertain you here like this from time to time. And the starting point should be that the two of us form a good relation," said Sawako as she lifted a piece of cake to her mouth.

Just what kind of starting point it might be, she did not take the trouble to say. What on earth did she have in mind? thought Michiko. Some plan, of course, that would probably bring good fortune.

"Are you someone who has particular beliefs?" asked Michiko.

Enjoying the tasty cake, apparently homemade, Michiko imagined her a member of some new religious cult that might be called the Congregation of Cheerful Cherubs or some such.

"Yes, I do believe in something—myself," said Sawako, misinterpreting the question.

"In yourself? In what way?"

The yellow cake fairly melted in her mouth, and she savored its delicate flavor.

"For example, just this way."

Sawako dropped her fork on the table and spread her two hands slightly apart.

"What's that?" Michiko, unable to grasp the significance of the gesture, fixed her eyes on Sawako, and saw that her mouth was smeared with whipped cream.

"Aren't we fond of each other?"

And Sawako, as if afraid to hear the answer to her own question, hastily removed the lid from the cardboard box at the end of the table, and began taking out the paper flower materials.

"Fond?" said Michiko, pursuing the matter nonetheless. Was she referring to the phantom third party—Takuzō?

Wearing a somewhat troubled expression, Sawako pinched between her fingertips a length of wire used for making paper flowers.

"Hold the wire this way. Then take a section and bend it into a hoop like this. Yes, that's right. It's thin wire, so it's easy to work with. Make only as many hoops as there will be flower petals."

Sawako handed some wire to Michiko who made it into hoops following the instructions. Being unused to it and therefore not very good at it, Michiko, glancing now and then to see how Sawako was doing it, bent over her work, trying somehow or other to do her best. Her hoops were not at all neatly curved.

After a while, sensing something like a vacuum before her, Michiko looked up. She found a persistence in Sawako's gaze which was fixed right on her. A moment ago nimbly bending the wire, her hands now were motionless; she seemed to be in a daze, and yet her eyes, vibrant, were looking full at her. Then, like a startled dove, she blinked and blurted out in a fluster, "Can you manage?"

That expression in Sawako's eyes duplicated the expression Michiko had seen twice before, and she met the other's gaze.

"Yes, I'm managing," she said, her eyes still fastened on Sawako.

"Well, then, let's go on to the next stage."

From the other side of the table Sawako's smiling face bent closer.

She fashioned five petals from a single length of wire, then connected them together one by one around a center by securing them with two or three turns of wire. Finally she wrapped the wire around in circles as a stem, and then used wire snips to clip off the two ends of the wire with an audible click.

All the while she was following these instructions, Michiko visualized the persistence Sawako had inadvertently revealed, and the expression in her sister's eyes likewise came to mind. The two were definitely of the same temperament.

During the time when she was in the home of her sister and brother-in-law Sanada Misao, Michiko recalled that she had from first to last felt that same expression. Looking around, Michiko would see that her sister had already averted her eyes. However, it happened that once in a while when her sister was slow to look away, their eyes would meet. The more Michiko tried to ignore her sister's stare, the more frequent those visual assaults became. What could she be looking at like that? Neither observation nor surveillance, it seemed rather that she was looking right through her at something. Her sister would have stared for fully an hour if Michiko had not become aware of it.

Her sister probably was not just looking at external appearances. Michiko took it that her sister was somehow looking at nothing other than her very soul. A person's soul is ascertained through her eyes. In order for Kaori to live, mused Michiko, another woman had to be killed. And for another woman to live, she herself had to be killed. The look in Kaori's eye had in an instant unconsciously retraced countless centuries and returned to primitive woman.

While Michiko was shaping the outline for her first flower, Sawako was making her third. When occasionally she looked up, Sawako gave Michiko a friendly wink as if to say everything is just fine.

The pleasantly warm room, the cheerful yellow curtains, the well vacuumed tatamis with nary a stray thread showing in the cracks between them—such an apartment as this gave credence to that wink.

"I'm so happy, really so happy," exclaimed Sawako, breaking the silence between them.

"What?" said Michiko as if she had misunderstood, though in fact she had understood perfectly.

"Doing something like this with someone. There's really more to it than just the thing itself—it brings such happiness, doesn't it."

Sawako, apparently again fearing the answer she might hear, began the next stage of her lesson.

Paper made of a synthetic material resembling traditional Japanese paper was removed from the box. There was purple and red and green and white and so on, thin almost to transparency, and velvety soft. She cut each piece of paper a little bigger than the wire petal frames, and attached them one by one to the frames with adhesive. In the center, a ready-made stamen was inserted. Then, bringing together the various ends to make a single base, she wrapped them around with blue paper cut into the shape of a calyx.

"Ah, that's it; all done," exclaimed Sawako cheerily, and, having finished her own part, she got up and went into the kitchen. After a few moments' clatter of pots and dishes, suddenly all was again silent. What could she be doing? thought Michiko, glancing toward the kitchen. All was silence, right up to the curtain partitioning off the kitchen.

"Please wait a bit longer," came a cheerful voice suddenly flying out.

And then the silence resumed.

Yes, the silence of that other time was also the same as this. Michiko vividly recalled the appearance of the rented house where her sister and Sanada Misao had been living. At her sister's request, Michiko was in the garden watering flowers with a sprinkling can. Loud noises came from upstairs where her sister was vacuuming. Every single noise reflected her sister's mood, and her restless and persistent rantings were clearly audible. Suddenly everything quieted down. It was as if nothing at all would resume. Facing this meaningful silence, Michiko for the longest time just blankly listened. Then something not heavy but not light either fell on her head, knocking her dizzy. For a moment she lost her balance but quickly recovered, and, rubbing her head, she picked up the thing that had fallen at her feet. It was a wet rag, as filthy as one used to wipe soot from ceiling beams. Looking up, there was her sister's face looking down at her.

I'm not going to say I'm sorry, her sister had said. Until you say I'm sorry, I won't say I'm sorry, she continued. I didn't throw the cleaning rag. It just fell. There's no I'm sorry about it, and even supposing I did throw it, there still wouldn't be any I'm sorry, and it is you who should say I'm sorry, and yes it was I who threw the cleaning rag but oughtn't it be you who say the I'm sorry?

Her sister's face looked as though she were disintegrating. It was the beginning of her insanity.

"Ouch!" came a shrill cry from the kitchen.

Michiko half rose to her knees.

"I've burned myself," said Sawako in an unexpectedly matter-of-fact voice.

Holding up her right hand, Sawako appeared from behind the kitchen curtain. She showed Michiko the tips of her thumb and forefinger.

"I've just been baking apples in the oven. When I took them out to look, they weren't done yet, so I turned the oven back on. Then, after five minutes went by, without thinking I grabbed the oven pan directly. Just look at how red they're getting."

Looking at the tips of her two fingers with a dazed look on her face, Sawako seemed actually to be pleased that her fingers were getting red.

Since yesterday I haven't eaten a single meal; I've stopped eating for two whole days now; look at how thin I've gotten, and do you know why I have stopped eating? Do you know? Do you know anything about me? See how thin I've gotten.

So her sister, as if pleased with herself, had said, thrusting forward a face made pitiful in those two days.

"I should have run cold water over the burns right away. How dumb of me."

As she said this, Sawako again disappeared into the kitchen. Over the sound of running water, Sawako's voice could be heard mumbling, Oh, my poor precious fingers my poor precious fingers, like some sort of incantation.

Michiko got up. If she stayed here any longer, she thought, Sawako seemed inclined to inflict a yet more serious injury on herself. Her very presence here had already wounded Sawako.

With such thoughts in mind, it was her sister standing right before her eyes.

You should say I'm sorry, Kaori went on. Slut! she screamed. Trollop! Backstabber!

So, that's the way it is. I have no reason to hurt anyone. However, if the fact that I am living does hurt somebody, there's nothing that can be done about it, Michiko had finally said.

"Oh, are you leaving already? And I've specially baked these apples," said Sawako, emerging from the kitchen.

"It's because my husband is home on Sunday. But let me take some apples back with me. Ah, they're still warm," said a flustered Michiko.

"Oh, you have a husband?" said Sawako with a wooden expression. After that the blood seemed to drain from her and she turned stony-faced. She fairly spat out her next words.

"Sunday evening and dinner with your husband. And every weekday it's dinner with a lover. You must certainly have many lovers. You must be greatly admired even by your husband. Any man would love to take care of you."

"No, that's not the case. Not at all, absolutely not at all," bristled Michiko, though she didn't know what she might say to present her case.

"You have such a talent for paper flowers. How I wish I had the same talent," said Michiko.

Michiko felt inclined to talk more about her own situation, but fell silent. Then she fixed her eyes on her companion.

You should say you're sorry, said Sawako.

I'm not doing anything to you, said Michiko.

But he's absolutely crazy about you, said Sawako.

Surely it's the fault of that woman.

That woman?

I am the woman who is witness, the woman who is right alongside me. Because that woman is strong. I am not strong, and that woman is strong.

"Do stay a bit longer. Stay until the two of us have eaten some baked apple." Sawako was all bright-eyed.

Michiko became a little flustered.

"Oh, but first, would you do me a favor? Open the cabinet there please, and grab the first-aid box. Just look, I can't manage it with these fingers of mine ..."

Sawako, holding up the two fingers where blisters had now already formed, motioned with her eyes toward the cabinet in the bathroom just off the dining room where the two of them were now standing.

Michiko stepped into the bathroom; on the right there was the toilet, and on the left the bathtub room. The door of the bathtub room was ajar, and perhaps because this was an old apartment it did not have the fashionable up-to-date modular-style tub. She could see the small rectangular tub of polished concrete for soaking and the area next to it for scrubbing down.

"There should be a cookie tin in that cabinet. Would you get it down please, and take out the burn ointment?" And while she was saying this, Sawako also stepped into the bathroom.

"This must be it," said Michiko.

"Yes, yes, that's it." Sawako imagined herself fortunate in winning Michiko's sympathy, but somehow or other her performance seemed to ring false.

As Michiko was getting the tin down from the bathroom cabinet, her eyes fell to the washstand where, near Sawako's toothbrush and cup and soap, she saw three used blades for a man's shaving razor. That there should be razor blades but no razor anywhere Michiko thought rather odd. As she was staring at them, Sawako's eyes also fell there.

For an instant a void inserted itself between the two of them.

"Mr. Sawamura's things," said Sawako barely audible, then immediately began spouting an explanation.

"That day a while ago when I first saw you, on the way back home I stopped in at Mr. Sawamura's. I told him what a fine person you are, and because that was the only thing I talked about, he seemed quite at a loss. You can see that I'm kind of an odd person, not like your ordinary woman. Why should I be jealous or anything of you? Really, those who have love have happiness. That day when I went to his apartment, I brought back with me as a memento three razor blades lying around in his bathroom. Though they were old, I could still use them."

"Memento?" returned Michiko, giving her a hard look.

Sawako reacted with an oddly blank expression.

"Why are you looking at me like that? When your eyes fix on me like that, it's really very beautiful."

"Memento?" repeated Michiko, who now considered Sawako's attitude to be not so much that of rival but as something quite the opposite.

"Oh, the ointment has to be applied right away." As Michiko held the tin out in front of her and removed the lid, Sawako lifted out the tube of ointment, and then stepped out of the bathroom.

"On that same day I too talked with Mr. Sawamura, by phone though," said Michiko, recalling that twice during the course of that day she had phoned him to discuss a number of things. She followed Sawako out of the bathroom.

Now finally, the phantom that existed between the two of them had been given a name by both parties—Sawamura Takuzō.

Sawako looked as though she was waiting for what Michiko would say next.

Yet Michiko said nothing at all—a fact which she knew would hurt Sawako. But if her simply being there was already hurting Sawako, then her present silence by comparison did not amount to much, she thought. If Sawako wanted to apply love as her balm for this hurt, that was her business.

"Would you bandage them up for me?" Sawako held out the two fingers, shiny with the greasy ointment.

Michiko took a bandage roll out of the first-aid tin and wrapped a length of it around Sawako's thumb and index finger.

"Aren't we fond of each other?" asked Sawako, repeating her earlier question.

No. How would it be simply to say no, thought Michiko, as she finished bandaging the fingers. Even if she didn't say it, silence itself would amount to the same thing. No, absolutely not.

"I have to be going now," said Michiko, without answering the question.

The answer Sawako awaited did not materialize, but floated midway between the two of them as they stood there.

Sawako said no more about her baked apples. She had apparently forgotten all about the two of them eating, but just stood there dumbly.

It can't be helped, there's nothing to be done about it, things cannot be changed.

Thinking such thoughts, Michiko looked at Sawako.

She had once looked at her sister with similar thoughts in mind. She looked at various other women. And always her look was returned with a malicious eye as if she were the assailant.

Every woman is probably connected with her inner feminine self. However, the power that comes from drawing it up varies, and there are people living who hardly ever draw it up. When one woman is in rivalry with another, it is certain that each has decided to rely on her own way of drawing upon that resource. That's probably how it is.

I'm sorry, she said, without the words' having left her mouth.

As for me, that's just the way I am.

Michiko had visited Edgewood Mental Hospital numerous times, and even when she was walking aimlessly along the property wall, it was this same sort of feeling.

I'm so sorry—even if she had said so to her rival, it would have been of no use.

Michiko picked up her handbag and went to the door. As she was putting on her shoes, she felt Sawako's unrelenting stare boring into her from behind. Finished with her shoes, she looked over her shoulder. Beyond where Sawako was standing, Michiko could see the remnants of the paper flower materials still scattered on the table.

"It's been so enjoyable. As you gradually get to know me better, it will be an even greater pleasure. Today is just the beginning. Thank you for coming," said Sawako with a smile, as she waved good-bye to Michiko.

When she emerged from the apartment, Michiko felt tired all over. She had a premonition that today's affairs were not yet over.

Ambiguous—isn't that just the way she is, thought Michiko. Ambiguous.

Leaving the public housing building, Michiko turned in the direction of the subway station. With still a good deal of time before she was to meet Keitarō for dinner out, she walked leisurely. She felt like drinking a cup of strong coffee. But this was a residential street lined both left and right with concrete-block property walls extending along all the homes as if by prearrangement. From above the walls could be seen the branches of lifeless garden trees. The leaves had mostly fallen from the deciduous trees and the colorless branches trembled in the wind. Wherever one went, there were always the same rows of houses. A cold wind struck her legs exposed below her overcoat. Not yet winter but no longer autumn, the cold of this halfway season, wrapped in dust and fumes, swirled about her.

Spotting a public pay phone, it occurred to her to call Takuzō. It was not that Sawako would be her topic. Like her two long phone calls the other day, she wanted to exchange thoughts by phone. Although—no, rather because—they had been together until late yesterday evening in a hotel, she wanted to exchange some thoughts with him that she had been nursing in her mind.

She dialed, but the line was busy. She waited a minute or so and dialed again. She was relieved when she heard the ringing tone, but it just kept on ringing and ringing. Just now the line had been busy, so he couldn't be out. What was he doing? Had he gone out during just that one minute? After listening to it ring thirty times or so, she hung up. And then she understood. That busy signal a moment ago was simply because someone had telephoned him. And that someone, she had a hunch, could have been none other than Muro Sawako. Once again, Michiko dialed the number and once again she got the busy signal. There was a pay phone in front of a bakery on the same side of the street as Sawako's apartment building, and the figure of her with receiver pressed to her ear crossed Michiko's mind, and soon the notion that anything's okay faded from her mind.

It occurred to her, once aboard the subway car, that Takuzō's lodgings were not far away.

In twenty minutes she arrived at Ginza station. On the spur of the moment she went into a snack bar and had a coffee. She soon left and wandered about. During the year construction had apparently finished on a number of stores along Ginza Avenue, either remodeled or built anew. The shops and stores, now so splendidly dressed up, were scarcely recognizable from those of five or six years ago when she had come to Tokyo on vacation. Well, Japan has suddenly become a wealthy nation, Keitarō would boastfully say.

So, that's the way it is. With this thought in mind, she strolled along Ginza Avenue.

It was still early for their six o'clock dinner date, but when she went into the restaurant he had decided upon, Keitarō was already there, sitting at a table for two with a newspaper spread out before him.

"Ah!" he exclaimed with an apparent sense of relief.

"What? How come you're so early?" said Michiko, as she stood there looking down at him, for she knew Keitarō's habit of being neither early nor late but right on time.

"Actually, I've been to Edgewood Hospital again. I went planning to spend a good deal of time there. As usual, however, it was a disappointingly short visit."

The apparent sense of relief in Keitarō's voice just now, so Michiko supposed, was certainly because he hadn't known what to do with the unexpected time on his hands.

"Isn't that just like you, standing over me forever like that—people will think we are a most ill-paired couple," he said, casting glances toward nearby tables.

"Ill-paired?" And with a smile, Michiko took her seat.

The dishes, which Keitarō apparently had already ordered, were served. He had eaten here once before on business, and because the duck had been particularly good, he had proposed coming here today so Michiko could try it.

"Well then, how was my sister?" asked Michiko, as she watched the waiter, who had brought a serving stand to the side of the table and was deftly slicing the duck.

"The food here is unusually good, so let's save the talk for afterwards." Keitarō pushed aside the very topic Michiko was expecting.

Plates of thinly sliced duck were set before them, accompanied by a gravy boat filled with sauce, then small bowls of salad were served. When they were ready to start eating Michiko remarked that the wine had not come, and Keitarō realized that he had forgotten to order one. Michiko supposed that his mind must at that point simply have drifted off to Edgewood Hospital.

"Having such a meal with you in a first-class Tokyo restaurant … I've been thinking about this for years…now I have fulfilled my ambition," said Keitarō, who, with some wine in him, had turned quite merry.

The time that Michiko had spent at Sawako's apartment from about two o'clock in the afternoon and the time that was now flowing by her here were, she was aware, altogether different in character. The two chafed so much that she could catch the grating sound of the one slowly rubbing against the other within herself. It was an instinctive movement to which she had become daily accustomed. Being alive was itself trying, sometimes rational and sometimes not, and so she seemed to be pitching this way and that.

For dessert, melon was served. Finally, when the coffee arrived, Keitarō opened up about Edgewood Hospital.

"Actually, I hadn't intended to go there. In preparation for next week's work, there were lots of materials I simply had to get in order, and so I intended to go to the library. But I just couldn't get out of my mind my previous failure at that hospital. The more I tried to develop effective plans for the coming week's work, the more intolerable were the distractions that prevented me from making those plans. That's the reason. But my visit to the hospital was, you might say, like pounding a nail into thin air or flailing one's arms at nothing—it was just an utter waste of time. And contrary to what I was hoping, my inquiries were nonchalantly but skillfully dodged—such is her kind of mental illness. And so, when all is said and done, I was outwitted this time, too.

"So how was my sister?"

"Kaori didn't come in."

"So you never even saw her?"

"Not quite. What you might call her proxy appeared. She introduced herself as Uji Kyōko and she had strangely clear skin. She said something like this: You probably think that this world is the only world, and yet there is another world which in fact affects this world, and I possess the power to perceive it, and I am the person who imparts to Kaori the power to develop this spiritual discipline, and you, please, do not try to interfere, and about this other world it exists in the human inner self—the inner self of women and the inner self of men—dwelling in us like gathering clouds, but when one pushes through to that other world and enters it ever more deeply, the blue sky opens up and … And on and on it went like that. I was flabbergasted."

Michiko remembered the strange feeling of something like a clammy wing fluttering around inside her stomach as if it were trying to escape, but the feeling did not linger, so she finished her coffee and got to her feet. For she was suddenly carried away by an urge to telephone Takuzō. It would be enough simply to fix the day for their next meeting.

"There's no reason to return so early—why not go to a movie or something," said Keitarō looking at his watch.

"I'll be going back soon, so please you go back first, because honestly I'll be back soon."

Whereupon a willful Michiko abruptly started out. I want to be alone for even just thirty minutes—that would be good, she thought. The wish to be alone welled up powerfully, and because of that even her intention to try to have that thirty minutes on the phone abated.

"If you're going to a movie, there's an interesting sci-fi playing," said Keitarō, cupping his hands to his mouth like a megaphone, since she was already some distance away heading toward the door.

"I'm sorry. Excuse me, please".

Michiko felt that her own voice was instantly drowned out by the street noise.

I really am sorry. It was not that she was speaking only to Keitarō. The longer she lived the more she might say that about all the festering wounds she was creating in this world.

Twenty-Two

~

"OH, THOSE HATEFUL DEMONS ARE HAUNTING me again and they never leave my side," said Murayama Kaori.

"But I drove those people off for you in good order," said Uji Kyōko.

"Those people? Who?"

"Demons and devils."

"Why were you so kind as to drive them off?"

"It wasn't particularly out of kindness."

"Oh, I see. They're not of this world."

"As for me, I didn't do it out of kindness or anything."

"I wonder what I'd do if you weren't here. If you weren't here, I'd probably be terribly lonely."

"Everybody is lonely."

"The more you hate, the lonelier you become."

"Everybody hates."

"Good heavens, really?"

"As I see it, the make-up of every human being is entirely visible. Completely visible."

"Who hates whom?"

"Everybody hates someone."

"Really? You're a genius!"

"No, I'm crazy."

"Oh?"

"Oh?"

"So everybody hates someone?"

"The energy involved is appalling. Anyone who fully amassed it could create an atomic blast in which the human race would perish in an instant."

"There isn't anyone who doesn't hate someone else?"

"No, not a single person."

"Do you hate me?"

"Only to the extent that you hate me."

"I only hate that other woman, not you. I've been injured by that woman's violence, and so I want to pay her back with the same violence."

"Yes, sometimes there's a reason for it and sometimes there's no reason for it, and yet everybody hates."

"How can you say that with such assurance?"

"Because I too have hated."

"You?"

"Within mankind there is something like a sea of dark clouds of hatred which is very common, and when a person hates, he falls into it. And then one can hear the hateful voices of those who are there. It's quite common, really. Everybody falls in. Indeed, it goes beyond just that."

"Hmm, I don't understand."

"People who don't understand simply do not understand."

"So how is it that you understand?"

"Because I'm a genius."

"That is often said by people who are crazy. One might say I myself am a genius."

"Yes, one might say that of a crazy person."

"But I seem to have come to a somewhat better understanding. It's similar to what I sometimes feel about being a genius because I'm crazy."

"Finally you too seem to have become crazy."

"And then? What about after that?"

"What is it you'd like to inquire about?"

"About the blue sky."

"If one hates to the extent possible, one can emerge into the blue sky."

"How come?"

"Because one hates the very fact of hatred."

"Oh, pushing through the dark clouds with both hands, one emerges out there."

"Exactly."

"I wonder if it's really true."

"It seems like it's a lie."

"Oh! Then it's not true?"

"Whenever I say that, people say I'm crazy."

"But I don't say that, so please enlighten me."

"I too somehow have the feeling that it seems to be a lie. As for me, there are ups and downs. There now seems to be a slight strangeness that has come over me. A time when I seem to have returned to normalcy. My head is spinning. Oh, my head is spinning." Eyes downcast, Kyōko held her head in her hands.

"Kyōko, Kyōko, it's true, you said!" cried Kaori, shaking her by the shoulder.

"You two are so noisy. I finally got to sleep, and now you've woken me up." Lying on her bedding next to them, Takeda Miyo abruptly sat up. "I was just having a nice dream," she said, rubbing her puffy eyes. "I was dreaming that I was alone floating in a big bathtub."

Kaori stood up. Looking down at the now motionless form of Kyōko, she passed around by her side and stood by the window. She pressed her nose against the unfrosted glass of the window's upper half and the area around her nose immediately turned white with her breath. It must be cold out. Low-lying clouds, countless, multilayered, went scudding by, and high above them was yet another layer of clouds. The dark pine woods spread out into the distance. Some birds, five or six of them, were perched at regular intervals along a telephone line. There was not a soul in the exercise yard.

Twenty-Three

ON A DARK SIDE STREET OFF A BUSY THOROUGHFARE Takuzō bade goodbye to Michiko with a handshake. Facing one other, each extended the right hand and squeezed. On Michiko's part it was an especially firm handshake. The other day, Takuzō was seized with strong ill-feeling toward Michiko, and that had thrown him into emotional turmoil. However else his own feelings might be changed toward her, still his feelings of love for her swelled up within him.

As they were shaking hands Michiko drew back a step or two, her high heels clicking on the pavement. Their hands were still clasped though their arms were now stretched straight apart.

"Well then, distant though we may be from each other, it's okay, because this grip will never be loosened."

So said Michiko, seemingly reverting to the game-playing of her childhood. She actually did put on a childish face, too.

After the hotel, they had gone to a bar and drank beer, which made them both a bit tipsy.

Quite unexpectedly, in this picture showing the two of them hand-in-hand, arm-in-arm, Takuzō somehow or other saw something like the model of an impossible union.

In the afterglow of desire, Michiko had become a degree yet more beautiful. The fire itself had burned out but there was still a glow, and though it was over, quite over, it seemed to burn on.

Takuzō was thinking about the chart of their relations—one straight line extending from one beyond to the next beyond, coming to a conclusion at that furthest beyond.

"You were thinking of something else just now," said Michiko, sensitive to his reactions.

"Not at all, I was thinking only of you. Just now when you stepped back, when you kept withdrawing, a picture …" Takuzō was trying to express what he deemed to be quite beyond verbal expression. And yet, he thought, it was not of her that he was thinking, but, after all, of something else perhaps.

"You do have so much on your mind. Although it's good that you're thinking of me here right now," said Michiko apparently somewhat displeased.

"Really? Well, yes, that's true, all right, but … Or rather, I'm poor at expressing myself," he said. And then he recalled his thoughts of the other day. He had aimed his arrow at Michiko as if aiming at a target, yet that arrow was charged with such an excess of love that it must have overshot the mark.

"Oh, how the red lights on that hotel over there float up before our eyes." And because Michiko pointed toward the hotel, their hands separated.

Takuzō, who was feeling depressed, immediately understood that Michiko, seeing the red hotel lights, might be trying to entice him.

"After you part from me now," he said, "where do you suppose you'll go? Wherever you go, it seems, those red lights will haunt you and walk along with you." When he thought of such a woman as her, he was conscious that both of them were somehow searching for their own separate direction, and he found it hard to leave.

"Well, life for a person like me is senseless and painful. And so, surely I'll be pursuing those red lights," said Michiko, laughing momentarily. To laugh about what she had said in all sincerity suggested she was trying to gloss over something.

Thereupon the two of them in fact walked off, each in a different direction.

Looking back at Michiko, who was now out of sight heading for the National Line station, Takuzō walked off in the direction of the subway station.

His thoughts toward Michiko saturated him, mind and body. With every step those thoughts flooded over him. Then, from deep within him, another thought came to the surface, a thought far removed in character from his earlier ones. This morning he had received a special delivery from Sawako which had stuck vaguely in his mind throughout the day.

> *Please come to my apartment on December 12th.*
> *During the day or in the evening, it doesn't matter which.*
> *Please don't fail to come. Because there is something*
> *you have to see.*
>
> *Hurriedly,*
> *Muro Sawako*

Such was the simple wording of her postcard.

This was probably the first time he had ever received a letter from Sawako, who always either telephoned or came directly to visit. It must be because she felt some particular reluctance this time, Takuzō had at first thought. The card was postmarked with yesterday's last mailing period, and December 12 was in fact today. Because he had quit his part-time job, his days were free, but every day in order to start a new life, he was out walking the streets looking for new lodgings and new work. The comfortable amount he had accumulated in savings was now drastically reduced because of his relationship with Michiko. Although he had to find them soon, both work and lodgings having a direct connection with her, he was not at all sure he could manage to do so. The more he thought about his own hopes, the fuzzier they became. The single thing that was clear to him was his ardent desire to continue his relation with her.

Takuzō had thought he might stop by at Sawako's following his date with Michiko, but with midnight approaching, he found that he had no enthusiasm for it. I'll make it for tomorrow, he suddenly decided as he descended the stairs to the subway, and he felt relieved.

Even so, he couldn't think what sort of reluctance might have compelled Sawako to send an express postcard. Why was it that, after Sawako and Michiko had first spotted each other at the coffee shop on that late November day, Sawako had since then visited him any number of times at his rooming house.

Granted that she felt some reserve, every time she dropped in for a little while she only just chatted for an hour or so then left. She wished for nothing more, according to what she herself said. Whenever something involving Michiko became the topic of conversation, Sawako always spoke admiringly of her. Speaking admiringly seemed to be Sawako's way of stimulating her own happiness. At such times Takuzō would be at a loss for a reply, and he would let her remarks stand as they were.

You might say of me that I'm a cheerful redcap. I offer a service and discerning people buy from me.

That's what Sawako had said, and the quip having come to mind she herself had a good chuckle.

There is something you have to see, her note said, though from another person's point of view it might be no more than just some silly feat. While Takuzō was immersed in these thoughts, he nodded off, swaying gently to and fro in the subway car.

By the time he recovered his alertness, he had already passed his stop. He changed to a train going in the opposite direction, finally getting off only to find that bus service had already terminated, and, as he walked back, he realized a very substantial amount of time had passed since parting from Michiko.

As he neared his rooming house, he could hear a telephone ringing somewhere. Entering the building, he realized that the ringing was coming from his own room. For some reason or other he thought it might be Okada Heisuke, but as he was hurriedly taking off his shoes, the ringing, which must have been going on a long time, stopped. It couldn't have been anyone other than Sawako, he thought, and that being the case it was all the better that it had stopped ringing. After a date with Michiko it was always like that: he had the feeling that every cell in his body was reliving the experience, impelling him to bed and sleep.

As he was washing his face in the bathroom, with his toothbrush, toothpaste, cup, soap and so on all lined up, his eyes fell to the shaving razor, which seemed to remind him of some place or other, but being sleepy he couldn't recall, and so with that he went into his room, rolled into bed, and soon was asleep.

He was awakened by the telephone. He had no idea how long he had been sleeping, but he felt he was being dragged out of a stupor.

"Hello?"

"Hello, might Mr. Sawamura Takuzō be at home, please?"

It was a woman's voice he didn't recognize.

"Yes this is Sawamura speaking," he said. He wanted to get back to bed as soon as he could.

"This is Miss Shirai from the Public Housing Office."

"Public Housing Office?"

"Would you be acquainted with Miss Muro Sawako?"

"Oh, her apartment?"

"Um … well … Miss Muro has died."

"What did you say?"

"It was suicide. That's what a policeman just now said it looked like. I've been trying to call you for some time, but no one answered, that's why I'm calling now so late. Your name in her address book is underlined in red, and the English words 'love love love' are written in red, and … oh, I'm so sorry, but this is no joke, and that's why I was wondering if you were someone close to her …"

"Suicide?" Takuzō was staggered. Was there not some mistake, or perhaps a fatal accident? Like a tape recorder in play-back mode, Sawako's voice during these past couple of weeks came to mind, and that voice, bright as a sparrow's chirp with never a hint of doubt, now instantly came under examination.

"In any event, sir, would you be able to come over here? I've telephoned the family home and until one of her family members arrives, I'd like to have someone here."

"I just don't understand. Is this all true?"

"If you could see it, you'd understand. She was in the bathtub with her wrists slashed. Blades were scattered all over."

"Blades?"

"They were razor blades."

"Oh? What kind of razor blades?"

Suddenly Takuzō felt as if struck by a powerful blow. Everything now took on a clear meaning, bright like an exploding flashbulb. Yet instantly darkness extended around him, and without being able to recall the things he understood just a moment ago, he was at an utter loss.

"One razor blade wouldn't be enough to make the cuts, she must have thought, so she used every blade she had."

"I'll be over there right away," said Takuzō and he hung up the phone.

He was already convinced that Sawako had indeed committed suicide. And yet to confirm such a conviction, he was for the moment, what with his mind in utter turmoil, incapable of detailed thought. Furthermore, it was not just this matter alone but also layer upon layer of impressions, which made thinking about them all the more painful.

He at once decided he had to inform Michiko.

After dialing her number he glanced at the clock on the table. It was a little before two in the morning. That being the case, he calculated he had been sleeping only for a short while before the phone call awakened him.

"Hello?" A man's voice answered.

Hearing the voice, Takuzō realized it was a time when her husband would of course be at home.

"Hello. My name is Sawamura. Is Mrs. Nobe at home, please? Excuse me for the lateness of the hour, but it's a matter of some urgency." He felt an unexpected animosity suffusing his own voice.

"It is indeed inexcusable to call at so late an hour," replied the husband sleepily to Sawamura's statement. His voice was thick and slow.

"My name is Sawamura Takuzō." By giving his full name he was clearly indicating that he had no guilty feelings about announcing exactly who he was.

"Urgent? So what's the matter? Anyway," he said, his voice gradually growing steadier, "she's sound asleep and even if I told her there was a phone call for her, she wouldn't wake up."

This remark told Takuzō that it was the husband who was being the wary one.

"Because when she falls asleep, she sleeps right through until morning," the husband continued.

With a vividness which fairly took his breath away, Takuzō suddenly pictured the figure of the pajama-clad husband standing in front of the telephone.

"It's that a friend has committed suicide," said Takuzō. He had no choice but to state the fact head on.

"Oh? A friend of Michiko's." The husband was thoroughly unperturbed. Or was it rather a pretense of being unperturbed?

"Her name was Muro Sawako. If you would be so kind as to convey this to Mrs. Nobe..."

Beyond this, Takuzō for his part decided to have no more to do with the husband. He was a very strong-willed person, and to that extent a man inclined to monopolize his wife—something which had not hitherto occurred to Takuzō.

And yet, the husband continued the conversation.

"Things like mental hospitals and suicides—recently Michiko has personally become familiar with such things."

"Mental hospitals? What's this about and who's involved?" Takuzō experienced unexpected feelings. Never once had he heard such things from the mouth of Michiko.

"Well, um, that's my business. Anyway," he said, "please hold on a minute," followed by the sound of the receiver's being set down.

Takuzō imagined a broad-shouldered man near forty walking slowly to the bedroom.

"Hello?" It was Michiko's voice.

"Nobe Michiko," said Takuzō."

By stating her full name, Takuzo hoped to elicit Michiko's general situation, though it would seem that the husband had planted himself close by.

"What's this about something urgent?" she began with friendly informality then, catching herself, she switched to a more formal "Could you tell me, please, what this matter is about?"

Takuzō realized that the husband had conveyed nothing to Michiko about the contents of their conversation. Even in so inconsequential a matter as conveying a message, that man had revealed his true character. Although Takuzō could understand the husband's manliness, yet at the same time his own failure to understand Sawako's true feelings, along with Miss Shirai's startling information of a moment ago, struck Takuzō hard.

"Miss Muro has committed suicide. Someone just now called from her apartment to inform me of it. The persons most closely connected with her are you and I. So I'm going over there. It would be well if you could come too, though I can't force you. However, since we're the most closely connected, what might they make of that? Something unusual for sure, don't you think? They've certainly made a connection between her death and us as the persons most closely involved with her."

Takukzō said it all in a single span.

There was no reaction, just silence, from the other end of the line. Or rather, Michiko was suppressing any reaction.

"Are you listening? Do you understand me? Shall I hang up, then?"

Nobe Michiko said nothing.

Takuzō also said no more.

"I'll go there," she finally said matter-of-factly.

He replaced the receiver. The entire exchange left him in a state of numb abstraction, but then, recovering his wits, he changed clothes, threw on an overcoat and hurried from his room.

He took the same route as the other day when he walked to Sawako's apartment. Even if he had encountered a passing taxi it would not have occurred to him to flag it down.

You've got some razor blades there, but do you mind if I take them back home with me? There are three of them, so I'll take all three. So Sawako had said when coming from the bathroom into Takuzo's room.

They're dull. There are probably some new ones right across from them, said Takuzō, seeing Sawako holding the three used blades in her small plump hand.

No, these are better. The ones your shaved off whiskers have stuck to. Don't you men know that us girls like to keep aside a lock of hair or a bit of beard of the men we love, she said with a giggle.

Really? I didn't know that, he had said, but what he meant was, whatever you like is fine with me. It was altogether different from when he had said to Michiko, I don't understand what you are saying.

Sawako wrapped the blades in toilet tissue and put them in her handbag.

Thinking back on it now, Takuzō realized that Sawako had come to his rooming house to visit the very evening of the day when he had had his first date with Michiko at that coffee shop, around the twentieth of November.

Sawako had most likely made her decision on that day.

She had probably thought all along that if she formed a physical relationship with Takuzō she would be able to feel secure. To the contrary, however, it was probably because of forming such a physical relationship that she may have become all the more confused. Then, after meeting Michiko firsthand, she most likely thought she should make her feelings clear to him. And in the end she did make them clear, tragically clear.

Pursuing his train of thought, however, it all seemed to be elaborate dissimulation. When she had said, us girls like to keep aside a lock of hair or a bit of beard of the men we love, that comment surely smelled of dissimulation. Yes, that was it, wasn't it: being on the border of consciousness and unconsciousness, she was capable of wonderful dissimilation.

"Hmm...yes," Takuzō muttered to himself as he walked along the slumbering streets, enlivened only by street lights and gate lamps.

His thoughts turned to subsequent events, and there were very painful things to have witnessed. He had the sensation of a double-bottomed trunk: having emptied it down to the first bottom, there was yet another where different things might suddenly appear, but the surroundings were so nebulous that he simply could not get them in his grasp.

More razor blades! I'm going to take them back home with me. In the four days since I've been here, four blades have piled up. So Sawako had said when she had come four days later.

Okay, sure, he had replied.

You're awfully kind.

Oh? How come?

They're such dangerous things, but you don't get alarmed and cry out, don't touch them!

Recalling which, he had the same feeling of a moment ago about opening up a double-bottomed trunk. Still, he brushed aside the past and drove away the details of the present.

You've only got one blade today. Even though I haven't come here for five days, the others have been thrown away. Does that mean you don't want me to take those things back with me? So Sawako had remarked on yet another day, picking up the one blade.

If you don't want me to, just say so.

I'm not saying no.

Just a single word from you and it would be okay with me to stop taking your razor blades once and for all.

Takuzō hadn't said a thing. He was taken aback somewhat, but he felt nothing peculiar in Sawako's customary and unchanging expression.

He walked up the hill toward the back of the public housing complex. He was reminded that about a month ago Sawako had been standing there with two children in tow.

Circling around to the front of the building, he saw people milling about in a vague atmosphere of confusion. At an hour when most windows should have been dark, all around they were lit up. He passed by the apartment doorways ranged along the first floor, and as he approached her apartment a chattering throng of people standing there looked intently his way.

He entered the apartment; three men and a woman were there. Takuzō bowed in greeting to them and the woman came up to him and silently motioned toward the bathroom.

"The outside door hadn't been locked," she explained, "so one of the children Miss Muro was so attached to came in and discovered the body." She was apparently the same woman who had called him a short while ago, for he recognized the voice.

He took a step into the bathroom and, from the open door of the bathtub area, blood-splattered surfaces everywhere assailed his eyes. The water in the bathtub was dyed with the blood that had drained from Sawako's body. And it was in this very water that Muro Sawako, now ashen white, lay in quiet repose, her head resting aslant in a corner of the tub, one arm thrown up over its edge. Since it was a small tub, she was settled with both legs drawn up against her chest. She had probably soaked one of her arms in the hot water and then cut it. She seemed to be wearing a pink negligee, though the water was so muddied with blood that her body was not visible. A frilly collar emerging at the surface of the water was bathed in blood. Aside from its pallor far whiter than her actual fair complexion, it was the same face she'd had while alive.

Even more than the death of a woman with whom he had had such a close relation, his failure to have taken notice of her signals tormented him. His eyes next chanced to fall on the blades in question. The police detective, following his inspection, had apparently neatly stacked them up on one corner of the sink, so many blades one could hardly count them all, but there was no mistaking they were indeed his used razor blades. For all that, there was no evidence of her having given any indication of their intended use, and so he was as before left in ambiguity.

At the living room table the three men—the detective, a police department medical officer, and a municipal medical examiner—were talking quietly as they prepared a report of their investigation. Takuzō was asked two or three questions, and when he inquired about any suicide note, the detective replied that none had been found. And thus, the ambiguity he felt became ever cloudier.

Which called to mind the message in that special delivery postcard, altogether forgotten since being informed of the death. Please come to my apartment on December 12th. During the day or in the evening, it doesn't matter which. Please don't fail to come. Because there is something you have to see.

That "something you have to see" was what he had just now seen, was it not?

Suddenly he felt a blazing hatred leaping up from these words. The unlocked apartment door was probably meant for him to enter.

There were footsteps and the door opened. Takuzō, figuring it was Michiko, started to raise himself, but it was a man who entered. Behind the man was another person, a woman, who also came in. A telephone call from Sawako's parents in her hometown had explained that the parents would not be able to arrive for a number of hours, and so in their place Sawako's cousin and his wife were hurrying here from the Tokyo suburb where they lived.

Having entrusted remaining matters to them, Takuzō stood up. As he was about to leave, he took another look into the bathroom. He had no sense of the battlefield carnage he had seen a moment ago; rather, serenity reigned—the serenity of a life-size doll lolling in red water. All that remained was the physical substance. The battlefield carnage was on the interior alone. And while even that was mere conjecture, Takuzō nevertheless thought this outcome a grotesque inconsistency from what Sawako had day after day been saying.

Emerging from the apartment, he wended his way through the crowd and stood at the side of the building. Spotting an adjacent vacant lot where some building or other had been cleared away, he decided to wait there for Michiko. He looked up at the sky, but neither moon nor stars were visible, leaving only the dull light of the gate lamps of homes surrounding the vacant lot to be swallowed up in the chilly air. That's just another one of those gate lamps—such was his impression of one red dot out there—but it was swaying slightly to and fro in the very middle of the vacant lot and he realized that in fact it was someone smoking a cigarette. It's a man, he thought at first, but then no, it seemed more like a woman, and after a while he recognized it as his beloved Michiko, whose face emerged dimly from the darkness dissipated from around that red dot of fire. Takuzō walked slowly in the direction of that face. As he approached, the outline of her body also emerged, as did the very sensation of her, the scent of her hair, and her slender wrists—every detail that for him made up the only woman, and revealed as well a harmony with his concept of the ideal woman.

"Sweetheart?" he said, and then for some reason or other thought to rephrase it as, "Nobe Michiko?"

And yet, however close he approached, the agony of his never reaching her stood between the two of them. That had never been so clear until this very moment.

"It's all over," said Michiko in a whisper.

Takuzō was speechless.

The meaning of that remark expressed the agony which he himself had felt just a moment ago, and even during the instant when he was coming to this understanding, he hoped Michiko might say that "it's all over" meant simply that the police had arrived so there would be a prompt disposition of the incident.

Since learning of the suicide, Takuzō was aware, although he had not really analyzed why, that this farewell was something he had brought on himself. Perhaps because of that, he recalled so fondly her lovely face, and changed his greeting as if she had now become a stranger.

"I got here about a half hour ago and I've been right here smoking the whole time," said Michiko on a different topic.

"It's just as well you didn't go in and look. It was pretty gruesome."

It occurred to Takuzō that the appalling sight of that corpse was perhaps not really so appalling after all.

"How did she die? Gas?" asked Michiko, tossing her cigarette butt by her foot and crushing it under her high-heel shoe.

In the vacant lot the concrete foundation of the former building protruded here and there, and dead grass appeared white as if frozen under the night air. Takuzō recalled that previously a wood-frame building stood here housing a small workshop. When he had last passed by here upon return from that night at Sawako's apartment, it still existed. Shaking off these irrelevant thoughts wandering relentlessly through his mind, he finally answered her question.

"She was sunk in the bathtub and her wrists were slashed. With razor blades."

"Razor blades? What razor blades?"

Silence.

Takuzō was unable to speak.

"Those blades—I think I know what blades they were," said Michiko mysteriously, then lapsed into silence. Finally she spoke again.

"When I said it's all over, did you understand?"

Michiko, apparently not wanting to hear the answer, turned around and started slowly across the vacant lot. After a few steps she turned back and went off in a different direction for a few steps. Completely wrapped in a long dark overcoat, both hands thrust in her pockets, eyes looking down at the ground, she paced back and forth.

"I don't know what your plans are, but for me it's all over," said Michiko, drawing near, though she seemed to be speaking more to herself than to him.

And it's the same for me, thought Takuzō, though the words did not leave his mouth.

"Me … I've mulled the thing over … again and again. And having mulled it over … I have come to be … disappointed in myself," said Michiko hesitantly.

Unexpectedly there was something that threw light upon her words. And I've been mulling over the same thing, too, he was thinking.

Takuzō was aware that the thing he kept recalling to mind as he had walked over here was precisely that.

"As for me, in all honesty, as long as I live, for sure it'll be just such …," Michiko mused aloud.

In the pit of his stomach Takuzō felt a sudden depression far greater than the disappointment Michiko was talking about.

I've mulled this over and over: that's what Takuzō had wanted to say to Okada Heisuke.

So what do you want to do about it, Heisuke would likely have asked, jokingly fixing his keen round eyes on him.

Me? I certainly can't change, Takuzō would probably have said.

Only to be expected; three times, four times, five times, mulling it over and over for a whole lifetime, Heisuke might have replied.

"We won't be meeting like this any more—is that it?" said Takuzō, knowing full well that "it's all over" also applied to himself.

"Yes. Here, now, it has ended," said Michiko without a trace of regret.

"I see. Well then, let's walk back. I'll walk you back as far as your apartment. By that time it'll probably be getting light out."

Takuzō started walking ahead.

"As for me … I have the feeling that … I'll be repeating the same thing … from now on, and into the future too," said Michiko again after a long pause.

"The same thing?" Takuzō considered the fact that he knew nothing of her past.

"Yes, exactly," said Michiko, without really responding to the question. There was a trace of laughter in her voice.

"You're laughing?" He glanced at her profile.

"Well, I guess I'm just that way."

"When we first met and went to that hotel you also said the same thing."

"Starting tomorrow, I'll look for another man."

"This is not the time to be talking of such cruel things. And yet, maybe that's a part of why I love you."

In his mind Takuzō changed his comment from "that's a part" to "that's an unrestrained part." And, he would like to have added, this is the first time I have ever met a woman devoid of all affectation.

"Starting tomorrow, I'll look for a man. Until I find him, even if it takes three years or four years, I'll search every day, yes, every day. For that purpose I'll wander the streets of this desert of a city. It didn't necessarily have to be you—as I said sometime before. A man who has only the ability to accept me—anybody will be fine. If I should happen to see one, I'll know it."

Michiko spoke this with a tenseness in her voice which up to now she had never once used. It was a voice that could also be taken to indicate she was trying hard to restrain something.

"Well, I won't be looking for another woman starting tomorrow." What Takuzo was saying—that Michiko alone was fine for him—somehow struck him as an eye-opening thought. Quite beyond the notion that she was the ideal woman for him, there was something else that seemed to come into view.

As for that, however, Michiko said not a word.

"It is I who am saying I'm sorry," she said. "It is not about anyone else nor is it about anything else. Even so, as for me this is not the end of it."

To which Takuzō also said nothing, and felt himself getting caught up in just his own thoughts. But even if they were just his own thoughts, his thoughts were of Michiko. Although the object of his thoughts was walking right alongside him, his thoughts did not stop there—they passed far beyond that.

Along the main thoroughfare the streetlights were uniformly ranged and, except for an occasional passing car, all was silent.

Although Takuzō had wanted to walk with her until night gave way to dawn, Michiko flagged down a taxi that chanced to pass by. Catching his eye seemingly with both coquetry and sorrow, she suddenly climbed in alone, leaving Takuzō standing there stunned.

As the taxi sped her away, that over-abundance of love, which Takuzō possessed from the time he was born, accompanied the woman who was receding into the distance and extended to wherever she went, while she who was receding into the distance savored still more the feeling that what she was doing was best.

- - -

Takeda Sachiko dialed the number.

"Hello, this is LifeLine. May I help you?"

"Hello? Oh, it's you. Will you please listen to me again today? Please listen. Oh, please listen ..."

~

About the Author

TAKAHASHI TAKAKO (1932–2013) earned bachelor's and master's degrees in French literature at prestigious Kyoto University, a remarkable achievement for a woman in the 1950s. There, she was influenced by the decadent poetry of Charles Baudelaire (1821-1867) and the writings of novelist and Catholic apologist François Mauriac (1885-1970). Christianity and depravity characterize both *The Wasteland* and many of Takahashi's other works.

About the Translator

BRITTEN DEAN earned his BA from Brown University in French and German literature and his MA and PhD from Columbia University in East Asian Languages and Cultures. During a 30-year career at California State University Stanislaus, he published extensively and taught a wide variety of courses in the fields of modern Chinese and Japanese history and culture. He lived for many years in East Asia, and now, professor emeritus, he resides in Charlottesville, Virginia.

Titles in the New Japanese Horizon Series

The Art of Being Alone: Tanikawa Shuntarō Poems 1952–2009
translated with introduction by Takako U. Lento (2011)

Indian Summer by Kanai Mieko (2012)
translated with introduction by Tomoko Aoyama and Barbara Hartley (2012)

Of Birds Crying by Minako Ōba
translated with introduction by Michiko N. Wilson and Michael K. Wilson (2011)

Pioneers of Modern Japanese Poetry
translated with introduction by Takako Lento (2019)

Red Ghost, White Ghost: Stories and Essays by Kita Morio
translated with introduction by Masako Inamoto (2018)

The Running Boy by Megumu Sagisawa
translated with introduction by Tyran Grillo (2019)

Single Sickness and Other Stories by Misuda Mizuko
translated with introduction by Lynne Kutsukake (2011)

The Wasteland by Takako Takahashi
translated with introduction by Britten Dean (2019)

eap.einaudi.cornell.edu/publications

www.ingramcontent.com/pod-product-compliance
Lightning Source LLC
Chambersburg PA
CBHW060804310726
48980CB00002B/233

9781939161109